A Little Maid
of New England

A Little Maid
of New England

Two Volumes in One

A Little Maid of Province Town
A Little Maid of Massachusetts Colony

ALICE TURNER CURTIS

DERRYDALE BOOKS
NEW YORK

This 1991 edition is published by Derrydale Books,
distributed by Outlet Book Company, Inc.,
a Random House Company,
225 Park Avenue South,
New York, New York 10003.

Printed and bound in the United States of America

Library of Congress Cataloging-in-Publication Data
Curtis, Alice Turner.
     A little maid of New England / Alice Turner Curtis.
       p.   cm.
     Contents: Contents: v. 1. A Little maid of Province Town — v.
   2. A Little maid of Massachusetts Colony.
     ISBN 0-517-06494-4
     1. United States—History—Revolution, 1775–1783—Juvenile
   fiction.   [1. United States—History—Revolution, 1775–1783 —
   Fiction.]   I. Title.
PZ7.C941Lmhj   1991
     [Fic]—dc20   91-12104
                                                                      CIP
                                                                       AC

8 7 6 5 4 3 2 1

CONTENTS

Introduction vii
A Little Maid of Province Town 1
A Little Maid of Massachusetts Colony 125

INTRODUCTION

WHAT WAS IT like to be a child in New England during the American Revolution? Now you can find out in this delightful book which includes two separate novels about the fascinating life and adventures of eight-year-old Anne Nelson, who lived in Massachusetts Colony during the Revolutionary War.

In *A Little Maid of Province Town,* Anne, who was recently orphaned, is rescued by a kindly couple, and immediately sets out on a series of spectacular and terrifying adventures that prove her to be a brave and bold spirit. She escapes from unfriendly Indians and dangerous wolves, makes an unexpected trip to Boston, and successfully carries an important secret message to the Colonial army.

Anne, along with her two good friends Amanda and Amos Cary, continues her astonishing adventures in *A Little Maid of Massachusetts Colony.* She goes on a trip with friendly Indians, escapes from imprisonment in a house in the woods, sees the splendors of Colonial Boston, and helps to capture an English privateer.

Anne Nelson is not just a child of her time, but a good-hearted and brave little girl who will be loved by everyone who reads about her. Like *The Secret Garden* and *Anne of Green Gables,* the "Little Maid" novels are among the timeless and classic books of childhood. We laugh and weep along with the stories, and remember them for years to come.

Alice Turner Curtis, who lived to be ninety-eight years old, was born in Sullivan, Maine, in 1860. She spent most of her adult life in Newburyport, Massachusetts. Her childhood home was near a shipyard on the Maine coast, and, as a little girl, she watched schooners being built and launched. From these early experiences come the vivid descriptions of ships and the sea that are so much a part of her books. A published poet at the age of thirteen, Curtis decided then and there to write books that other girls would enjoy reading. And so she did. Her first book, *Marjorie's Way,* was published in 1904. In addition to all the books in the "Little Maid" series, she also wrote the "Yankee Girl" series, historical novels set in the Civil War era. *A Little Maid of Province Town* was the first of what were to become many successful "Little Maid" books. With the exception of *A Little Maid of Massachusetts Colony,* which continues the story of little Anne Nelson, each of the many other "Little Maid" titles introduces a new little girl within the general historical setting of the Revolutionary War. The other "Little Maid" books include *A Little Maid of Vermont, A Little Maid of Bunker Hill,* and *A Little Maid of Narragansett Bay.*

Anne Nelson is truly the Nancy Drew of the Revolutionary War, and her daring adventures make a delightful and memorable journey back to the early days of America's history.

LOIS HILL
New York
1991

A Little Maid
of Province Town

CONTENTS

ONE ANNE NELSON 5

TWO ANNE WINS A FRIEND 13

THREE ANNE'S SECRET 21

FOUR ANNE AND THE WOLF 27

FIVE SCARLET STOCKINGS 35

SIX CAPTURED BY INDIANS 41

SEVEN OUT TO SEA 47

EIGHT ON THE ISLAND 55

NINE THE CASTAWAYS 61

TEN SAFE AT HOME 67

ELEVEN CAPTAIN ENOS'S SECRETS 73

TWELVE AN UNEXPECTED JOURNEY 79

THIRTEEN ANNE FINDS HER FATHER 87

FOURTEEN A CANDY PARTY 95

FIFTEEN A SPRING PICNIC 105

SIXTEEN THE MAY PARTY 111

SEVENTEEN THE SLOOP *PEGGY* 117

CHAPTER ONE

——— 🍂 ———

ANNE NELSON

"I DON'T KNOW what I can do with you, I'm sure!" declared Mistress Stoddard, looking down at the small girl who stood on her doorstep gazing wistfully up at her.

"A man at the wharf said that you didn't have any little girls," responded the child, "and so I thought——"

" 'Twas Joe Starkweather told you, I'll be bound," said Mrs. Stoddard. "Well, he's seven of his own to fend for."

"Seven little girls?" said Anne Nelson, in an almost terror-stricken voice, her dark eyes looking earnestly into the stern face that frowned down upon her. "And what would become of them if their mother should die, and their father be lost at sea?"

"Sure enough. You have sense, child. But the Starkweathers are all boys. Well, come in. You can take your bundle to the loft and leave it, and we'll see what I can find for you to do. How old are you?"

"Eight last March," responded Anne.

"Well, a child of eight isn't much use in a house, but maybe you can save me steps."

"Yes, indeed, Mistress Stoddard; I did a deal to help my father about the house. He said I could do as much as a woman.

I can sweep out for you, and lay the table and wash the dishes, and bring in the wood and water, and——" there came a break in the little girl's voice, and the woman reached out a kindly hand and took the child's bundle.

"Come in," she said, and Anne instantly felt the tenderness of her voice. "We are poor enough, but you'll be welcome to food and shelter, child, till such time as some of your own kinsfolk send for thee."

"I have no kinsfolk," declared Anne; "my father told me that."

"Come you in; you'll have a bed and a crust while I have them to give you," declared the woman, and Anne Nelson went across the threshold and up to the bare loft, where she put her bundle down on a wooden stool and looked about the room.

There was but a narrow bed in the corner, covered with a patchwork quilt, and the wooden stool where Anne had put her bundle. The one narrow window looked off across the sandy cart tracks which served as a road toward the blue waters of Cape Cod Bay. It was early June, and the strong breath of the sea filled the rough little house, bringing with it the fragrance of the wild cherry blossoms and an odor of pine from the scrubby growths on the low line of hills back of the little settlement.

It was just a year ago, Anne remembered, as she unwrapped her bundle, that she and her father had sailed across the harbor from Ipswich, where her mother had died.

"We will live here, at the very end of the world, where a man may think as he pleases," her father had said, and had moved their few household possessions into a three-roomed house near the shore. Then he had given his time to fishing, leaving Anne alone in the little house to do as she pleased.

She was a quiet child, and found entertainment in building sand houses on the beach, in wandering along the shore searching for bright shells and smooth pebbles, and in doing such simple household tasks as her youth admitted. A week before her appearance at Mrs. Stoddard's door, John Nelson had gone out in his fishing boat, and now he had been given up as lost. No sign of him had been seen by the other fishermen, and it was generally believed by his neighbors that his sloop had foundered and that John Nelson had perished.

Some there were, however, who declared John Nelson to be a British spy, and hesitated not to say that he had sailed away to join some vessel of the British fleet with information as to the convenience of the harbor of Province Town, and with such other news as he had brought from Ipswich and the settlements nearer Boston. For it was just before the war of the American Revolution, when men were watched sharply and taken to task speedily for any lack of loyalty to the American colonies. And John Nelson had many a time declared that he believed England meant well by her American possessions—a statement which set many of his neighbors against him.

" 'Mean well,' indeed!" Joseph Starkweather had replied to his neighbor's remark. "When they have closed the port of Boston, so that no ship but the king's warships dare go in and out? Even our fishing boats are closely watched. Already the Boston people are beginning to need many things. Americans are not going to submit to feeding British soldiers while their own men go hungry."

But now Joseph Starkweather was the only man who interested himself in the lonely child. Day after day of that first week of her father's absence Anne had stayed close to the little house, looking hopefully out across the harbor for a sight of his boat; and day after day Joseph Starkweather had come lounging down the beach to speak with the child, to ask her what she had for breakfast, and if she slept safe and unafraid.

"The meal is gone," she told him one morning, "and I do not sleep now—I wait and listen for my father." And then it was that he told her she must seek another home.

"You are too young to stay alone," he said; "pick up a bundle of your clothes and go to Mrs. Stoddard on the hill. She hasn't a chick or child of her own. Like as not you'll be a blessing to her." And Anne, used to obedience and sorrow, obeyed.

There was nothing of much value in the small house, but on the day after Anne's entrance as a member of the Stoddard family, Captain Stoddard loaded the poor sticks of furniture on a handcart, and pulled it through the sandy tracks to his cottage door.

"It's the child of an English spy you're giving shelter to," he had said, when Martha Stoddard had told him that Anne was to

7

live with them, "and she'll bring no luck to the house." But his wife had made no response; the dark-eyed, elfish-looking child had already found a place in the woman's heart.

"I don't eat so very much," Anne announced as Mrs. Stoddard gave her a bowl of corn mush and milk when she came downstairs.

"You'll eat what you want in this house, child," answered her new friend, and Anne ate hungrily.

"Now come to the door, Anne, and I'll brush out this tangle of hair of yours," said Mrs. Stoddard; "and after this you must keep it brushed and braided neatly. And bring down your other frock. I'll be doing some washing this afternoon, and I venture to say your frock is in need of it."

The first few days in the Stoddard family seemed almost unreal to Anne. She no longer watched for her father's boat, she no longer wandered about the beach, playing in the sand and hunting for shells. Her dresses were not now the soiled and ragged covering which had served as frocks, but stout cotton gowns, made from a skirt of Mrs. Stoddard's, and covered with a serviceable apron. A sunbonnet of striped cotton covered the dark head, and Anne was as neat and well-dressed as the other children of the settlement. To be sure her slender feet were bare and tanned, and hardened by exposure; but there was not a child in the neighborhood who wore shoes until the frost came, and Mrs. Stoddard was already making plans for Anne's winter footgear.

"I'll trade off something for some moccasins for the child before fall," she had resolved; "some of the Chatham Indians will get down this way when the beach plums begin to ripen, and will be glad of molasses, if I am lucky enough to have it."

For those were the days when the little coast settlements had but few luxuries, and on Cape Cod the settlers were in fear of the British. Province Town was especially exposed, and at that time there were but thirty houses; and the people had no established communication with the outside world. The sea was their thoroughfare, as a journey over the sandy country from Province Town to Boston was almost impossible. News was a long time in reaching the little settlement of fishermen. But they knew that King George III had resolved to punish Boston for destroying his cargoes of tea, and had made Salem the seat of government in the place of Boston. Warships from England hovered about the coast, and the children of Province Town were quick to recognize these unwelcome craft.

"Mistress Stoddard," said Anne one morning, when she had returned from driving the cow to the enclosed pasturage at some little distance from the house, "Jimmie Starkweather says there is a big ship off Race Point, and that it is coming into harbor here. He says 'tis a British ship, and that like as not the men will land and burn down the houses and kill all the cows." Anne looked at Mrs. Stoddard questioningly.

"Nonsense!" responded the good woman. "Jimmie was but trying to make you afraid. 'Twas he sent thee running home last week in fear of a wolf that he told you was prowling about."

"But there is a ship, Mistress Stoddard. I went up the hill and looked, and 'tis coming along like a great white bird."

"Like enough. The big ships go up toward Boston and Salem on every fair day. You know that well, child."

"This seems a different kind," persisted Anne; and at last Mrs. Stoddard's curiosity was aroused, and with Anne close beside her she walked briskly up to the hill and looked anxiously across the blue waters.

" 'Tis much nearer, now," said Anne. "See, it's coming to— 'twill anchor."

"Sure enough," answered Mrs. Stoddard. "Jimmie Stark-weather is a wise lad. 'Tis a British man-of-war. Trouble is near at hand, child."

"Will they kill our cow?" questioned Anne. "Jimmie said they would, and eat her," and Anne's voice trembled; for the small brown cow was the nearest approach to a pet that the little girl had. It seemed a loss hardly to be borne if "Brownie" was to be sacrificed.

"It's like enough they will," replied Mrs. Stoddard. "They'll be sending their boats ashore and taking what they can see. Run back to the pasture, Anne, and drive Brownie down the further slope toward the salt meadow. There's good feed for her beyond the wood there, and she'll not wander far before nightfall, and she will not be quickly seen there."

Anne needed no urging. With another look toward the big

ship, she fled back along the sandy road toward the pasture, and in a short time the brown cow, much surprised and offended, was being driven at a run down the pasture slope, around the grove of scrubby maples to the little valley beyond.

Anne waited until Brownie had sufficiently recovered from her surprise to begin feeding again, apparently well content with her new pasturage, and then walked slowly back toward the harbor. The village seemed almost deserted. The children were not playing about the boats; there was no one bringing water from the spring near the shore, and as Anne looked out toward the harbor, she saw two more big ships coming swiftly toward anchorage.

"Poor Brownie!" she said aloud, for if there was danger in one ship she was sure that three meant that there was no hope for the gentle brown cow which she had just driven to a place of safety.

Before night a boatload of British sailors had landed, filled their water barrels at the spring, bought some young calves of Joseph Starkweather and returned quietly to their ships.

"They seem civil enough," said Captain Stoddard that night as he talked the newcomers over with his wife. "They know we could make no stand against them, but they treated Joseph Starkweather fairly enough."

Anne listened eagerly. "Will they take Brownie?" she asked.

"Indeed they won't if I can help it," answered Mrs. Stoddard; "we'll not drive the creature back and forth while the British are about. I can slip over the hill with a bucket and milk her night and morning. She's gentle, and there's no need of letting the pirates see how sleek and fat the creature is."

"And may I go with you, Mistress Stoddard?" asked Anne.

"Of course, child," answered Mrs. Stoddard, smilingly.

After Anne had gone up to the loft to bed Captain Stoddard said slowly: "She seems a good child."

"That she does, Enos. Good and careful of her clothes, and eager to be of help to me. She saves me many a step."

" 'Tis John Nelson, they say, who has brought the Britishers into harbor," responded Captain Enos slowly. "Joseph Stark-weather swears that one of the sailors told him so when he bargained for the calves."

"Anne's not to blame!" declared Mrs. Stoddard loyally, but there was a note of anxiety in her voice; "as you said yourself, Enos, she's a good child."

"I'll not be keeping her if it proves true," declared the man stubbornly. "True it is that they ask no military duty of any man in Province Town, but we're loyal folk just the same. We may have to barter with the British to save our poor lives, instead of turning guns on them as we should; but no man shall say that I took in a British spy's child and cared for it."

"They'd but say you did a Christian deed at the most," said his wife. "You're not a hard man, Enos."

"I'll not harbor a traitor's child," he insisted, and Mrs. Stoddard went sorrowfully to bed and lay sleepless through the long night, trying to think of some plan to keep Anne Nelson safe and well cared for until peaceful days should come again.

And Anne, too, lay long awake, wondering what she could do to protect the little brown cow which now rested so securely on the further side of the hill.

CHAPTER TWO

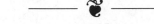

ANNE WINS A FRIEND

"COME, ANNE," CALLED Mrs. Stoddard at so early an hour the next morning that the June sun was just showing itself above the eastern horizon.

"Yes, Mistress Stoddard," answered the little girl promptly, and in a few minutes she came down the steep stairs from the loft.

"It is early to call you, child," said the good woman kindly, "but the captain has made an early start for the fishing grounds, and I liked not to leave you alone in the house in these troublous times; and so eat your porridge and we'll go and milk Brownie."

Anne hastened to obey; and in a few moments the two were making their way up the slope through the fragrant bayberry bushes, and breathing in the sweet morning air. No one else seemed astir in the little settlement. Now and then a flutter of some wild bird would betray that they had stepped near some low-nesting bird; and the air was full of the morning songs and chirrupings of robins, red-winged blackbirds, song sparrows, and of many sea-loving birds which built their nests among the sandhills, but found their food upon the shore.

Anne noticed all these things as they walked along, but her

thoughts were chiefly occupied with other things. There was one question she longed to ask Mrs. Stoddard, yet almost feared to ask. As they reached the summit of the hill and turned for a look at the beautiful harbor she gained courage and spoke:

"Mistress Stoddard, will you please to tell me what a 'spy' is?"

"A spy? And why do you wish to know, Anne?" responded her friend; "who has been talking to you of spies?"

"Is it an ill-seeming word?" questioned the child anxiously. "The Cary children did call it after me yesterday when I went to the spring."

"Did they that!" exclaimed Mrs. Stoddard angrily, "and what reply did you make, Anne?"

The little girl shook her head. "I said nothing. I knew not what they might mean. Does it mean an orphan child, Mistress Stoddard?" And the little girl lifted her dark eyes appealingly.

"I will tell you its meaning, Anne, and then you will see that it has naught to do with little girls. A 'spy' is like this: Suppose some one should wish to know if I kept my house in order, and what I gave the captain for dinner, and could not find out, and so she came to you and said, 'Anne Nelson, if you will tell me about the Stoddard household, and open the door that I may come in and see for myself, I will give thee a shilling and a packet of sweets'; then, if you should agree to the bargain, then you could be called a spy."

"But I would not do such a thing!" declared Anne, a little flash of resentment in her dark eyes. "Do the Cary children think me like that? I will throw water on them when next we meet at the spring—aye, and sand."

"Nay, Anne," reproved Mrs. Stoddard, but she was not ill-pleased at the child's spirit. "Then you would be as bad as they. It does not matter what they may say: that is neither here nor there. If you be an honest-thinking child and do well they cannot work harm against you."

As they talked they had walked on and now heard a low "Moo!" from behind a bunch of wild cherry trees.

"There's Brownie!" exclaimed Anne, "but I do wish she would not 'moo' like that, Mistress Stoddard. The British might hear her if they come up this far from shore."

" 'Tis only to remind me that it is time she was milked," said Mrs. Stoddard. "You can play about here, child, till I have finished."

Anne did not wander far. There was something else she wished to know, and when the bucket was filled with foamy, fragrant milk, of which Mrs. Stoddard bade the child drink, she said:

" 'Tis near a month since my father went. The Cary children also called after me that my father was a 'traitor'; is that an ill-seeming word?"

"The little oafs!" exclaimed Mrs. Stoddard, "and what else did they say?"

" 'Twill not make you dislike me, Mistress Stoddard?" questioned the child. "I honestly do not know why they should so beset me. But they called me 'beggar' as well, whatever that may be; though I'm sure I am not it, if it be an ill-seeming word."

Mrs. Stoddard had set down her milking pail; Brownie was quietly feeding near by; there was no one to see, and she put her arm about the little girl and drew her near. It was the first outward show of tenderness that she had made toward the child, and as Anne felt the kindly pressure of her arm and looked up into the tender eyes her own face brightened.

"We'll sit here for a bit and rest, child," said Mrs. Stoddard, "and be sure I think only well of you. Thou art a dear child, and I will not have aught harm thee or make thee unhappy."

Anne drew a long breath, and snuggled closely to her good friend's side. A great load was lifted from her sad little heart, for since she had come to Province Town she could remember but few kindly words, and to have Mistress Stoddard treat her with such loving kindness was happiness indeed. For a moment she forgot the taunts of the Cary children, and sat silent and smiling, her head resting against Mrs. Stoddard's shoulder. There was a peaceful little silence between the two, and then Anne spoke.

"I would wish to know what 'traitor' might mean, Mistress Stoddard?"

"Very like to 'spy,' " answered Mrs. Stoddard. "The children meant that your father had told the British that they could find good harbor and provisions here. That, like a spy, he had opened the door of a friend's house for silver."

15

Anne sprang from the arm that had encircled her, her cheeks flushed and her eyes blazing. "Now!" she declared, "I *will* throw water upon them when I go to the spring! All that the bucket will hold I will splash upon them," and she made a fierce movement as if casting buckets full of wrath upon her enemies. "And sand!" she continued; "while they are wet with the water I will throw sand upon them. 'Tis worse to say things of my father than of me."

"Come here, child," said Mrs. Stoddard. "We will not let words like the Cary children speak trouble us. And you will remember, Anne, that I shall be ill-pleased if I hear of water throwing at the spring. Come, now, we'll be going toward home."

Anne made no response, but walked quietly on beside her companion. When they reached the hilltop they paused again before going down the slope toward home.

"Look, Anne! Are not the fishing boats all at anchor? What means it that the men are not about their fishing? We'd best hurry."

Captain Enos met them at the door. He gave Anne no word of greeting, but said to his wife, "The British tell us to keep ashore. They'll have no fishing. They know full well how easy 'tis for a good sloop to carry news up the harbor. They are well posted as to how such things are done."

"But what can we do if we cannot fish?" exclaimed Mrs. Stoddard. " 'Tis well known that this sandy point is no place for gardens. We can scarce raise vegetables enough to know what they mean. And as for corn and wheat, every grain of them worth counting has to be bought from the other settlements and paid for in fish. If we do not fish how shall we eat?"

The captain shook his head. "Go about your play, child," he said, turning toward Anne, and the little girl walked slowly away toward a bunch of scrubby pine trees near which she had established a playhouse. She had built a cupboard of smooth chips, and here were gathered the shells she had brought from the beach, a wooden doll which her father had made her, and the pieces of a broken earthenware plate.

She took the doll from its narrow shelf and regarded it closely. Her father had made it with no small skill. Its round head was covered with curls carved in the soft wood; its eyes were colored with paint, and its mouth was red. The body was more clumsily made, but the arms and legs had joints, and the doll could sit up as erect as its small mistress. It wore one garment made of blue and white checked cotton. It was the only toy Anne Nelson had ever possessed, and it had seemed more her own because she had kept it in the little playhouse under the pines.

"Now, you can go up to the house and live with me," she said happily, "and now you shall have a truly name. You shall be Martha Nelson now. I know my father would want you to be called Martha, if he knew that Mrs. Stoddard put her arm around me and called me a 'dear child,' " and Anne smiled at the remembrance.

She did not speak of her father before the Stoddards, but she could not have explained the reason for her silence. She had wondered much about him, and often watched the harbor yearningly, thinking that after all the old sloop might come sailing back, bringing the slender, silent man who had always smiled upon her, and praised her, and had told her that some day she should have a Maltese kitten, and a garden with blossoming trees and smooth paths. Anne did not forget him, and now as she regarded her wooden doll a great longing for a sight of his dear face made her forget everything, and she leaned her head against a little pine and cried silently. But as she cried the remembrance of the taunts of the Cary children came into her thoughts, and she dried her eyes.

" 'Tis near the hour when they go to the spring," she said, laying the doll carefully back in its former resting place. "I will but walk that way that they may not think me afraid of their ill-seeming words." And with her dark head more erect than usual, Anne made her way down the path, her brown feet sinking ankle deep in the warm sand at every step.

The Cary children, a boy and a girl, both somewhat Anne's seniors, were already filling their buckets at the spring. Jimmie Starkweather was there, and a number of younger children ran shouting up and down the little stream which flowed from the spring across the road.

As Anne came near, Jimmie Starkweather called out: "Oh,

Anne Nelson! The Indians from Truro are camping at Shankpainter's Pond. I've been over there, near enough to see them at work, this morning. My father says they'll be gone as soon as they see the British vessels. We'll not have time to buy moccasins if they go so quickly."

Anne's eyes rested for a moment upon Jimmie, but she did not speak. She could hear the Carys whispering as they dipped their buckets in the spring, and as she came nearer, their voices rose loudly: "Daughter of a spy! Beggar child! Beggar child!"

But their taunts vanished in splutterings and pleas for mercy; for at their first word Anne had sprung upon them like a young tiger. She had wrenched the bucket of water from the astonished boy and flung it in his face with such energy that he had toppled over backward, soused and whimpering; then she had turned upon his sister, sending handful after handful of sand into the face of that astonished child, until she fled from her, wailing for mercy.

But Anne pursued her relentlessly, and Captain Enos Stoddard, making his mournful way toward the shore, could hardly believe his own senses when he looked upon the scene—the Cary boy prostrate and humble, while his sister, pursued by Anne, prayed for Anne to stop the deluge of sand that seemed to fill the air about her.

"I'll not be called ill-seeming names!" shrieked Anne. "If thou sayest 'traitor' or 'spy' to me again I will do worse things to you!"

Captain Stoddard stood still for a moment. Then a slow smile crept over his weather-beaten face. "Anne!" he called, and at the sound of his voice the child stopped instantly. "Come here," he said, and she approached slowly with hanging head. "Give me your hand, child," he said kindly, and the little girl slipped her slender fingers into the big rough hand.

"So, Jimmie Starkweather, you'll stand by and see my little girl put upon, will you!" he exclaimed angrily. "I thought better than that of your father's son, to stand by and let a small girl be taunted with what she cannot help. It speaks ill for you."

"I had no time, sir," answered the boy sulkily; "she was upon them both in a second," and Jimmie's face brightened; "it was fine, sir, the way she sent yon lubber over," and he pointed a scornful finger toward the Cary boy, who was now slinking after his sister.

"Here, you Cary boy!" called the captain, "come back here and heed what I say to you. If I know of your opening your mouth with such talk again to my girl here," and he nodded toward Anne, "I'll deal with you myself. So look out for yourself."

"I'll see he keeps a civil tongue, sir," volunteered Jimmie, and Captain Enos nodded approvingly.

"Now, Anne, we'd best step up home," said the captain. "I expect Mistress Stoddard will not be pleased at this."

Anne clung close to the big hand but said no word.

"I am not angry, child," went on the captain. "I like your spirit. I do not believe in being put upon."

"But Mistress Stoddard told me I was not to throw water and sand," responded Anne, "and I forgot her commands. I fear she will not like me now," and remorseful tears dropped over the flushed little cheeks.

"There, there! Do not cry, Anne," comforted the captain; "I will tell her all about it. She will not blame you. You are my little girl now, and those Cary oafs will not dare open their mouths to plague you."

Mrs. Stoddard, looking toward the shore, could hardly credit what she saw—the captain, who but yesterday had declared that Anne should not stay under his roof, leading the child tenderly and smiling upon her!

"Heaven be thanked!" she murmured. "Enos has come to his senses. There'll be no more trouble about Anne staying."

CHAPTER THREE

ANNE'S SECRET

MRS. STODDARD SAID nothing to Anne of the trouble at the spring, and when Anne would have explained her part in it, her friend said quickly: "Captain Enos is not displeased with you, Anne. He thinks the Cary children not well taught at home, and says for you not to play with them," so that Anne had gone happily back to her playhouse, and told "Martha" that there was no one so good as Mistress and Captain Stoddard, "except my dear father," the little girl had added loyally.

"Now, Martha, you must be a good and quiet child," she advised, "for after this you will live in the house with me. You can come out here to play with me, but every night you are to sleep in my bed; and it may be, Mistress Stoddard will let you rest in the kitchen now and then, and you may go with me over the pasture hill to see Brownie."

The big British ships lay quietly at anchor for several days. The men came ashore in boatloads, washed their clothes at the spring, bought such provisions as the little settlement could offer, and wandered about the shore. The citizens treated them not uncivilly, for since the men of Province Town were unable to make any resistance to those they felt to be their country's foes, they knew it to be best to be silent and accept the authority they had not the strength to defy. So the fishing boats swung at anchor in the harbor, and the men lingered about the landing, or fished for plaice fish and sole from their dories near shore.

"We'll be poor indeed when frost comes," complained Mrs. Stoddard; "my molasses keg is near empty now, and the meal barrel not half full. If those Britishers do not soon leave the harbor so that the men can get back to the fishing, this place will know hunger, for our larder is no poorer than our neighbors'."

"Yes," agreed Captain Enos, "the whole coast is feeling the king's displeasure because we will not pay him taxes to fill his pockets, and make slaves of us. I wish we had some news of our Boston friends. The Freemans are well to do, but with Boston beset on all sides with British soldiers they may be hard pressed."

" 'Twill come to worse yet, be sure," predicted Mrs. Stoddard gloomily.

It was but a few days after this when with joyful songs the British sailors made ready to sail, and on a bright July morning the vessels, taking advantage of a fair wind, bent their sails and skimmed away up the coast.

"They are bound for Boston," declared Captain Enos, "and 'tis soon enough they'll be back again. The Boston folk will not let them come to anchor, I'll be bound."

Hardly had the ships got under headway before the fishermen were rowing out to their sailboats, and soon the little fleet was under sail bound off Race Point toward the fishing grounds.

"Now, Anne, you had best go after Brownie and bring her back to her old pasture. I like not the long tramp morning and night to milk the creature," said Mrs. Stoddard, and she watched Anne, with the wooden doll clasped in her arm, go obediently off on her errand.

A little smile crept over her face as she stood in the doorway. "Captain Enos would like well that Anne be called Anne Stoddard," she said aloud; "he begins to recall good traits in her father, and to think no other child in the settlement has the spirit that our girl has. And I am well pleased that it is so," she concluded with a little sigh, "for there will be poor days ahead for us to bear, and had the captain not changed his mind about

Anne I should indeed have had hard work to manage," and she turned back to her simple household tasks.

Anne went slowly up the sandy slope, stopping here and there to see if the beachplums showed any signs of ripening, and turning now and then to see if she could pick out Captain Enos's sail among the boats going swiftly out toward the open sea.

As she came in sight of the little grove of maples her quick eyes saw a man moving among them. Brownie was quietly feeding, evidently undisturbed. Anne stopped, holding Martha very tightly, her eyes fixed upon the moving figure. She was not afraid, but she wondered who it was, for she thought that every man in the settlement had gone to the fishing grounds. As she looked, something familiar in the man's movements sent her running toward the grove.

"It is my father. I know it is my father," she whispered to herself. As she came down the slope the man evidently saw her, for he came out from the wood a little as if waiting for her.

"Anne, Anne!" he exclaimed, as she came near, and in a moment his arm was around her and he was clasping her close.

"Come back in the wood, dear child," he said. "And you have not forgotten your father?"

Anne smiled up at him happily. "I could never do that," she responded. "See, here is my doll. Her name is Martha Stoddard Nelson."

"An excellent name," declared the man smilingly. "How neat and rosy you look, Anne! You look as if you had fared well. Be they kind to you?"

"Oh, yes, father. They say now that I am their little girl. But I am not," and Anne shook her head smilingly. "I am my own father's little girl; though I like them well," she added.

The two were seated on a grassy hummock where no eye could see them; but from time to time John Nelson looked about furtively as if expecting some one to appear.

"You are not a 'traitor' or a 'spy,' are you, father?" questioned the child. "When the Cary children did say so I chased them from the spring, and Captain Enos said I did well. But I did think you lost at sea, father!"

The man shook his head. "Try and remember what I tell you, child, that you may know your father for an honest man. The day

I left harbor on my fishing trip I was run down by one of those British vessels. The sloop sank, and they threw me a rope and pulled me on board. It was rare sport for their sailors to see me struggle for my very life." The man stopped and his face grew very grave and stern. "Then they said they were coming into Cape Cod Harbor, and that I should be their pilot. They said they would make a good bonfire of the shanties of the settlement. And then, child, I misled them. I laughed and said, "Tis a settlement of good Royalists if ever there was one.' They would scarce believe me. But they came into harbor, and when the men proved civil and refused them nothing, then they credited what I said. But they told me they were bound for Dorchester Harbor, and there they would make a good English soldier of me. I said nothing, but this morning, in the confusion of making sail, I slipped overboard and swam ashore, bound that I would have a look at my girl and know her safe and well."

"And now, father, shall we go back and live in the little house by the shore? Mistress Stoddard has kept our things safely, and she has taught me many useful things," said Anne proudly.

"No, child. For me to stay in this settlement would bring trouble upon it. Those ships will return here, and if I were found among the men here, then, indeed, would their anger be great. They must think me drowned, else they would indeed make a bonfire of every house along the shore."

"But what will you do, father? You must stay with me now."

"No, dear child. I must make my way up the cape to the settlements and join the Americans. My eyes are opened: 'tis right that they should protect their homes. I will have some information for them, and I no longer have any place here. The Stoddards are good to you, Anne? They task thee not beyond thy strength? And they speak pleasantly to thee?"

"They are ever kind, father; they do smile on me, and Captain Enos does always give me the best piece of fish at table; and he told the Cary children that I was his little girl, and that I was not to be plagued. But he is not my own father," answered Anne, "and if you must go up the cape I will go with you. The nights are warm and pleasant, and I shall like well to sleep out-of-doors with the stars shining down on us. And if you go with the Americans I will go too. They will not mind one little girl!"

Her father smoothed the dark hair tenderly and smiled at the eager, upturned face.

"You love me, Anne, and I'll not forget that I have a dear, brave daughter waiting for me. I'll be the braver and the better man remembering. But you cannot go with me. I shall be scant fed and footsore for many a long day, and I will not let you bear any hardship I can keep from you. It will be a joy to me to know you safe with Mistress Stoddard; and if I live they shall be repaid for all they do for you. They are indeed kind to you?" he again questioned anxiously.

"They are indeed," responded Anne, seriously.

"Now I must begin my journey, Anne. And do not say that you have seen me. Keep in your heart all I have told you. I shall come for you when I can. But you are to be happy and not think of me as in danger. A brave man is always quite safe, and I wish you to believe that your father is a brave man, Anne."

"Am I not to tell Mistress Stoddard?"

"Tell no one, Anne. Remember. Promise me that when they speak of me as drowned you will say no word!"

"I will not speak, father. But if they do say 'traitor' or 'spy' I am not to bear it. Captain Enos said I need not."

A little smile came over the man's face and he nodded silently. Then he kissed his little daughter and again promising that it should not be long before he would come for her, he turned and made his way through the wood, and soon Anne could no longer see him.

For a long time the little girl sat silent and sorrowful where he had left her. She had forgotten all about the little brown cow; her wooden doll lay neglected on the grass beside her. But after a little she remembered the errand on which she had been sent, and, picking Martha up, started off to drive Brownie back to the pasture near home.

Anne was so quiet that day that at night Mrs. Stoddard questioned her anxiously. "Have those Cary children been saying hateful words to you again, child?" she asked.

"No, I have not been to the spring," answered Anne.

"Has Jimmie Starkweather been telling thee more foolish tales of a big wolf that comes prowling about at night?" continued Mrs. Stoddard.

"Oh, no, Mistress Stoddard. And indeed I do not think Jimmie Starkweather would frighten me. You know his father has seen the wolf. 'Twas near Blackwater Pond."

"Then, child, I fear you are ill. Your face is flushed and you left your porridge untasted. Would you like it better if I put a spoonful of molasses over it?"

Anne nodded soberly. Molasses was not to be refused, even if she must live without her brave father; and so she ate her porridge, and Mrs. Stoddard patted her on the shoulder, and told her that the beach plums would soon be ripening and then she should have a pie, sweet and crusty. And if the captain did well at the fishing, and the British ships kept their distance, she should have some barley sugar, a great treat in those days.

"We'll be getting you some sort of footgear before long, too," promised Mrs. Stoddard. "I have enough wool yarn in the house to knit you a good pair of warm stockings. 'Tis an ugly gray; I wish I could plan some sort of dye for it to make it a prettier color."

"But I like gray," said Anne. "Last winter my feet were cold, and ached with the chilblains. My father knew not how to get stockings for me, and cut down his own, but they were hard to wear."

"I should say so!" said Mrs. Stoddard; "a man is a poor manager when it comes to fending for children's clothes. 'Tis well I am provided with some warm garments. When the frost comes you shall learn to knit, Anne; and if we be in good fortune you shall do a sampler." And Anne, comforted and somewhat consoled by all these pleasant plans for her future happiness, went to sleep that night with the wooden doll closely clasped in her arms, wishing her father might know how good Mistress Stoddard was to her.

CHAPTER FOUR

ANNE AND THE WOLF

"A PIE OF beach plums, sweet and crusty," Anne repeated to herself the next day as she carried Martha out to the playhouse, and rearranged her bits of crockery, and looked off across the harbor.

"I do wish they would ripen speedily," she said aloud. "Indeed those I tasted of yesterday had a pleasant flavor, and I am sure Mistress Stoddard would be well pleased if I could bring home enough for a pie. I will take the small brown basket and follow the upper path, for the plum bushes grow thickly there," and Martha was carefully settled in her accustomed place, and Anne ran to the house for the brown basket, and in a few moments was following a sandy path which led toward the salt meadows.

She stopped often to pick the yellowing beach plums, and now and then tasted one hopefully, expecting to find the sweet pungent flavor which the children so well loved, but only once or twice did she discover any sign of ripeness.

"I'll cross the upper marsh," she decided; " 'tis not so shaded there, and the sun lies warm till late in the day, and the plums are sure to be sweeter. I hope my father finds many to eat

27

along his journey. I wish I had told him that it was best for me to go with him. We could have made little fires at night and cooked a fish, and, with berries to eat, it would not have been unpleasant."

The July sun beat warmly down, but a little breath of air from the sea moved steadily across the marshes filled with many pleasant odors. Here and there big bunches of marsh rosemary made spots of soft violet upon the brown grass, and now and then little flocks of sand-peeps rose from the ground and fluttered noisily away. But there was a pleasant midsummer stillness in the air, and by the time Anne had crossed the marsh and reached the shade of a low-growing oak tree she began to feel tired and content to rest a time before continuing her search for ripe beach plums.

"I wish I had put Martha in the basket," she thought as she leaned comfortably back against the scrubby trunk of the little tree; "then I could have something to talk to." But she had not much time to regret her playmate, for in a second her eyes had closed and she was fast asleep. There was a movement in the bushes behind her, a breaking of twigs, a soft fall of padded feet, but she did not awaken.

A big animal with a soft, gray coat of fur, with sharp nose and ears alertly pointed, came out from the woods, sniffed the soft air cautiously, and turned his head warily toward the oak tree. The creature was evidently not alarmed at what he saw there, for he approached the sleeping child gently, made a noiseless circle about her, and then settled down at her feet, much as a big dog might have done. His nose rested upon his paws and his sharp eyes were upon the sleeping child.

In a little while Anne awoke. She had dreamed that Jimmie Starkweather had led a beautiful, big gray animal to Mistress Stoddard's door, and told her that it was a wolf that he had tamed; so when she opened her eyes and saw the animal so near her she did not jump with surprise, but she said softly, "Wolf!"

The creature sprang to its feet at the sound of her voice, and moved off a few paces, and then turned and looked over its shoulder at Anne.

"Wolf!" Anne repeated, brushing her hair from her eyes and

pulling her sunbonnet over her head. Then she reached out for the plum basket, and stood up. Still the animal had not moved.

"I do believe it is tame," thought Anne, and she made a step toward her visitor, but the gray wolf no longer hesitated, and with a bound it was off on a run across the marsh, and soon disappeared behind a clump of bushes.

"I wish it had stayed," Anne said aloud, for there had been nothing to make her afraid of wild creatures, and Jimmie's stories of a big wolf ranging about the outskirts of the settlement had not suggested to her that a wolf was anything which would do her harm, and she continued her search for beach plums, her mind filled with the thought of many pleasant things.

"I do think, Mistress Stoddard, that I have plums enough for a pie," she exclaimed, as she reached the kitchen door and held up her basket for Mistress Stoddard's inspection.

" 'Twill take a good measure of molasses, I fear," declared Mrs. Stoddard, "but you shall have the pie, dear child. 'Twill please Captain Enos mightily to have a pie for his supper when he gets in from the fishing; and I'll tell him 'twas Anne who gathered the plums," and she nodded smilingly at the little girl.

"And what think you has happened at the spring this morning?" she went on, taking the basket from Anne, who followed her into the neat little kitchen. "Jimmie Starkweather and his father near captured a big gray wolf. The creature walked up to the spring to drink as meek as a calf, and Mr. Starkweather ran for his axe to kill it, but 'twas off in a second."

"But why should he kill it?" exclaimed Anne. "I'm sure 'tis a good wolf. 'Twas no harm for it to drink from the spring."

"But a wolf is a dangerous beast," replied Mrs. Stoddard; "the menfolk will take some way to capture it."

Anne felt the tears very near her eyes. To her, the gray wolf had not seemed dangerous. It had looked kindly upon her, and she had already resolved that if it ever were possible she would like to stroke its soft fur.

"Couldn't the wolf be tamed?" she questioned. "I went to sleep near the marsh this morning and dreamed that Jimmie Starkweather had a tame wolf." But for some reason, which Anne herself could not have explained, she did not tell her good friend of the wild creature which had come so near to her when she slept, and toward whom she had so friendly a feeling, and Mrs. Stoddard, busy with her preparations for pie-making, did not speak further of the wolf.

There was a good catch of fish that day, and Captain Enos came home smiling and well pleased.

"If we could hope that the British ships would keep out of harbor we could look forward to some comfort," he said, "but Starkweather had news from an Ipswich fisherman that the 'Somerset' was cruising down the cape, and like as not she'll anchor off the village some morning. And from what we hear, her sailors find it good sport to lay hands on what they see."

The appearance of the beach-plum pie, warm from the oven, turned the captain's thoughts to more pleasant subjects. " 'Tis a clever child to find ripe beach plums in July," he said, as he cut Anne a liberal piece, "and a bit of tartness gives it an excellent flavor. Well, well, it is surely a pleasant thing to have a little maid in the house," and he nodded kindly toward Anne.

After supper when Anne had gone up to her little chamber under the eaves, and Captain Enos and Mrs. Stoddard were sitting upon their front doorstep enjoying the cool of the evening, Captain Enos said:

"Martha, Anne calls you Mistress Stoddard, does she not?"

"Always," answered his wife. "She is a most thoughtful and respectful child. Never does she speak of thee, Enos, except to say 'Captain.' She has been in the house for over two months now, and I see no fault in her."

"A quick temper," responded Captain Enos, but his tone was not that of a person who had discovered a fault. Indeed he smiled as he spoke, remembering the flight of the Cary children.

"I would like well to have the little maid feel that we were pleased with her," continued the captain slowly. "If she felt like calling me 'Father' and you 'Mother,' I should see no harm in it, and perhaps 'twould be well to have her name put on the town records as bearing our name, Anne Stoddard?" and Captain Enos regarded his wife questioningly.

"It is what I have been wishing for, Enos!" exclaimed Mrs. Stoddard, "but maybe 'twere better for the child to call us 'Uncle' and 'Aunt.' She does not yet forget her own father, you see, and she might feel 'twere not right to give another his name."

Captain Enos nodded approvingly. "A good and loyal heart she has, I know," he answered, "and 'twill be better indeed not to puzzle the little maid. We'll be 'Uncle' and 'Aunt' to her then, Martha; and as for her name on the town records, perhaps we'll let the matter rest till Anne is old enough to choose for herself. If the British keep on harrying us it may well be that we fisherfolk will have to go further up the coast for safety."

"And desert Province Town?" exclaimed Mrs. Stoddard, "the place where your father and mine, Enos, were born and died, and their fathers before them. No—we'll not search for safety at such a price. I doubt if I could live in those shut-in places such as I hear the upper landings are."

Captain Enos chuckled approvingly. "I knew well what you would say to that, Martha," he replied, "and now we must get our sleep, for the tide serves early tomorrow morning, and I must make the best of these good days."

"Captain Enos was well pleased with the pie, Anne," said Mrs. Stoddard the next morning, as the little girl stood beside her, carefully wiping the heavy ironware. "And what does thee think! The captain loves thee so well, child, that it would please him to have thee call him Uncle Enos. That is kind of him, is it not, Anne?" and Mistress Stoddard smiled down at the eager little face at her elbow.

"It is indeed, Mistress Stoddard," replied Anne happily; "shall I begin tonight?"

"Yes, child, and I shall like it well if you call me 'Aunt'; 'twill seem nearer than 'Mistress Stoddard,' and you are same as our own child now."

Anne's dark eyes looked up earnestly into Mistress Stoddard's kind face. "But I am my father's little girl, too," she said.

"Of course you are," answered her friend. "Captain Enos and I are not asking you to forget your father, child. No doubt he did his best for you, but you are to care for us, too."

"But I do, Aunt Martha; I love you well," said Anne, so naturally that Mrs. Stoddard stopped her work long enough to give her a kiss and to say, "There, child, now we are all settled. 'Twill please your Uncle Enos well."

As soon as the few dishes were set away Anne wandered down the hill toward the spring. She no longer feared the Cary children, and she hoped to see some of the Starkweather family and hear more of the gray wolf, and at the spring she found Jimmie with two wooden buckets filled and ready for him to carry home to his waiting mother.

"You missed the great sight yesterday, Anne," he said, as she approached the spring. "What think you! A wolf as big as a calf walked boldly up and drank, right where I stand."

" 'Twas not as big as a calf," declared Anne; "and why should you seek to kill a wild creature who wants but a drink? 'Tis not a bad wolf."

Jimmie looked at her in surprise, his gray eyes widening and shining in wonder. "All wolves are bad," he declared. "This same gray wolf walked off with Widow Bett's plumpest hen and devoured it before her very eyes."

"Well, the poor creature was hungry. We eat plump hens, when we can get them," answered Anne.

Jimmie laughed good-naturedly. "Wait till you see the beast, Anne," he answered. "Its eyes shine like black water, and its teeth show like pointed rocks. You'd not stand up for it so boldly if you had but seen it."

Anne made no answer; she was not even tempted to tell Jimmie that she had seen the animal, had been almost within arm's reach of it.

"I must be going," she said, "but do not harm the wolf, Jimmie," and she looked at the boy pleadingly; "perhaps it knows no better than to take food when it is hungry."

"I'd like its skin for a coat," the boy answered, "but 'tis a wise beast and knows well how to take care of itself. It's miles away by this time," and picking up the buckets he started toward home, and Anne turned away from the spring and walked toward the little pasture where Brownie fed in safety.

She stopped to speak to the little brown cow and to give her a handful of tender grass, and then wandered down the slope and along the edge of the marsh.

"Maybe 'twill come again," she thought, as she reached the little oak tree and sat down where she had slept the day before.

"Perhaps if I sit very still it will come out again. I'm sure 'tis not an unfriendly beast."

The little girl sat very still; she did not feel sleepy or tired, and her dark eyes scanned the marsh hopefully, but as the summer morning drifted toward noon she began to realize that her watch was in vain.

"I s'pose Jimmie Starkweather was right, and the gray wolf is miles away," she thought, as she decided that she must leave the shadow of the oak and hurry toward home so that Aunt Martha would not be anxious about her.

"I wish the wolf knew I liked him," the little girl said aloud, as she turned her face toward home. "I would not chase him away from the spring, and I would not want his gray fur for a coat," and Anne's face was very sober, as she sent a lingering look along the thick-growing woods that bordered the marsh. She often thought of the wolf, but she never saw it again.

CHAPTER FIVE

──── ❦ ────

SCARLET STOCKINGS

"GOOD NEWS FROM Truro, Captain Enos," said Joseph Stark-weather, one morning in August, as the two neighbors met at the boat landing. "There'll be good hope for American freedom if all our settlements show as much wit and courage."

"And what have Truro men done?" demanded Captain Enos. "They are mostly of the same blood as our Province Town folks, and would naturally be of some wit."

Joseph Starkweather's eyes brightened and twinkled at his neighbor's answer.

"'Twas the sandhills helped them," he answered. "You know the little valleys between the row of sandhills near the shore? Well, the British fleet made anchorage off there some days since, and the Truro men had no mind for them to land and spy out how few there were. So they gathered in one of those little valleys and, carrying smooth poles to look like muskets, they marched out in regular file like soldiers over the sandhill; then down they went through the opposite depression and around the hill and back, and then up they came again, constantly marching; and the British, who could be seen getting boats ready to land, thought better of it. They believed that an immense force of American soldiers had assembled, and the ships hoisted sail and made off. 'Twas good work."

"Indeed it was," responded Captain Enos. "I could wish that we of this settlement were not so at the mercy of the British. Our harbor is too good. It draws them like a magnet. I do think three thousand ships might find safe anchorage here," and Captain Enos turned an admiring look out across the beautiful harbor.

"Have you any news of John Nelson?" questioned Joseph Starkweather.

"How could there be news of a man whose boat sunk under him well off Race Point in a southerly gale?" responded Captain Stoddard.

Joseph approached a step nearer his companion and said: "He was on one of the British ships, Enos; he was seen there, and now news comes by way of a Newburyport fisherman that 'twas no fault of John Nelson's. The Britishers ran down his boat and took him on board their ship, and the news goes that when the fleet anchored off here Nelson escaped; swam ashore in the night, the story goes, and made his way to Wellfleet and joined the Americans at Dorchester who are ready to resist the British if need be."

Captain Enos's face brightened as he listened. "That is indeed good news!" he said. "I am glad for our little maid's sake that her father is known to be a loyal man. But 'tis strange he did not seek to see Anne," he continued thoughtfully.

"John Nelson loved the little maid well," declared Joseph Starkweather. "He had but poor luck here, but he did his best. The Newburyport man tells that the British are in great anger at his escape, and vow that the settlement here shall pay well for it when they make harbor here again."

"We have no arms to defend the harbor. 'Tis hard work to rest quiet here," said Captain Enos; "but it is great news to know that our little maid's father is a loyal man. We like the child well."

" 'Twas I sent Anne to your house, Enos," responded Joseph. "My own is so full that I dared not ask Mistress Starkweather to take the child in; and I knew your wife for a kind-hearted woman."

"It was a good thought, Joseph," responded the captain, "and Anne seems well content with us. She has her playhouse under the trees, and amuses herself without making trouble. She is a helpful little maid, too, saving Mistress Stoddard many a step. I must be going toward home. There was an excellent chowder planned for my dinner, and Martha will rejoice at the news from Truro," and the captain hurried toward home.

Halfway up the hill he saw Anne, coming to meet him. "Uncle Enos! Uncle Enos!" she called, "Brownie is lost! Indeed she is. All the morning have I gone up and down the pasture, calling her name and looking everywhere for her, and she is not to be found."

"Well, well!" responded Captain Enos; " 'tis sure the Britishers have not stolen her, for there is not one of their craft in sight. The cow is probably feeding somewhere about; we'll find her safe in some good pasturage. Is the chowder steaming hot and waiting?"

"Yes, Uncle Enos," replied Anne, slipping her hand into the captain's, "but Aunt Martha is greatly concerned about Brownie. She fears the Indians may have driven her off."

"We'll cruise about a little after dinner," answered the captain. "I don't like to think that the Indians would show themselves unfriendly just now," and his pleasant face grew stern and serious.

But his appetite for the chowder was excellent, and when he started out to search for Brownie he was sure that he would find her near the marsh or perhaps in the maple grove further on, where the cattle sometimes wandered.

"Now, Anne, I have an errand for you to do," said Mrs. Stoddard, as the captain started on his search. "I've just remembered that the Starkweather children had good stockings last year of crimson yarn. Now it may be that Mrs. Starkweather has more on hand, and that I could exchange my gray, as she has stout boys to wear gray stockings, for her scarlet yarn; and then we'll take up some stockings for you."

Anne's face brightened. "I should well like some scarlet stockings," she said.

"I mean you to be warmly clad come frost," said Mrs. Stoddard. "Now see that you do the errand well. Ask Mrs. Starkweather, first of all, if she be in good health. It is not seemly to be too earnest in asking a favor. Then say that Mistress Stoddard has enough excellent gray yarn for two pair of long stockings, and that she would take it as a kindness if Mistress Starkweather would take it in exchange for scarlet yarn."

"Yes, Aunt Martha, I will surely remember," and Anne started off happily.

As she passed the spring a shrill voice called her name, and she turned to see Amanda Cary, half hidden behind a small savin.

"Come and play," called Amanda. "I am not angry if you did chase me. My mother says you knew no better!"

Anne listened in amazement. Knew no better! Had not Captain Enos approved of her defense of herself, and were not the Cary children the first to begin trouble with her! So Anne shook her head and walked sedately on.

"Come and play," repeated the shrill voice. "My brother and Jimmie Starkweather are gone looking for our cow, and I have no one to play with."

"Is your cow lost, too?" exclaimed Anne, quite forgetting Amanda's unkindness in this common ill fortune.

Amanda now came out from behind the savin tree; a small, thin-faced child, with light eyes, sandy hair and freckles.

"Yes, and we think the Indians have driven them off. For the Starkweathers' cow is not to be found. 'Twill be a sad loss, my mother says; for it will leave but three cows in the town."

"But they may be found," insisted Anne. "My Uncle Enos has gone now to look for Brownie."

"'Uncle Enos'!" repeated Amanda scornfully. "He's not your uncle. You are a waif. My mother said so, and waifs do not have uncles or fathers or anybody."

"I am no waif, for I have a father, and my Uncle Enos will tell your mother not to say such words of me!" declared Anne boldly, but she felt a lump in her throat and wished very much that she had not stopped to talk with Amanda.

"I don't see why you get angry so quick," said Amanda. "You get angry at everything. I'd just as soon play with you, if you are a waif."

"I wouldn't play with you anyway," said Anne; "I have an errand to do, and if I had not I would rather never play than play with such a hateful, ill-speaking child as you are," and Anne

38

hurried on her way toward the Starkweathers' low-built, weather-beaten house near the shore.

"I shall be glad indeed to get rid of some of my scarlet yarn," declared Mrs. Starkweather, "and you can take home a skein or two of it and tell Mistress Stoddard that her little girl does an errand very prettily. I could wish my boys were as well-mannered."

Anne smiled, well pleased at the pleasant words.

"Uncle Enos says there is no better boy than Jimmie," she responded. "He says he is a smart and honest lad—a 'real Stark-weather,' he calls him," she responded.

"Does he so?" and the woman's thin face flushed with plea-sure at this praise of her eldest son. "Well, we do prize Jimmie, and 'tis good news to know him well thought of, and you are a kindly little maid to speak such pleasant words. Mistress Stod-dard is lucky indeed to have you."

"I call her Aunt Martha now," said Anne, feeling that Mrs. Starkweather was nearly as kind as Mrs. Stoddard, and quite forgetting the trouble of Brownie's loss or of Amanda's teasing in the good woman's pleasantness.

"That is well," replied Mrs. Starkweather. "You will bring her much happiness, I can well see. I could wish you had come to me, child, when your father went; but the Stoddards can do better for you."

"Should I have called you 'Aunt'?" Anne asked a little wistfully.

"Indeed you should, and you may now if Mistress Stoddard be willing. Say to her that I'd like well to be Aunt Starkweather to her little maid."

So Anne, with her bundle of scarlet yarn, started toward home, much happier than when she had rapped at Mrs. Starkweather's door.

Amanda was still sitting at the spring. "Anne," she called shrilly, "may I go up to your house and play with you?"

Anne shook her head, and without a backward look at the child by the spring kept on her way toward home. She had much to tell her Aunt Martha, who listened, well pleased at her neigh-bor's kind words.

"And Amanda Cary said that their cow was lost, and the

Starkweathers' cow, too. Amos Cary and Jimmie are off searching for them now, and do fear the Indians have driven them off," said Anne.

" 'Twill be bad fortune indeed if that be true," replied Mrs. Stoddard, "for we are not as well provisioned for the winter as usual, and it would be a worrisome thing to have the Indians bothering us on shore and the British to fear at sea. But I'll take up your stockings today, Anne. The yarn is a handsome color, and well spun."

"I think I will not leave Martha at the playhouse after this," said Anne thoughtfully; "something might happen to her."

Mrs. Stoddard nodded approvingly, and Anne brought the wooden doll in.

"Like as not your Uncle Enos will make you a wooden chair for the doll when the evenings get longer," said Mrs. Stoddard. "He's clever with his knife, and 'twill give him something to busy his hands with. I'll call his attention to the doll."

"My!" exclaimed Anne, "I do think an aunt and uncle are nice to have. And a father is, too," she added quickly, for she could not bear that any one should think that she had forgotten her own father.

"Yes, indeed, child; and there's good news of your own father. He was on the British ship and escaped and made his way to Wellfleet to join the American soldiers."

"Oh, Aunt Martha!" and the little girl sprang up from her little stool and grasped her good friend's gown with eager hands, and then told her the story of her father's visit. "But I could not tell it before," she said.

"Indeed you are a loyal little maid," replied Mrs. Stoddard approvingly, "and you must always keep a promise, but see to it that you promise nothing quickly. I think the better of John Nelson that he took great risk to make sure his little daughter was safe and well cared for. The captain will think it good news, too."

"My father will come back some day," declared Anne, and Mrs. Stoddard agreed cheerfully.

"To be sure he will," she said, "but do not think of that too much, dear child. See, I have the stitches all cast on, and your scarlet stockings are really begun."

CHAPTER SIX

❦
——— ❦ ———

CAPTURED BY INDIANS

THE MORE ANNE thought about Brownie the more fearful she became that some harm had befallen the pretty brown cow.

"Her foot may have caught in those twisted roots on the hill," thought the little girl, "or perhaps the Indians have fastened her in the woods. I do believe I could find her, and save Uncle Enos the trouble," and the more Anne thought of it the more eager she became to search for Brownie; and, on the day that the scarlet stockings were begun, Anne resolved to walk up the hill and look about for the missing cow.

As she trudged along she thought of many things, of the gray wolf, which had disappeared completely, having probably made its way up the cape to better hunting grounds; and she thought a great deal about her father, and of the day he had come to tell her of his safety. But Anne did not think much about the Indians. The cape settlements had been on friendly terms with the Chatham Indians for some time, and the people of Province Town were more in peril from the freebooters of the sea than from Indians.

Anne had climbed the hill, passed the grove of scrubby pines, and stood looking across the sand dunes toward the open

41

sea. She had looked carefully for Brownie, but there was no trace of her. But Anne was sure that, at the edge of the pine woods, some creature had been near her. She had lived out-of-doors so much that her ears were quick to distinguish any sound. At first she had wondered if it might not be the wolf, and, as she stood looking across the sand, she almost hoped that it might be. "Perhaps I could tame it and have it live at our house," she thought, and then remembered what Aunt Martha had said: that it would be a hard winter, "and wolves eat a good deal, I suppose," decided Anne, "so 'twill not be wise to tame it."

Had she looked behind her she would not have felt so secure. An Indian woman had been following Anne, and was now within arm's reach of her. And Anne had just come to her decision in regard to the wolf, when a blanket fell over her head, was quickly twisted about her, and she felt herself lifted from the ground. Then she heard a chatter of voices in a strange tongue, and realized that she was being carried away from the pine woods. She tried to free herself from the blanket, and tried to call out; but she could not move, and her voice made only a muffled sound. She heard a laugh from the squaw who was carrying her so easily, and in a moment felt herself dropped on the soft sand, and held down firmly for a moment. Then she lay quietly. She knew, though she could not see, that a canoe was being launched. There was talk among a number of people near her, and then she was lifted and put into the canoe, and again firmly held by a strong arm. Then came the smooth dip of paddles, and Anne knew that she was being taken away from home, and she felt the tears on her cheeks. She did not try to scream again, for there had been a rough twist of the blanket about her head when she cried out before, and she was held too firmly to struggle. She could hear the guttural voices of the Indians, and, after what seemed a long time, she realized that her captors were making a landing. She was again dropped on sand, and now the blanket was unwound and Anne stood up. She found herself facing three Indian women. Two of them frowned at her, but the younger smiled and nodded, and patted Anne's shoulder.

The two elder squaws began to talk rapidly, but the one who stood beside Anne remained silent. The canoe was lifted from the beach by the two, as they talked, and carried up toward the rough pastureland. Anne's companion took her by the hand and led her after the others.

"I want to go right home," Anne announced. "You must take me right back to Captain Stoddard's." The young squaw shook her head, still smiling, and Anne realized that her companion could not understand what she said. The little girl stopped short, and then the smile faded from the squaw's face; she gave her an ugly twitch forward, and when Anne still refused to move a stinging blow on the cheek followed. Anne began to cry bitterly. She was now thoroughly frightened, and began to wonder what would become of her.

The squaws hid the canoe carefully, covering it up with vines and brush, and then started along the shore. Anne and her companion now kept close to the other two. And the three squaws talked together. Now and then they would stop, and shading their eyes with one hand, look seaward as if watching for some expected boat, but none appeared. Anne's bare feet began to ache. She believed they would be blistered, but the women paid no attention to her. Anne knew that they were very near the Truro beach. She could see the big waves dashing up in a long curving line, and as they came round a high cliff of sand they came suddenly upon a big fishing boat drawn up on the beach. Two sailors stood by it. In an instant the squaws had turned to flee, dragging Anne with them. But she screamed, and threw herself down on the sand. The sailors came running toward them, and the Indian women fled.

"It's a white child," exclaimed one of the men, picking Anne up, and wiping her face with a big soft handkerchief. "What were they doing with you, child?" And leaning against his friendly arm, Anne told her story, and showed her bruised feet.

" 'Tis lucky for you we put ashore," said the man. "We'll take you home, little maid, safe and sound."

"You are not from Province Town?" Anne ventured to ask, looking up into the kind blue eyes.

"We are good English sailors, my girl," the other man answered her question, "and we borrowed this boat from a settler up shore to get fish for His Majesty's ship *Somerset*; but we'll take you safe home, never fear."

The blue-eyed man lifted Anne into the boat, and the two men were soon pulling strongly at the oars.

" 'Tis a stiff pull to Province Town, but the tide's with us, William," said the last speaker.

Anne sat very quiet. She was wondering if Aunt Martha had missed her, and if Uncle Enos would blame her for having wandered to the outer beach. She looked up to see the sailor whom his companion called "William" smiling at her.

"Do not be afraid," he said kindly; "the folks at home will be glad to see you, and you'll not be scolded."

Anne tried to smile back. She wanted to ask him if he had any little girls of his own; but she remembered that he was an Englishman, and decided that it was best not to say anything.

"Can you walk across the pasture if we set you ashore near here?" asked the sailor, when they had reached the smooth beach near where Anne had been seized by the Indians. "You'll not be troubled again, and we cannot well round the point tonight."

"I can get home from here. I see the pine woods," Anne agreed, and the men ran the boat well up on the beach, and William lifted her out.

" 'Tis hard for those tender feet," he said, "but be quick as you can. My name is William Trull, if your folks ask who 'twas that fetched you home, and my mate's name here is Richard Jones."

"Thank you; my name is Anne Nelson," Anne replied.

She turned back and waved her hand to them when she had reached the land above the shore, and saw them push off their boat and row away. It was very hard now to walk over the rough ground, and Anne felt very tired and unhappy. She kept steadily on, and was soon in sight of home. Mistress Stoddard and Captain Enos were both standing in the doorway looking anxiously toward her.

"Well, well, Anne, and do you think you should stay away like this? And what has become of your sunbonnet?" questioned Mrs. Stoddard.

"Indians!" wailed Anne. "Indian women, Aunt Martha! They carried me off," and, with Mrs. Stoddard's arm about her, and Captain Enos listening in angry amazement, Anne told the story of her adventure.

" 'Twas an evil thing!" declared the captain. "I'm thankful the English sailors were on shore. I'll remember their names."

Mrs. Stoddard bathed the tired feet, and Anne was quite hungry enough to relish the hot corn bread, even though she had no milk to drink with it.

"We must be careful about letting the child wander about alone," Captain Enos said, after Anne was safe in bed that night. " 'Twould be ill fortune indeed if harm befell her."

"I'll keep her more at home," replied Mrs. Stoddard. "She is to begin knitting now, and that will give her amusement indoors."

" 'Tis said that English soldiers are coming into Boston by land and sea," said Captain Enos. "We Province Town people are exempt from military service, but we are loyal to the American forces, and some of us think the time is near when we must let you women stay here by yourselves," and Captain Enos looked at his wife questioningly.

"We'd do our best, Enos, be sure of that," she answered bravely, "and I'd have Anne for company, if you're needed in Boston."

"If we stood any chance of getting there," complained Captain Enos, "without the Britishers making us prisoners. No boat gets by them, I'm told."

"Talk no more of it tonight, Enos. Mayhap things may be settled soon, and these unhappy days well over," and Mistress Stoddard stepped to the door and looked out on the peaceful little settlement. "We have great cause to rejoice this night that our little maid is safe at home," she said.

"I'll make a good search for Brownie tomorrow," declared Captain Enos, "but I fear now that the Indians have her."

The good couple decided that it would be best to say as little of Anne's adventure as possible, and to tell her not to talk of it to her playmates.

"I'll caution the mothers," said Mrs. Stoddard, "but 'tis no use for our little people to frighten themselves by wondering about Indians. Maybe they will not come near us again, and they'll not dare to make another mistake." So but little was made of Anne's escape from the squaws, although the children now stayed at home more closely, and Anne did not often stray far from Aunt Martha.

CHAPTER SEVEN

———— 🍎 ————

OUT TO SEA

CAPTAIN ENOS AND the boys returned without having found any trace of the missing cattle, and the villagers felt it to be a loss hardly to be borne that three of their six cows should have disappeared. The men went about their fishing even more soberly than before, and the women and children mourned loudly.

Amanda Cary waited at the spring each day for Anne's appearance. Sometimes the two little girls did not speak, and again Amanda would make some effort to win Anne's notice.

"Your father is a soldier," she declared one morning, and when Anne nodded smilingly, Amanda ventured a step nearer. "You may come up to my house and see my white kittens if you want to," she said.

There could be no greater temptation to Anne than this. To have a kitten of her own had been one of her dearest wishes, and to see and play with two white kittens, even Amanda's kittens, was a joy not lightly to be given up. But Anne shook her head, and Amanda, surprised and sulky, went slowly back toward home.

The next morning, as Anne went toward the spring, she met Amanda coming up the hill, carrying a white kitten in her arms.

47

"I was just going up to your house," said Amanda. "I was bringing up this white kitten to give to you."

"Oh, Amanda!" exclaimed Anne, quite forgetting her old dislike of the little girl, and reaching out eager hands for the kitten which Amanda gave to her.

"My mother said that we could not afford to keep two kittens," Amanda explained, "and I thought right off that I would give one to you."

"Thank you, Amanda," and then Anne's face grew sober, "but maybe my Aunt Martha will not want me to keep it," she said.

"I guess she will," ventured Amanda. "I will go with you and find out, and if she be not pleased I'll find some one to take it."

The two little girls trudged silently along over the sandy path. Anne carried the kitten very carefully, and Amanda watched her companion anxiously.

"If Mistress Stoddard says that you may keep the kitten may I stay and play a little while?" she asked as they came near the Stoddard house.

"Yes," answered Anne, "you may stay anyway, and I will show you my playhouse."

Amanda's thin freckled face brightened. "If she won't let you keep the kitten you may come over to my house every day and play with mine," she said; and almost hoped that Mistress Stoddard would not want the little white cat, for Amanda was anxious for a playmate, and Anne was nearer her age than any of the little girls of the settlement.

Mrs. Stoddard was nearly as much pleased with the kitten as Anne herself, and Amanda was told that she was a good little girl, her past unkindness was forgotten, and the two children, taking the kitten with them, went out to the playhouse under the pines. Amanda was allowed to hold the wooden doll, and they played very happily together until disturbed by a loud noise near the shore, then they ran down the little slope to see what was happening.

"It's Brownie!" exclaimed Anne.

"And our cow and the Starkweathers'," declared Amanda. "Where do you suppose they found them?"

Jimmie Starkweather drove Brownie up to the little barn, and Mrs. Stoddard came running out to welcome the wanderer.

"Where did they come from, Jimmie?" she questioned.

"A Truro man has just driven them over," explained Jimmie; "he found them in his pasture, and thinks the Indians dared not kill them or drive them further."

"It's good fortune to get them back," said Mrs. Stoddard. "Now you will have milk for your white kitten, Anne. Since the English sailors rescued you from the Indians, they've not been about so much."

The kitten was almost forgotten in petting and feeding Brownie, and Amanda looked on wonderingly to see Anne bring in bunches of tender grass for the little brown cow to eat.

"I cannot get near to our cow," she said; "she shakes her horns at me, and sniffs, and I dare not feed her," but she resolved to herself that she would try and make friends with the black and white animal of which she had always been afraid.

"Come again, Amanda," said Anne, when Amanda said that she must go home, and the little visitor started off happily toward home, resolving that she would bring over her white kitten the very next day, and wondering if her own father could not make her a doll such as Anne Nelson had.

"Thee must not forget thy knitting, Anne," cautioned Mrs. Stoddard, as Anne came in from a visit to Brownie, holding the white kitten in her arms; " 'twill not be so many weeks now before the frost will be upon us, and I must see to it that your uncle's stockings are ready, and that you have mittens; so you must do your best to help on the stockings," and Mrs. Stoddard handed the girl the big ball of scarlet yarn and the stocking just begun on the shining steel needles.

"Remember, it is knit one and seam," she said. "You can sit in the open doorway, child, and when you have knit round eight times we will call thy stint finished for the morning. This afternoon we must go for cranberries. We will be needing all we can gather before the frost comes."

Anne put the kitten down on the floor and took the stocking, eyeing the scarlet yarn admiringly. She sat down in the open doorway and began her stint, her mind filled with happy thoughts. To have Amanda speak well of her dear father, to know that Brownie was safe in the barn, to possess a white kitten of her own, and, above all, to be knitting herself a pair of scarlet stockings made Anne feel that the world was a very kind and friendly place. The white kitten looked at the moving ball of yarn curiously, and now and then made little springs toward it, greatly to Anne's amusement, but in a few moments she found that her progress was slow, and the white kitten was sent off the broad step to play by itself on the sandy path.

From time to time Mrs. Stoddard would come to look at Anne's knitting, and to praise the smoothness of the work.

"Your uncle says you are to have stout leather shoes," she said. "Elder Haven tells me that there will be six weeks' school this autumn and it be good news."

"Shall I go to school, Aunt Martha?" questioned Anne, looking up from her knitting.

Mrs. Stoddard nodded, smiling down at the eager little face. "Indeed you will. 'Twill be the best of changes for you. Like as not Elder Haven will teach thee to write."

"I know my letters and can spell small words," said Anne.

"I'll teach thee to read if time allows," answered Mrs. Stoddard. "Your Uncle Enos has a fine book of large print; *Pilgrim's Progress* it's named, and 'tis of interest. We will begin on it for a lesson."

That afternoon found Anne and Mrs. Stoddard busily picking cranberries on the bog beyond the maple grove. Jimmie Starkweather and Amos Cary were also picking there, and before the afternoon finished, Amanda appeared. She came near Anne to pick and soon asked if Anne was to go to Elder Haven's school.

"Yes, indeed," answered Anne, "and maybe I shall be taught writing, and then I can send a letter, if chance offers, to my father."

"You are always talking and thinking about your father," responded Amanda; "if he should want you to leave the Stoddards I suppose you would go in a minute."

Anne's face grew thoughtful. Never had she been so happy and well cared for as at the Stoddards'; to go to her father would perhaps mean that she would go hungry and half-clad as in the old days, but she remembered her father's loneliness, how he had always tried to do all that he could for her, and she replied slowly, "I guess my father might need me more than Aunt Martha and Uncle Enos. They have each other, and my father has only me."

Amanda asked no more questions, but she kept very close to Anne and watched her with a new interest.

"I wish I could read," she said, as, their baskets well filled, the two girls walked toward home. "I don't even know my letters."

"I can teach you those," said Anne eagerly. "I can teach you just as my dear father did me. We used to go out on the beach in front of our house and he would mark out the letters in the sand and tell me their names, and then I would mark them out. Sometimes we would make letters as long as I am tall. Would you like me to teach you?"

"Yes, indeed. Let's go down to the shore now," urged Amanda.

"We'd best leave our berries safely at home," replied Anne, who did not forget her adventure with the Indian squaws, and was now very careful not to go too far from the settlement, and so it was decided that they should hurry home and leave their baskets and meet on the smooth sandy beach near Anne's old home.

Anne was the first to reach the place. She brought with her two long smooth sticks and had already traced out an enormous A when Amanda appeared.

"This is 'A,' " she called out. " 'A' is for Anne, and for Amanda."

"I know I can remember that," said Amanda, "and I can make it, too."

It was not long before a long row of huge letters were shaped along the beach, and when Amos came down he looked at them wonderingly.

"Amos, can you spell my name?" asked his sister.

"Of course I can!" replied the boy scornfully. "I'll mark it out for you," and in a short time Amanda was repeating over and over again the letters which formed her name.

After Amos had marked out his sister's name in the sand he

started along the shore to where a dory lay, just floating on the swell of the incoming tide.

"Amos is going to fish for flounders," said Amanda; "he catches a fine mess almost every afternoon for mother to cook for supper. He's a great help."

"Want to fish?" called out Amos as the two little girls came near the boat and watched him bait his hooks with clams which he had dug and brought with him.

"Oh, yes," said Anne; "do you think I could catch enough for Uncle Enos's supper?"

"Yes, if you'll hurry," answered the boy; "climb in over the bow."

The barefooted children splashed through the shallow curl of the waves on the beach, and clambered over the high bow of the dory. Amos baited their lines, and with a word of advice as to the best place to sit, he again turned to his own fishing and soon pulled in a big, flopping, resisting flounder.

"The tide isn't right," he declared after a few minutes when no bite came to take the bait. "I'm going to cast off and pull a little way down shore over the flats. They'll be sure to bite there. You girls sit still. You can troll your lines if you want to. You may catch something."

So Anne and Amanda sat very still while Amos sprang ashore, untied the rope from the stout post sunk in the beach, pushed the boat into deeper water, and jumped in as it floated clear from the shore.

It was a big, clumsy boat, and the oars were heavy; but Amos was a stout boy of twelve used to boats and he handled the oars very skillfully.

"The tide's just turning," he said; " 'twill take us down shore without much rowing."

"But 'twill be hard coming back," suggested Amanda.

"Pooh! Hard! I guess I could row through any water in this harbor," bragged Amos, bending to his oar so lustily that he broke one of the wooden tholepins, unshipped his oar, and went over backward into the bottom of the boat, losing his hold on the oar as he fell. He scrambled quickly back to his seat, and endeavored to swing the dory about with one oar so that he could reach the one now floating rapidly away. But he could not get within reach of it.

"You girls move forward," he commanded; "I'll have to scull," and moving cautiously to the stern of the boat he put his remaining oar in the notch cut for it and began to move it regularly back and forth.

"Are you going inshore, Amos?" questioned his sister.

"What for?" asked the boy. "I've got one good oar, haven't I? We can go along first-rate."

"It's too bad to lose a good oar," said Amanda.

"Father won't care," said Amos reassuringly; " 'twa'n't a good oar. The blade was split; 'twas liable to harm somebody. He'll not worry at losing it."

The dory went along very smoothly under Amos's sculling and with the aid of the tide. Amanda and Anne, their lines trailing overboard, watched eagerly for a bite, and before long Anne had pulled in a good-sized plaice, much to Amos's satisfaction. He drew in his oar to help her take out the hook, and had just completed this task when Amanda called out:

"Amos! Amos! the oar's slipping!"

The boy turned quickly and grabbed at the vanishing oar, but he was too late—it had slid into the water. They were now some distance from shore and the tide was setting strongly toward the mouth of the harbor. Amos looked after the oar and both of the little girls looked at Amos.

"What are we going to do now?" asked Amanda. "We can't ever get back to shore."

CHAPTER EIGHT

ON THE ISLAND

AMOS MADE NO answer to his sister's frightened exclamation. He was well used to the harbor, as he often went fishing with his father, and had been on cruises of several days. Tide and wind both took the boat swiftly toward Long Point, a low, narrow sand beach, which ran out into the harbor.

"We'll run straight into Long Point if the wind don't change," said Amos.

Anne had held fast to her line and now felt it tugging strongly in her grasp.

"I've caught something!" she exclaimed, "and I don't believe I can ever pull it in."

Amos reached across and seized the line. "Gee!" he exclaimed, "I'll bet it's a cod," and he pulled valiantly. It took all the boy's strength to get the big fish into the boat. "I'll bet it weighs ten pounds," declared Amos proudly, quite forgetting in his pleasure over the big fish that the boat was still moving swiftly away from the settlement.

"Amos, Amos, just see how fast we are going," said Amanda; "we'll be carried right out to sea."

"Well, then some vessel will pick us up and bring us back,"

answered her brother, "but it looks now as if we would bring up on Long Point, and we can walk home from there easy enough. It's only a couple of miles."

"Perhaps we could get home before they missed us," suggested Anne, hopefully.

Amos nodded; he was still busy with the big fish, but in a few moments he began to look anxiously ahead.

"The wind's pulling round to the southeast," he said. "I guess we sha'n't hit Long Point after all."

"We're going right into Wood End," declared Amanda, "or else to House Point Island. Oh, Amos, if we land on that island nobody will ever find us."

"It will be better to land anywhere than to be carried beyond Race Point," said Amos; "the wind is growing stronger every minute."

The three children no longer felt any interest in their fishlines. Amos had drawn his line in when they started off from shore, and Amanda had let go of hers when the first oar was lost. Anne was the only one who had kept a firm hold on her line, and now she drew it in and coiled it carefully around the smooth piece of wood to which it was fastened.

"I'll get this boat ashore some way," declared Amos boldly; "if we run near any land I'll jump overboard with the painter and pull the dory to shore. I'll get up in the bow now so's to be ready."

Neither of the little girls said anything. Amanda was ready to cry with fear, and Anne was watching the sky anxiously.

"The sun is all covered up with clouds," she said, and before Amos could answer there came a patter of raindrops. The wind, too, increased in force and the waves grew higher. Anne and Amanda crouched low in the boat, while Amos in the bow peered anxiously ahead.

Within the curve of the shore of Race Point lay House Point Island, where Amos hoped they might land. It was a small island partly covered with scrubby thickets but no tall trees, and with shallow water all about it. Amos was sure that he could pull the clumsy boat to shore if the wind would only set a little in that direction. The September afternoon was growing late, the sky was now completely overcast, and the rain falling steadily.

"We're getting near the island," said Amos. "I'll slide overboard in a minute, and all you girls need do is keep still till I tell you to jump," and Amos, the painter of the dory in one hand, slipped over the high bow of the boat and struck out for shore. He was a strong swimmer, and managed to change the course of the boat so that it swung in toward the shallow water, and in a few minutes Amos got a foothold on the sand, and pulled strongly on the rope until the boat was well out of the outward sweep of the current.

"Now jump out," he commanded; "you on one side, Anne, and Amanda on the other, and take hold of the side and help pull the boat ashore."

The two girls obeyed instantly, and the three dripping children struggled up the beach, pulling the dory beyond reach of the tide.

"We must be sure this boat is safe," said Amos; "if we can get it up a little further, we can tip it up on one side and crawl under and get out of the rain."

The codfish, plaice and flounder Amos took out carefully and carried to a large rock further up the beach. "We'll have to eat those fish if we stay here very long," he said.

It grew dark early and the children, under the shelter of the boat, peered out at the rushing waves, listened to the wind, and were very glad that they were on shore, even if it was an island and miles away from home.

"Nobody can find us tonight," said Anne, "but prob'ly tomorrow morning, first thing, my Uncle Enos and your father will take a boat and come sailing right down after us."

"How will they know where we are?" whimpered Amanda. "We'll have to stay here always; I know we shall."

"If we do I'll build a brush house," said Amos hopefully, "and there's lots of beach plums grow on this island, I've heard folks say; and we'll cook those fish and I'll bet I can find mussels along the shore."

"We can't cook anything," said Anne, "for we can't make any fire."

"I can make a fire when things get dry," said Amos; "how do you suppose Indians make fires when they are off like this? An Indian doesn't care where he is because he knows how to get

57

things to eat and how to cook them, and how to make a shelter. I've wished lots of times that I'd had the chances to learn things that Indians have."

The boat proved a shelter against the wind, and the long night wore slowly away. Amos slept soundly, but neither Anne nor Amanda could sleep, except in short naps from which they quickly awakened. The storm ceased in the night and the sun came up and sent its warm beams down on the shivering children, who crept out from the dory and ran and jumped about on the sand until they were quite warm and very hungry.

Amos went searching along the shore for the round dark-shelled mussels which he knew were good to eat, and Anne and Amanda went up toward the thick-growing bushes beyond the sandbanks to look for beach plums.

"Look, Anne! Look! Did you ever see so many on one bush?" exclaimed Amanda, and the bush was indeed well filled with the appetizing fruit.

"We must take a lot to Amos," said Anne, "for he is getting mussels for us now."

"Yes, indeed," agreed Amanda; "do you suppose they will come after us this morning, Anne?"

"Of course they will, first thing," replied Anne hopefully, so that Amanda grew more cheerful, and when they got back to the boat with aprons full of beach plums and found Amos waiting for them with a fine lot of fresh mussels they quite forgot to be troubled or unhappy. The sun was shining brightly, the blue water looked calm and smooth, and the wind had entirely gone. They ate the plums and mussels hungrily.

"We'd better look around a little," said Amos, when they had finished, "and see if we can find a good place for a brush house. We ought to build it near the shore so that we can keep a watch for any passing boat."

"Won't father find us today?" asked Amanda anxiously.

"Can't tell," replied her brother; "anyway we want to get ready to build a house, for we might have to stay here a week."

"I believe you want to stay a week, Amos Cary!" exclaimed his sister.

"I'd just as soon stay as not," said Amos, "if I can find some rotten wood like the Indians use to start a fire; but it isn't much use to look for it until things begin to dry up."

Amos, followed closely by the little girls, went up the bank and toward a place where grew a thicket of small pines. "We can break off a lot of these branches and carry them down to the shore," he said, "and fix some beds of them under one side of the dory. It will be better than sleeping on the sand."

They made several trips back and forth to the boat with armfuls of pine boughs until they each had quite a pile, long and wide enough for a bed, and high enough to keep them well off the sand. But Amos was not satisfied.

"This sandbank makes a good back for a house," he said; "now if we could only build up sides, and fix some kind of a roof, it would make a fine house."

"Won't the dory do for one side?" asked Anne.

"No," said Amos, "but we can pile up heaps of sand here on each side of our beds, right against this sandbank, and that will make three sides of a house, and then we'll think of something for the roof."

So they all went to work piling up the sand. It was hard work, and it took a long time before the loose sand could be piled up high enough for Anne and Amanda to crouch down behind.

"I'm dreadful hungry," said Amanda, after they had worked steadily for some time; "let's rest and eat some mussels and beach plums," and Amos and Anne were both quite ready to stop work.

"It must be past noon now," said Amos, looking at the sun, "and there hasn't a boat come in sight."

Anne had begun to look very serious. "My Aunt Martha may think that I have run away," she said, as they sat leaning back against the piles of warm sand.

"No, she won't," Amos assured her, "for they'll find out right off that Amanda and I are gone, and father's dory, and it won't take father or Captain Enos long to guess what's happened; only they'll think that we have been carried out to sea."

The little girls were very silent after this, until Amos jumped up saying: "I've just thought of a splendid plan. We'll pile up sand just as high as we can on both sides. Then I'll take those fishlines and cut them in pieces long enough to reach across

59

from one sand heap to the other, and tie rocks on each end of the lines and put them across."

"I don't think fishlines will make much of a roof," said Amanda.

"And after I get the lines across," went on Amos, not heeding what his sister had said, "we'll lay these pine boughs across the lines. See? We can have the branches come well over each side and lap one row over another and make a fine roof," and Amos jumped about, greatly pleased with his own invention.

They all returned to piling up sand and before sunset had made walls taller than their heads, and Amos had put the lines across and the covering of pine boughs, so that it was nicely roofed in.

"It will be a lot better than sleeping under the dory," said Anne, as they looked proudly at the little shelter, "and there's pine boughs enough left for beds, too!"

"We can get more tomorrow," said Amos, "and we'll have a fire tomorrow if I can only find some punk, and cook those fish."

"But I want to go home tomorrow," said Amanda; "I know my mother wants me. We've got a boat; can't you make an oar and row us home, Amos?"

"There isn't anything to make an oar out of," answered Amos.

They made their supper on more mussels and beach plums, and then lay down on their beds of boughs in the little enclosure. They could see the moon shining over the water, the big dory hauled up in front of their shelter, and they all felt very glad that they were not drifting out at sea.

Amos had many plans in his head, and was eager for another day to come that he might carry them out, but Amanda and Anne went to sleep hoping only that the next day would see one of the big fishing boats of Province Town come sailing up to the island to take them safely home.

CHAPTER NINE

———— ❦ ————

THE CASTAWAYS

"My, it was cold last night," shivered Amanda, as she and Anne went toward the spring of fresh water which bubbled up near the shore for their morning drink. "I do wish Amos would plan some way to get us home today."

"How can he?" asked Anne; "he hasn't any oars, and see what a long way it is across the water to Long Point. He couldn't swim that far."

"Yes, he could, too," declared Amanda, "and when the tide is out the water is so shallow that you can see the yellow sand shining through. He could swim some and walk some, and he'd get over there all right; then he could walk home and tell father and Captain Enos and they would come right after us."

"Why doesn't he go then?" questioned Anne. "I do know that my Aunt Martha is sadly worried; it is full two days since we set forth."

"Amos likes to stay here," said Amanda, lowering her voice to a whisper; "he thinks it is fun to live as Indians do, and he doesn't want to go home. If he gets enough to eat he'll stay and stay, and then he can tell Jimmie Starkweather of being wrecked on an island."

"Couldn't we get across to Long Point?" asked Anne.

"No. We can't swim, and 'twould be foolish to try," answered Amanda.

"We'll have cooked fish for dinner," said Amos as they ate beach plums for breakfast. "I'm sure I can find some punk somewhere on this island, and while I am looking for it you girls gather all the dry twigs you can find, make a good-sized hole in the sand and fill it up with dry stuff that will take fire quickly, and I'll show you how Indians cook."

"I'd rather have some Indian meal mush," replied Amanda; "can't you swim across to Long Point, Amos, and hurry home and send some one after us?"

Amos looked at her in astonishment, and then smiled broadly. "I know a better way than that," he said, and without waiting to answer the girls' eager questions he ran off toward the thicket of pines.

"We'll dig the hole in the sand, and then find some dry wood," said Anne; "anything cooked will taste good, won't it?"

"Amos knows some way to get us home," said Amanda, "and he's got to tell us what it is, and start just as soon as he cooks his old fish. I wonder what it is!"

Now that Amanda saw a prospect of getting home she felt more cheerful and so did Anne; and they gathered dry brush, bits of bark and handfuls of the sunburned beachgrass until the hole in the sand was filled, and there was a good-sized heap of dry brush over it.

"Do you suppose Amos can really make a fire?" asked Anne.

"I guess he can," said Amanda. "Amos is real smart at queer things like that, that other boys don't think about."

"I've found some!" shouted Amos, as he leaped down the bank; "just a little bit, in the stump of an old oak tree up here. Now wait till I get the tholepins, and you'll see," and he ran toward the dory and returned with a pair of smooth, round tholepins, and sat down on the sand in front of the brush heap. The precious piece of punk was carefully wrapped in a piece of the sleeve of his flannel blouse.

"I had to tear it off," he explained, when Amanda pointed to the ragged slit, "for punk must be kept dry or it isn't a bit of use."

He now spread the bit of flannel on the sand in front of him, and kneeling down beside it began to rub the tholepins across each other as fast as he could move his hands. Anne and Amanda, kneeling on each side of him, looked on with anxious eyes.

"There's a spark!" at last shouted Amanda.

The spark fell on the dry punk, in an instant the punk caught and there were several sparks, then Amos held a wisp of dry grass in front of it and blew vigorously, and the smouldering punk flamed up, the grass caught, Amos thrust it under the dry brush, and in less than a minute the whole mass was burning briskly. The children all jumped about it in delight.

"My, I wish we could have had a fire like that last night, when I was so cold," said Amanda.

"We'll keep it burning now," said Amos. "I've always wanted to start a fire this way. I think it's better than flint and tinder," for in those days the wooden splint matches were not known in the settlement, and fires were started by rubbing flint and steel together until a spark caught.

"We are going home this afternoon," said Amanda, so firmly that Amos looked at her in surprise.

"What for?" he asked. "I think it's fine here. We've got a house and a fire, and we'll have fish enough to last——"

"We are going home," interrupted Amanda; "it's horrid here, and everybody will be afraid we are drowned."

A little smile crept over Amos's freckled face. " 'Twill indeed be a tale to tell Jimmie Starkweather," he said, looking admiringly at the brush-covered shelter, and then at the brisk fire. " 'Tis a shipwreck such as no boy in the settlement has had."

Amos asked no more questions, but sent the girls after more dry brush, while he dug another hole in the sand. Then with a long stick he pushed the hot wood and coals from the first hole into the second, and carefully laid the big plaice fish on the hot sand, pushed a thick covering of hot sand over it, and started a new fire on top of it.

" 'Twill be baked to a turn," he said to his sister and Anne; " 'tis the way the Indians cook fish and mussels and clams. I have seen them."

"We'll go home as soon as we can eat it," said Amanda;

" 'twill be low tide by that time, and if you have no better plan for us, Amos, Anne and I will wade to Long Point."

"Wade!" repeated Amos scornfully; "you'd be drowned."

"Then tell us your plan," urged Amanda, while Anne looked at him pleadingly. She had thought much about her father as she lay awake under the roof of pine boughs, and wondered if some word from him might not have reached the settlement. She thought, too, about the scarlet stockings, and wished herself back in the little brown house on the hill. So she said, "We must go home, Amos."

"I wish you girls had stayed home," muttered Amos; "if some of the boys had come we'd have had a good time here; but girls always want to go home. Well, I'll get you to Long Point without swimming," and again Amos smiled, for he had a secret of his own that he knew would greatly surprise Amanda and Anne.

It was not long before he began scraping the hot embers from the sand under which the fish was cooking. Then he poked the hot sand away, and there lay the plaice, steaming and smoking, and sending out an appetizing odor.

"There!" said Amos proudly, as he managed to cut off a piece with his jackknife for each of the girls, "that's as good fish as you ever tasted."

"It's the best," said Anne, and Amanda ate hungrily. Indeed the children were all so hungry that they devoured the entire fish.

"If you'll stay till tomorrow I'll cook the cod," said Amos, but both Amanda and Anne said they wanted to go home. So Amos with their help pushed and dragged the dory into the water, and then telling the girls to stay right by the boat until he returned, started off up the beach to where he had found the mussels. In a few minutes they saw him running back.

"Look, Amanda!" exclaimed Anne, "he's found an oar!"

The little girls could hardly believe it possible; but Amos was smiling and seemed to think it was a great joke.

"I found it yesterday morning, the very first thing, when you were off after beach plums," he explained, "and I hid it, because I knew if I told you I'd found an oar you'd want to start for home right off; and as long as we were here I wanted some fun out of it. Now jump in, and I'll scull you over to Long Point in no time."

The girls were too glad at the idea of really starting for home to blame Amos for keeping them on the island so long, but Anne thought to herself that she was sure that none of the Stark-weather boys would have hidden the oar. "Amos is smart, but he's selfish," she decided, as the boy bent to the big oar and sent the clumsy boat toward Long Point.

" 'Tis a good oar, better than the one I lost," said Amos, "and I do think 'twas lost from one of the English ships. There's a big 'S' burned into the handle. Mayhap it belonged to the *Somerset.* If so I'm glad they lost it."

" 'Twas the *Somerset* ran down my father's boat and nigh drowned him," said Anne, "and the sailors lent him no help, but laughed to see him struggle till he reached near enough their ship to clamber up."

"I wish I could be a soldier like your father," said Amos, and at this Anne looked upon him more kindly.

"Scull faster, Amos," urged Amanda; "the sun is not two hours high, and 'tis a long walk through the sand before we can get home. I do hope we'll get there before milking time that I may have a drink of warm milk."

When the boat touched the sandy shore of Long Point, Anne and Amanda scrambled over the bow and urged Amos to hurry.

"I must make the boat safe," he said; " 'twould be a sad loss to have the tide take her out. And I'll hide this good oar, too. Tomorrow Jimmie Starkweather and I will sail down and tow her back, and maybe take a look at the island," and Amos looked back regretfully to the shores they had just left.

The dory was drawn up beyond reach of the tide, the oar hidden under the sand, and the children started on their walk toward home. The distance was but two miles, but walking through the loose sand was hard and tiresome.

"I slip back a step every step I take," said Anne; "look, the sun is nearly out of sight now."

"The milk will be strained and set ere this," said Amanda mournfully; "there's not even a beach plum grows on this point, and the long grass cuts my feet whenever I come near it."

"You could have had another baked fish by this time if you would have stayed on the island," said Amos complainingly.

After this the children plodded on in silence for a long time. The harvest moon rose beyond the harbor and smiled down upon them. There was a silvery glint all over the water, and as they came round one of the big piles of sand, which are so often seen along the coast of Cape Cod, they all stopped and looked out across the harbor. It was Amos who pointed toward a big ship riding at anchor, perhaps a mile from the shore.

"There's the *Somerset* back again," he said. "I wonder if there's any harm done at the settlement?"

CHAPTER TEN

——— 🍎 ———

SAFE AT HOME

IT WAS LATE in the evening when the three tired, hungry children reached the settlement. Amanda and Amos ran up the path to their door and Anne plodded on toward Mrs. Stoddard's, nearly a half mile from the Cary house.

There was not a light to be seen in the village, but Anne could see the shining lanterns on the *Somerset* sending narrow rays of light across the water. But she was too tired to think of the British ship, or of anything except how good it would be to sleep in a real bed again.

At Mrs. Stoddard's door she stood for a moment wondering if she could not creep in and upstairs without waking Uncle Enos and Aunt Martha; she tried the door softly, but it was bolted, so she rattled the latch and called, "Aunt Martha! Uncle Enos!" a sudden fear filling her heart that they might not hear her and that she might have to sleep on the doorstep.

But in an instant she heard steps hurrying across the kitchen floor, the big bolt was pulled back, the door swung open, and Anne was warmly clasped in Aunt Martha's arms. Uncle Enos hurried close behind her, and Anne was drawn into the kitchen with many exclamations of wonder and joy.

"Light a candle that we may look at her," said Aunt Martha, "and start up a fire. 'Tis a chilly night, and the child must have some warm porridge."

It was not long before the fire was burning brightly, a kettle of hot water bubbling cheerfully, that Anne might have a warm bath to rest and soothe her tired limbs, and Anne, sitting on Aunt Martha's lap, was eating a bowl of hot porridge and telling the story of her adventures.

"House Point Island, eh?" said Uncle Enos; " 'tis lucky there was an island just there, even so low a one as that. In a hundred years or so the tides and waves will sweep it away."

Anne told of the brush-covered shelter, of Amos making a fire and cooking the fish, and of their journey home, while her kind friends listened eagerly.

"We feared the boat had been carried out to sea and that our little maid was lost," said Aunt Martha, "and the men have looked for you all about the shore. The *Somerset* is in harbor and its crew are doing much mischief on shore, so that we have had much to disturb us. What a tangle of hair this is for me to brush out," she added, passing a tender hand over Anne's dark locks.

How good the warm water felt to Anne's bruised feet; and she was sure that nothing ever tasted so good as the porridge. The rough hair was brushed into smooth braids, and it was a very happy little girl who went to sleep in the upper chamber with her wooden doll beside her, and the white kitten curled up on the foot of her bed.

"I'm glad I'm not a little Indian girl," was Anne's last thought before she went to sleep.

It was late the next morning when she awoke. Her soiled and torn clothes were not to be seen, but a dress of clean cotton and a fresh pinafore lay on the wooden stool.

"My, it's nice to be clean," thought Anne, remembering the uncomfortable efforts that she and Amanda had made to wash their faces in water from the island spring.

"It's near noon, dear child," said Mrs. Stoddard, as Anne came into the kitchen. "You shall have a boiled egg for your breakfast, and I am cooking a fine johnnycake for you before the fire. You must be nigh starved. To think of that Amos Cary hiding the oar instead of fetching you straight home."

"But he worked all the time to make a house for us, and to cook the fish," explained Anne, "and he speaks well of my father. I like him better than when he called me names."

"Of course you do, child; and I did not think him so smart a boy as he proves. 'Twas no small thing to start a fire as he did."

" 'Twas Amanda made him come home," said Anne; "she told him we would walk through the water to the Point, and then he said he would fetch us."

"Your Uncle Enos thinks Amos may make a good sailor," said Aunt Martha. "Indeed, if it were not for these British ships hovering about our shores it is likely that Skipper Cary would have been off to the Banks and taken Amos with him."

The "Banks" were the fishing grounds off the island of Newfoundland, and for several years the Cape Cod fishermen had made summer cruises there, coming home with big cargoes of fine fish which they sold in the Boston market at excellent prices. These fishing grounds were called the "Banks" because of the heavy banks of fog which settled down in that region.

After Anne had finished her breakfast she went to Mrs. Stoddard's big workbasket, and took out her knitting-work.

"May I not knit a long time today, Aunt Martha?" she asked. "My feet ache sorely, and I should like well to knit."

"That is right," answered Mrs. Stoddard, nodding her approval. "Your Uncle Enos drove Brownie over the hill where the sailors from the *Somerset* will not be like to see her, and we will both stay indoors today and knit. Maybe we shall begin to read today, also."

"After I have knit a good stint," said Anne, "for 'twill be time for stockings soon."

It was a happy morning for the little girl. She worked steadily and carefully until Captain Enos came up from the shore for his noon meal.

"Well, well," he said smilingly, "now this seems good—to see our little maid safe at home by the window with her knitting. I saw Mistress Starkweather as I came home, and she bade me tell you she should walk this way to see you this afternoon. 'Tis a great day for Amos," continued the captain; "he tells all the boys in the village of his great adventure in rounding Long Point and living two days on an island. You'd think he'd seen Terra del Fuego, to say the least."

"And what is Terra del Fuego?" asked Anne wonderingly.

" 'Tis a far island, Anne, in warm southern seas, such a

distance as few Cape Cod sailors ever go; though we go to most places, I will say," he added with a hearty laugh.

"Amos and Jimmie Starkweather were all for sailing off this morning to bring the dory home," he continued, "but a boatload of the *Somerset*'s men stopped them and sent them ashore, threatening to dismast any sloop that put up a sail in this harbor without their permission."

Anne knit steadily on, thinking of her father, and wondering if these men on board the *Somerset* had any knowledge of him. But she asked no questions, knowing that Captain Enos would tell her if any news came.

The scarlet stockings had made good progress when Mistress Starkweather was seen coming up the sandy path. Anne ran to the door to meet her, and the good woman kissed her heartily. "To think of the danger you were in, dear child," she said, as Anne led her into the sunny kitchen and drew out the most comfortable chair for her.

"Amos was not afraid," said Anne, "but Amanda and I did wish ourselves home."

"I'll warrant that boy would not be afraid of the water, storm or no storm," said Mrs. Stoddard, drawing her own chair near to her neighbor's; "yet Captain Enos tells that he fled from our Anne here when she threw water at him," and the two women smiled, remembering the little girl's loyal defense of her absent father.

"School is to begin next Monday, if all goes well," continued Mrs. Starkweather, "and beside that the minister declared we must all come more punctually to church. Last Sunday there were but seven in the meetinghouse," and Mrs. Starkweather's face grew sober.

"I shall not have time to learn to read long words before Monday," said Anne anxiously.

"I planned to teach the child a little before school begins," explained Mrs. Stoddard, "from Captain Enos's *Pilgrim's Progress*. His mother bought the book in Boston, and he treasures it."

"And no wonder," replied Mrs. Starkweather; "beside the Bible there are few books in any household in the settlement. I doubt if the minister can lay claim to a half dozen. He has his knowledge in his head."

"And so should all people have," said Mrs. Stoddard. "Anne, go to the big red chest in my bedroom and take out the book that lays there and fetch it to me. Mayhap Mistress Starkweather would like to see it."

Anne quickly obeyed. The big red chest was one that Captain Enos had carried when he went on whaling voyages. It had handles of twisted rope, and a huge padlock swung from an iron loop in front. Anne lifted the top and reached in after the book; but the chest was deep; there were only a few articles on the bottom of the chest, and she could not reach it. So she pushed the lid back until it rested against the wall, and stepped into the chest, stooping down to pick up the book. As she leaned over, bang—down came the lid to the chest, shutting Anne closely in. For an instant the child was too frightened to move, as she lay on her face in the big chest; then she tried to sit up, and found she could not. She tried to call "Aunt Martha," but her voice sounded thick and muffled.

In the kitchen the two neighbors sat waiting for Anne and the book.

"Anne! Anne!" called Mrs. Stoddard. "Why, the child is usually so spry. I wonder what keeps her," and she went into the bedroom.

"Did Anne slip out while we talked?" she called back to Mrs. Starkweather. "She's not here."

Just then there came a sound from the chest. "Pity's sake!" exclaimed Mrs. Stoddard. "I do believe Anne is in the chest," and she hastened to swing back the big lid and to lift the half-stifled child out.

"Did you ever!" she said. "How came you in the chest, child?"

"I got in to get the book and the lid fell on me," half whispered Anne, clinging to Mrs. Stoddard's skirts.

"Well, well, child, there is no harm done," said Mrs. Stoddard, "but 'tis not a safe thing to get into chests. I will get the book. I thought your arms were longer," and Mrs. Stoddard reached into the sea chest and drew out a long black-covered

71

book. "It has many pictures," she said. "I wonder I have not shown it to Anne before."

Mrs. Starkweather looked at the book admiringly, and Mrs. Stoddard took Anne in her lap that they might all enjoy the pictures together.

"Look," she said; "here is Christian setting forth on his journey, and here are Obstinate and Pliable, two of his neighbors, following him to urge him to come home."

Anne looked at the picture eagerly. She had never seen pictures in a book before, and it seemed very wonderful to her.

"It is a good story," said Mrs. Starkweather. "True, it is said to be but a dream, but I read it in my youth and liked it well. It has been a treat to see it, Mrs. Stoddard. 'Tis seldom I have so carefree an afternoon. Six boys to look after keep me busy," and the good woman rose from her chair and with cordial words of goodbye started for home.

"I wish I could read this book," said Anne, turning the leaves over carefully and wondering what the pictures meant.

"So you shall. We'll read a little now. Come, you shall spell out the words, and I will speak them for you and tell you their meaning."

An hour later when Captain Enos stepped into the kitchen he declared that he thought school had begun there; and while Mrs. Stoddard hurried about to prepare supper Uncle Enos continued Anne's reading lesson.

"Perhaps I can read this book after I go to school," said Anne.

"That you can," answered the captain.

"And I will learn to write," said Anne, "and it may be I could send a letter to my dear father."

"That is a good child," said Captain Enos, patting the dark head; "learn to write and we'll set about starting the letter to your father as soon as you have it ready."

"I shall have much to tell him," said Anne, smiling up into Uncle Enos's kind face.

"And he'll have a good deal to tell you," replied Captain Enos. "I wish I could see him myself. I'd like news of what's going on in Boston."

CHAPTER ELEVEN

———— 🍎 ————

CAPTAIN ENOS'S SECRETS

THE PLAYHOUSE UNDER the pines was almost forgotten as the days grew colder, and the fall rains came, with high winds; and Anne's scarlet stocking was now long enough for Aunt Martha to "set the heel" and begin to shape the foot. School had begun in Elder Haven's sitting room, with fourteen scholars, and Anne was learning to write.

"Master Haven says I write my own name nicely," she said at the end of the first week, "and that by the time school closes he thinks I can write a letter."

Captain Enos nodded approvingly. He and Anne were sitting before a bright fire of driftwood in the pleasant kitchen, while Mrs. Stoddard had gone to Mrs. Starkweather's for more scarlet yarn. Anne was knitting busily; her wooden doll sat on the floor, and the white kitten was curled up close to the little girl's feet. Captain Enos had several pieces of smooth cedar wood on a stool near his chair, and was at work upon one with his sharp jackknife.

"Well, well!" he said, looking up from his whittling. "That will please thy father, Anne. And learn as fast as you can, for I see a fair chance of sending a letter to Boston, when one is ready; and then thy father could soon get it."

"Oh, Uncle Enos!" exclaimed Anne, "if there be a chance to send a letter could you not write for me? It may be when I can write there will be no chance to send a letter."

Captain Enos nodded. "You are a wise child," he said. "My writing isn't the plainest in the world, but I'll do my best. I have some sheets of good smooth paper in my sea chest, and a good quill pen, too. Elder Haven fixed the pen for me from the feather of a wild goose I killed on the marshes last spring. But I do not think there is such a thing as ink in the house; but I can make a fair ink with the juice of the elderberry and a fair lot of soot from the chimney. So think up what you wish to tell your father, Anne, and if it storms tomorrow we'll write the letter."

"How will you send it, Uncle Enos?" asked Anne, forgetting to knit and turning eager eyes toward the captain.

"Sshh!" said Captain Enos. " 'Tis a secret—hardly to be whispered. But there is a good-hearted sailorman on board the British ship. We have had some talk together on the shore, and he told me that he liked thy father; and that he did not blame him for escaping from the ship."

Anne nodded smilingly, and reached down and picked up her wooden doll.

"Has the sailorman any little girl?" she asked.

"That he has," said Captain Enos. "He told me that he had two small maids of his own in Plymouth, England, far across the ocean; and he asked if I knew aught of John Nelson's little girl."

"That's me!" said Anne, holding the wooden doll tight.

"Yes," said Captain Enos, "and he said that he might find a chance to send some word to thy father that you were a good and happy child. Then I told him, Anne, that you planned to write a letter, and he said he'd take it to Boston, and then 'twould soon reach thy father."

"I wish I could hear the sailorman speak of my father," said Anne, "and tell me of his little girls in England."

"Mayhap you can, child. He comes ashore after water each day. A stout man he is, with reddish hair and good honest blue eyes. He tells me his name is William Trull. If you see such a man you may speak to him."

"Uncle Enos! That is the sailorman who saved me from the Indian women, and brought me safe home," exclaimed Anne. "Do you not remember?"

"Indeed I do, Anne. And I thought the name would mean something to you," replied Captain Enos.

Anne smiled happily. It was good news to hear from the sailorman, and to know that he was a friend of her father's.

"What are you making, Uncle Enos?" asked Anne, as the captain put down one smooth bit of wood and picked up another.

Captain Enos pointed to Anne's wooden doll and whispered, "I'm afraid Martha Stoddard Nelson will hear. Put her down behind your chair and come over here, and I'll tell you."

Anne set the doll down carefully, with its head turned away from Captain Enos, and tiptoed across the little space between them.

"I'm making a chair for Martha Stoddard Nelson," whispered Captain Enos, "for a surprise. And you mustn't tell her a word about it till it is all ready for her to sit in."

Anne laughed. To have a secret with Uncle Enos was about the most delightful thing she could imagine; and to have it mean a fine cedar chair for her doll to sit in was the best kind of a secret.

"You mustn't let Martha Stoddard Nelson face toward me more than you can help," went on Uncle Enos. "You don't think she has noticed what I am doing, do you?"

"No," whispered Anne. "I'll be very careful, and let her stay upstairs a good deal until the chair is finished."

"That will be a good plan," said Uncle Enos, "and there comes your Aunt Martha. I hear her at the door."

Anne ran to open the door and Mrs. Stoddard came in smiling and rosy from her walk in the sharp wind. The white kitten jumped up and came running toward her, and the good woman looked about the cheerful room as if she thought it the finest place in the world.

"I have more scarlet yarn," she said, sitting down near Captain Enos, "and I have a present for thee, Anne; something that Mistress Starkweather sent thee with her love," and Mrs. Stoddard handed Anne a small package.

"It's a box!" declared the little girl, taking off the paper in which it was wrapped, "and see how sweet it smells."

" 'Tis of sandalwood," said Captain Enos. "There must be many such in the settlement, for 'twas but a few years ago that some of our men came back from a voyage to Ceylon, and fetched such boxes in their chests."

"Open it, Anne," said Mrs. Stoddard, and Anne carefully took off the cover.

"Look, look!" she exclaimed, holding out the box toward Aunt Martha; "what are these shining things; all pink and round?" and she picked up a string of pink coral beads and held them up.

"Coral beads!" said Aunt Martha. "Mistress Starkweather said that she thought when her husband brought them home she would keep them for a little girl of her own; but since she has but six boys, she says she knows of no little girl to whom she would rather give them than to thee, Anne. And you must go down tomorrow before school begins and thank her properly."

"Coral beads!" repeated Anne, holding up the pink beads and touching them softly. "May I put them around my neck, Aunt Martha?"

"Indeed you may, child. See, here is a clasp of bright gold to hold them," and Mrs. Stoddard fastened the beads around Anne's neck.

" 'Tis a fine gift," said Captain Enos admiringly, "and shows a kind heart in Mistress Starkweather."

"I wish my father could see," said Anne. "When he knows about my scarlet stockings and leather shoes, and the white kitten, and that I go to school and have coral beads, he will think I am the luckiest girl in the world."

"We will write him all that," said Captain Enos.

Just then the wooden latch of the kitchen door rattled and the door swung open.

"It's Amanda!" exclaimed Anne, and Amanda Cary stepped inside and carefully closed the door behind her.

"See, Amanda!" exclaimed Anne happily, "I have had a fine present. Mistress Starkweather gave me these," and she touched the pink beads, "and this!" and she pointed to the sweet-smelling box of sandalwood.

Amanda's thin face brightened. "I've got some coral beads just like yours," she said. "My father got them 'way off across the ocean. When I grow older and times are better, my mother says I shall have a white dress and can wear my coral beads then."

The two little girls played with the doll and kitten and Captain Enos kept on with his work.

"I wish I had a doll," he heard Amanda say. "I have asked Amos to make me one, but he is not clever at whittling out things."

Captain Enos nodded to himself smilingly. Since Anne and Amos and Amanda had been carried down the harbor to House Point Island together, and he had heard how pleasant Amanda had been to Anne, he had liked the Cary children better, and had quite forgiven their old-time teasing ways. After Amanda had started for home he called Anne to him and said, "I have another secret!"

"Yes!" said Anne, with a gay little laugh.

"Would you like to make Amanda Cary a present?" he questioned.

"I could not give her my doll," answered Anne, her bright face growing sober. " 'Tis all I have that my father made."

"But if I make another doll, a fine wooden doll, as near like yours as I can, would you like to give that to Amanda?" asked Uncle Enos.

"Oh, yes! Yes, indeed," said Anne, the smiles all coming back again.

"Then 'tis a secret till I have the doll finished," said Captain Enos; "then maybe you can make a dress for it, and give it to Amanda, just as she gave you her white kitten."

Anne was very happy over this secret; it seemed even better than the new wooden chair for Martha Stoddard Nelson.

"I never gave anybody a present," she said, "but I know it must be the finest thing in the world to give somebody a gift," and she looked up into Uncle Enos's kindly face questioningly.

"You are a good child, Anne," he said, "and I will make the wooden doll as soon as time offers. Now take thy beads and box and Martha Stoddard Nelson to thy room, and I will bring in some wood for Aunt Martha. Then 'twill be time for a bite of supper."

Anne carried her treasures upstairs to the little room. There was a stand in the room now, one that had belonged to her father. It had two drawers, and in one of them Anne carefully put the sandalwood box with the pink coral beads.

"I guess I have more lovely things than any little girl," she said to herself, as she slowly closed the drawer. "There's my doll, and my white kitten, and my scarlet stockings, which I shall have finished tomorrow, and my leather shoes, and these coral beads and the box!" But Anne gave a little sigh and then whispered, "and if my dear father could only know all about them, and that I am to give a doll to Amanda." She looked out of the small window toward the beautiful harbor, and wished that she might go sailing over it to Boston, to find her father and bring him safe to Province Town. "I wish King George knew how much trouble he was making with his old warships," Anne whispered to the wooden doll.

CHAPTER TWELVE

———— ❦ ————

AN UNEXPECTED JOURNEY

"I HAVE A fine dish of ink all ready," said Captain Enos the next morning, "but 'tis too clear a morning to sit in the house and write letters. There are good cod coming into the harbor, and I must row out and catch what I can while the weather is good."

"Can we not write the letter tonight?" asked Anne. "Aunt Martha has some fine pitch knots to burn that will make the kitchen light as day."

"We'll see, come night," replied Captain Enos.

The two were walking down the sandy path together—Captain Enos bound for the shore, and Anne started for Mistress Starkweather's to thank her for the coral beads.

"Be a good child," said Captain Enos, as he turned from the path and left Anne to go on alone.

As the little girl came near the spring, she saw a man rolling a water cask toward it, and toward the shore she could see several other men, whom she knew came from the British ship. She looked closely at the man at the spring, and as she passed near him, noticed that his hair was red. He smiled and nodded as Anne went by, and then she saw that he had pleasant blue eyes, and she stopped and said: "Have you forgotten the little girl you saved from the Indians?"

"No, indeed!" replied the big man heartily; "and so you are John Nelson's little girl. And you are not afraid of a Britisher?"

"Oh, no!" said Anne, in surprise; "you have two little maids in England."

"That I have, safe with their mother. But I should like well to see their bright faces, and your father would like to see you, child. You do not forget him?"

"No," said Anne soberly. "We plan to write him a letter for you to take."

"Speak not so loud," cautioned the man; "the other sailors may hear. And get your letter ready soon, for, come a fair wind, we'll be off up the coast again to Boston Harbor."

"Do your little girls write you letters?" asked Anne.

The big man shook his head. "No, they are not yet taught to write," he said. "It may be I'll be sailing back come spring, and then I'll tell them about the little maid I saw in Province Town."

"Tell them my name is Anne," said she eagerly. "I wish I could go to Boston and find my father. I must hurry now, but I wish I knew the names of your little girls."

"They have good names," said the big man. "Each one is named for a grandmother. One is Betsey and the other Hannah."

"I'll remember," said Anne, and she said "Goodbye" and went quickly on toward Mrs. Starkweather's.

"I do wish I could go and find my father," she thought as she walked along. "I know he'd like to see me better than a letter. I wish I had asked William Trull to take me in the big ship. But maybe Aunt Martha would not wish me to ask him."

All day Anne thought about the letter that Captain Enos had promised to write for her; and when supper was over and the kitchen began to grow dusky with the shadows of the October evening, she ran out to the little shed and came tugging in a big root of pine.

"May I put this on the fire, Aunt Martha?" she asked, "that Uncle Enos may see to write?"

" 'Tis a pine knot," said Mrs. Stoddard. "We shall need many such for light and heat before the long winter goes. But put it on, child. 'Tis a good plan to write thy father."

The pine knot blazed up brightly, and Captain Enos drew the table near the open fire, and, with Anne perched on a high stool beside him, and Mrs. Stoddard busy with her knitting, while the white kitten purred happily from its comfortable place under her chair, the letter was begun. Word for word, just as Anne told him, Captain Enos wrote down about the stockings and shoes, the school and the kitten, the pink beads and William Trull, and at last Anne said: "That is all, only that I want to see him and that I love him well," and Captain Enos finished the letter, and Anne went upstairs to bed.

"I have a plan to take a cargo of fish to Boston, Martha," said Captain Enos, as soon as Anne had gone. "The *Somerset* will sail on the first fair wind. I can fill the sloop with good cod by the time she is out of gunshot; and I'll venture to say they will bring a good price in Boston Town."

"But how can you make safe landing there, Enos?" asked his wife anxiously.

"I'll manage," replied the captain smilingly, "and it may be I can get some news of Anne's father."

" 'Twould be a brave cruise," said Mrs. Stoddard. "I should like well to go with thee, Enos."

Captain Enos laughed heartily. "And so would Anne, I dare say," he replied. "Maybe when spring comes and the British have been sent home I'll take you and Anne to Boston on a pleasure trip. If I get a good price for my fish, I'll bring you home a warm shawl, Martha."

"Mind not about me, Enos, but get some good wool cloth, if you see the chance, to make Anne a dress. She likes bright colors, and the Freemans will tell you where to purchase, and you may see some plaid or figured stuff that has good wearing in it. Three yards of good width will be a plenty."

"There's but little trading in Boston these days," replied Captain Enos; "there's a blight on the land, until we can make England give us fairer treatment. I do believe 'twill come to open war in Boston."

As they talked, Captain Enos was busy shaping the wooden doll which Anne was to give Amanda.

"I must finish this before I begin to plan for Boston," he said. "What did we do for pleasure, Martha, before Anne came to live with us? Why, we had not even a white kitten. And 'twas little enough I thought of whittling out dolls."

"Or I of knitting scarlet stockings," answered his wife. "Anne knits her stint each day, and will soon have hers done, but her second pair I am knitting for the child. November is close at hand, and then she must be warmly clad."

"Her leather shoes are ready," said Captain Enos, with a satisfied nod.

The next morning Captain Enos gave the letter to William Trull, who promised to find a chance of forwarding it to John Nelson.

"What think you, Anne?" said Mrs. Stoddard when the little girl came home from school that day. "The *Somerset* is getting under way, and your Uncle Enos says 'tis like enough that your father will have the letter before the week ends."

"I wish I could see him read it," said Anne.

"And your Uncle Enos has a bold plan, child. He is filling up his sloop with fine cod to take to the Boston market, and if this wind holds, he will go sailing up the coast tomorrow morning. Mayhap he'll be in Boston before the *Somerset*."

"But they will fire their big guns at him and sink the sloop!" said Anne fearfully.

"Your uncle will not give them a chance," answered Mrs. Stoddard. "He will put in and out among the islands and keep out of their sight."

"May I not go with him, Aunt Martha? I could see my father then."

Mrs. Stoddard shook her head. " 'Twould not be wise, child. Your uncle would not wish it. There would be but little chance of finding your father. Your uncle plans to make but a short stay and get home as soon as may be. It is no time to be coasting about, with British ships ready to sink any craft they see. Here, see!" and she held something up in her hand.

"Oh, Amanda's doll!" exclaimed Anne, "and you have made a fine dress for her. Can I take it down now?" And the little girl took the wooden doll which Captain Enos had whittled out and looked at it admiringly.

"Yes, run along," replied Mrs. Stoddard. " 'Twill be a great surprise for Amanda."

Anne hurried down the hill and along the shore toward the Cary house, holding the doll carefully under the little shawl of gay plaid which Mrs. Stoddard had pinned about her shoulders. The sand no longer felt warm about her bare feet.

"I shall be wearing my new stockings and shoes soon," she thought, as her feet felt the cold dampness.

Amanda saw her coming and ran out to meet her, a white kitten close at her heels.

"See, the British ship is going!" exclaimed Amanda, and the two little girls turned and watched the big ship under full sail moving off across the harbor.

"Amanda," said Anne, "you know you gave me the nice white kitten?"

"Yes," replied Amanda. "Has it run away?"

"Oh, no; it is just as contented as can be," said Anne. "Only ever since you gave it to me I have wished I could give you something."

Amanda's face flushed and she dug her bare toes into the sand. She was remembering how unkind she and Amos had been to Anne, and was wishing that Anne would not thank her for the kitten.

"And now I have a present for you," went on Anne, taking the wooden doll from beneath the little plaid shawl.

"Your doll!" exclaimed Amanda in surprise.

Anne shook her head smilingly.

"No," she said, "your doll. See, it is new. And it is larger than mine. Take it," for Amanda's hands were behind her, as if she did not mean to take the gift.

"It's yours. Uncle Enos made it, and Aunt Martha made the dress," and Anne held the doll toward her friend.

Then Amanda's hands unclasped and reached forward eagerly.

"It's a fine doll," she said. "I do think, Anne, it is full handsomer than yours. Come, that I may show it to my mother. I shall name it for you, Anne. I have already named it. I shall call it Lovely Anne Nelson. Indeed I shall. I never had a gift before." And Amanda held the doll tight and smiled happily at Anne, as she reached out to draw her into the house that Mrs. Cary might see the doll.

When Anne started for home, Amanda walked along beside her for a little way. When they neared the spring she put her arm about Anne's neck and kissed her on the cheek.

"There!" she exclaimed; "now you know how dear you are. I was bad to you, Anne Nelson, right here at this very spring; and I set Amos on to tease you. And now you have given me a gift."

"But you gave me the kitten," answered Anne, "and I chased you away from the spring with sand and water."

"But now we like each other well," said Amanda. "You like me now, Anne?"

"Yes," replied the little girl. "I would not give you a gift if I did not like you well," and the two little girls smiled at each other happily and parted, Amanda to run home to her doll, while Anne went more slowly up the hill, thinking of the trip Uncle Enos was about to make and wishing that she could go with him.

"I could wear my scarlet stockings and new shoes for my father to see," she thought, "and I would be no trouble to Uncle Enos. There are two bunks in the sloop's cabin, and I would be company for him."

The more Anne thought about this cruise to Boston the more she longed to go. Captain Enos was late to his supper that night.

"I have a fine cargo of fish," he said, "and I shall go out on the morning tide, before you are awake, little maid," with a nod to Anne. "Next spring you and Aunt Martha shall go with me and see the fine town of Boston, with its shops and great houses. The British soldiers will be gone by that time, and it may be we will have our own government. There will be good days for us all then."

"I want to go now," said Anne, and Captain Enos laughed and shook his head.

"Run away to bed now, child," said Aunt Martha, as soon as the supper dishes were washed, "and take these stockings up-stairs with you. I toed off the last one while you were at Amanda Cary's."

So Anne said goodnight, and Captain Enos gave her a

goodbye kiss, telling her to take good care of her Aunt Martha while he was away, and went slowly upstairs. But she did not undress and go to bed. She sat down on the little wooden stool, her mind full of a great resolve. She sat there quietly until she heard Captain Enos and Mrs. Stoddard go to bed. Then she moved softly to the little table under which stood her new shoes. Taking these and her scarlet stockings, she crept softly down the stairs. Crossing the kitchen gently, she slid back the bolt, and let herself out into the night.

There was a fresh wind from the southwest, and the little girl shivered a little as she ran toward the shore. The sloop was anchored some little distance from shore; Captain Enos would row out in his dory to her. As Anne reached the shore and looked out at the sloop she almost lost courage.

"I don't see how I can ever get out there without a boat," she exclaimed aloud.

"Out there?" The voice sounded close at her elbow, and Anne gave a jump and looked around.

"What do you want to get out to Captain Enos's boat for?" asked Jimmie Starkweather.

"Oh, Jimmie!" exclaimed the little girl, "what are you doing down on the shore in the night?"

"Night! Why, it's not much after dark," answered the boy. "Father has been out fishing all day, and I have just pulled the dory up, and was going home when I heard you. What do you want to go out to the sloop for?"

"Jimmie, my father is in Boston and I do want to see him," said Anne. "Captain Enos is going to sail early tomorrow morning for Boston, and I want to go out and sleep in the cabin tonight. Then I will keep as quiet as I can till he is nearly in Boston, and then I will tell him all about it, and he will take me to see my father."

Jimmie shook his head.

"Doesn't Captain Enos want you to go?" he asked.

"He says I may go next spring," answered Anne, "but if you row me out to the sloop, Jimmie, 'twould be no harm. You could tell Aunt Martha tomorrow, and I would soon be home. But 'tis a long time since I saw my father. You see yours every day."

There was a little sob in Anne's throat and Jimmie wondered if she was going to cry. He hoped she wouldn't.

"Jump into the dory," he said. "I'll get a good lesson from my father, I'll warrant, for this; but jump in. And mind you tell Captain Enos that I told you to go home, but that you would not."

"Yes, Jimmie," said Anne, putting her shoes and stockings into the boat, and then climbing in herself. The boy sprang in after her, pushed off the dory, and in a short time had reached the sloop.

"Now go straight to the cabin and shut the door," cautioned Jimmie, and Anne obeyed, creeping into the top bunk and pulling a rough blanket over her.

She heard the sound of Jimmie's oars, as he pulled toward shore, felt the motion of the tide, as the big sloop rose and fell, and soon was asleep and dreaming that her father and William Trull were calling her a brave little maid.

Jimmie had many misgivings after he reached shore, and made up his mind to go straight to Captain Stoddard and tell him of Anne's plan. Then he remembered that Anne had trusted him with her secret. "I guess I'll have to let her go," he decided.

CHAPTER THIRTEEN

———— 🍎 ————

ANNE FINDS HER FATHER

It was just daybreak when Captain Enos, carrying a basket of provisions for his cruise, made his way to the shore and pushed off his dory.

"Not a soul stirring," he said, as he stepped aboard the sloop, fastened the dory, which he intended to tow, and then carried the basket of food to the little cabin.

As he pushed open the door Anne awoke, but she did not stir, and Captain Enos did not look in the direction of the upper bunk. She heard him hoisting the big mainsail, then came the rattle of the anchor chain, the sloop swung round, and Anne knew that at last she was really on her way to find her father.

"I must keep very still," she whispered to herself, "or Uncle Enos might 'bout ship and sail straight back to Province Town." So she did not move, though she wished very much that she might be out on deck with Captain Enos, feeling the salt breeze on her cheeks and enjoying the sail. She knew by the way the sloop tipped that they were going very fast. "Seems as if it was sailing right on its side," thought Anne. "If it tips much more I do believe I'll slide out of this berth."

"A fine wind, a fine wind!" Captain Enos said with a satisfied nod, as his boat went flying along. "I'll make Boston Harbor before nightfall at this rate, in time to get my fish ashore by dusk, if I can slide into a landing without the British stopping me. My cargo will be welcome," and Captain Enos smiled to himself as he thought of the praise he would get from his friends and acquaintance for his brave venture in such troublous times.

Toward noon Anne carefully let herself down from the bunk, and peered out through the door, which Captain Enos had left open. She could see the low sandy shores of Cape Cod, and here and there a white-sailed boat. "I guess we must be 'most to Boston," she thought. "The sun is way up in the middle of the sky, and I am so hungry." She came a little nearer to the cabin door and put her head out. "Uncle Enos!" she said softly.

But the captain was singing to keep himself company, and did not hear the faint voice. His head was turned a little away from Anne, but just as she was about to call again his song came to an end and he turned his glance ahead.

"Bless my soul!" he exclaimed.

"It is I, Uncle Enos!" said Anne, stepping out of the cabin.

The captain was almost too surprised to speak. Anne clambered along the side of the sloop until she was close beside him, and reaching out took fast hold of his rough coat sleeve, and repeated:

"It is I, Uncle Enos."

"Where on earth did you come from?" he exclaimed.

Anne pointed toward the cabin.

"How did you get there?" questioned Captain Enos. "Weren't you abed and asleep when I left the house this morning?"

"No, Uncle Enos," said Anne, creeping a little closer. "I slept in the top bunk in the sloop."

"Well, this is a nice affair. I can't take you back now. I'll make Boston Harbor before dusk with this wind. But how came you in the sloop?"

"Jimmie Starkweather rowed me out last night after you were sound asleep. And he is going to tell Aunt Martha all about it this morning. He told me to tell you that he didn't want me to go aboard, but that I would," said Anne.

Captain Enos's face was very sober, but he did not say any harsh word.

"What did you hide in the sloop for, child?" he asked.

"To go to Boston with you, Uncle Enos, and find my father," said Anne.

Then the captain's face grew even more sober.

"Then you do not like living with us?" he said. "But I thought you seemed happy, Anne. Your Aunt Martha will miss you, child. But if your heart is so set on being with your father I must do my best to find him for you. How a soldier can manage to care for a small girl like you is more than I can tell," and the captain sighed.

"I brought my scarlet stockings and new shoes to show him," said Anne.

Captain Enos nodded.

"And I can tell him about my kitten and the coral beads, and about going to school."

"Did you not bring the coral beads?" asked the captain.

Anne shook her head.

"Oh, no," she answered. "I heard you tell Aunt Martha that you would be away but a day or two, and I thought I could tell my father about the beads."

"Then you mean to go home with me?" asked the captain, a little smile creeping about his mouth.

"Why, yes," said Anne. "I do but want to see my father and tell him all the pleasant things that have befallen me."

"Well, well," said Captain Enos, "now I must scold you, Anne. Your Aunt Martha will not be pleased at this."

"But you are not angry?" asked Anne. "I do see little wrinkles about your eyes that mean you will soon smile. And it is long since I have seen my father."

"We must make the best of it now," said the captain, "but I do blame the Starkweather boy for setting you out to the sloop. He should have sent you straight home, and let me know of your plan."

Anne looked at Captain Enos in surprise.

"Jimmie could not help my coming," she said. "I should have found some way to get to the sloop. And he would not tell a secret."

"So you did not mean to run away from us?" said Captain Enos. "I am glad of that, but how I will manage with you in Boston I know not, nor if I can find your father."

Captain Enos's sloop ran safely in among the islands, sailed across Boston Harbor without being noticed, and made fast at a wharf well known to Captain Enos, and where he was welcomed by an old acquaintance. Before dusk he had sold his cargo of fish at a good price, and Anne, wearing her scarlet stockings and new shoes, and holding fast to the captain's hand, walked with him up the street to the house of the man who had been at the wharf when the sloop came in.

"They are good people, born in Wellfleet," said the captain to Anne, as they walked along, "and I shall ask them to keep you over night. I shall sleep in the sloop, and tomorrow we will find out all we can about your father."

The Freemans, for that was the name of Captain Enos's friends, gave Anne a warm welcome. Their house seemed very large and grand to the little girl. There was a carpet on the sitting-room floor, the first Anne had ever seen, and pictures on the walls, and a high mantel with tall brass candlesticks.

The room in which she slept seemed very wonderful to Anne. The bed was so high that she had to step up from a footstool to get in it, and then down, down she went in billows of feathers. In the morning one of the Freeman girls came in to waken her. She was a girl of about fifteen, with pretty, light, curling hair and blue eyes. She smiled pleasantly at Anne, and told her that there was a basin of warm water for her to bathe her face and hands in.

"I will brush out your hair for you, if you wish," she said kindly.

But Anne said she could brush her own hair. Rose Freeman waited till Anne was quite ready for breakfast and went down the broad flight of stairs with her. Anne watched her new friend admiringly.

"She looks just like her name, just like a rose," she said to herself, and resolved that she would remember and walk just as Rose did, and try and speak in the same pleasant way.

Before breakfast was finished Captain Enos came up from the wharves. He smiled as he looked at Anne's bright face and smooth hair, and nodded approvingly. Then he and Mr. Freeman began to talk about the soldiers, and the best way to find John Nelson.

"Come, Rose," said Mr. Freeman; "the captain and I will walk up near King's Chapel and see what we can find out, and you and the little maid can come with us."

Rose went upstairs and came down wearing a little brown jacket and a hat of brown silk with a green feather on it. In her hands she brought a blue cape and a blue hat with a broad ribbon bow.

"Mother says you are to wear these," she said to Anne, with a little smile. " 'Tis a cape and hat that I wore when I was a little girl, and I would like to have you wear them."

"I never wore a hat before," said Anne.

"It is very becoming," said Rose, and the little party started out.

Mr. Freeman stopped here and there to ask questions, and Anne, holding fast to Rose Freeman's hand, looked wonderingly at the houses and the people. They went into a shop, and Captain Enos bought a fine warm brown shawl to take home to Mrs. Stoddard, and asked Rose Freeman to help Anne select a pretty stuff for a dress. The girls decided upon a small plaid of dark blue and brown, and the stuff was carefully wrapped up and Captain Enos took the package.

"I have news at last," said Mr. Freeman, who had been talking with a man at the door of the shop. "We will walk up to the Common and see if we cannot get sight of your father. He was here yesterday."

Anne listened eagerly, almost forgetting Rose Freeman, whose hand she still held tightly, in the thought that her dear father might be very near and that she would soon see him.

They walked toward the Common, and Mr. Freeman told the others to stand near the big elm while he went to make inquiries. He was gone but a few moments, when Rose Freeman felt Anne's hand slip from her own, and saw the little girl running swiftly across the grass calling out, "Father! Father!"

John Nelson heard the voice and stopped.

"Anne, Anne!" he answered, and in a moment the little girl

in scarlet stockings and blue cape and hat was gathered into the close clasp of the dark, slender man.

Then how much there was to say! How eagerly Anne told him all the pleasant news! How warmly Captain Enos shook his hand, and called him a brave fellow; and John Nelson tried to thank the captain for all his kindness to Anne.

Anne held fast to his hand as they walked together to the wharf where the sloop lay. Captain Enos said that he must start for home the next morning, and there was a great deal for them all to talk about. Rose Freeman and her father left them at the wharf, after Captain Enos had promised that he would bring Anne to their house in time for supper.

"I have a plan, John," said Captain Enos. "When we have settled with the British, and that must be soon now, you must come to Province Town and live with us. How would you like that, Anne?"

Anne smiled happily.

"Best of anything!" she declared.

"I need help with my fishing," went on Captain Enos, "and there's an empty loft next to Anne's room, where you can sleep. So think of Anne's home as yours, John. You'd not break Mistress Stoddard's heart by taking away the child?"

"It was good fortune led her to your door," said John Nelson gratefully. "I can see for myself that she is content and happy. And I'll be a fortunate man to come into your house, Enos Stoddard."

"How soon will you come, father?" asked Anne, hopefully.

"I think 'twill not be longer than another spring before the British leave us in peace," replied her father. "But we need more soldiers to let them know we are ready for war."

Captain Enos nodded. "There's a half dozen good Province Town men ready to come, and as many more from Truro, if a dozen would help," he found a chance to whisper.

"We'll talk of this later," said Anne's father. "I only hope you'll get safe back to Province Town harbor from this trip."

"No fear," laughed Captain Enos. "General Gage is doing his best to starve Boston out. Maybe we Province Town men can do the cause of Liberty good service if we can bring in loads of fish for the people."

"It's hard to have British troops quartered on us," replied Nelson. "General Gage is taking rough measures with everybody who opposes him. Dr. Joseph Warren tried to stop the fortifications on Boston Neck, but 'twas no use. And word is being sent to settlements to be ready to furnish men. We've got supplies in Concord, and Americans have been drilling for some time. We'll be ready for war if war comes. I've a message for the Newburyport men to be ready to join us, but I see no way of getting out of Boston. You're a brave man, Captain Stoddard, to come into harbor."

Captain Enos's face brightened as he listened to John Nelson.

"I'd find no trouble in slipping down the coast to Newburyport," he said eagerly.

"Maybe," responded Nelson, "tho' there's no need for my telling you that there's British craft cruising all about, and a man caught with a message to 'rebels,' as they call us, stands no chance."

"I'd keep my message to myself," answered Captain Enos.

"So you could, a message by word of mouth; but this is written, and has a drawing as well. I have it under the lining of my coat. But there's no way for me to get out of the town. I'm well known by many of the English."

"Let me take it." Captain Stoddard's voice was eager. " 'Tis ill luck that we Province Town men are to have no part in this affair. I'll get the paper safe to Newburyport. Tell me to whom I am to give it."

But John Nelson shook his head. "You'd be caught, and maybe sent to England," he answered.

"I'll not be caught. And if they catch me they'd not find the papers," he promised, and before they parted Nelson had agreed to deliver the package that day. "I'll give it to Anne," he promised. "It will not do for me to meet you again. There are too many eyes about. Let Anne walk along, with that tall girl yonder, about sunset toward the South Meeting House, and I'll give it to her."

Captain Stoddard nodded, and walked away.

"Anne," he said when they met in the Freemans' sitting room just before dinner, "you can be of great help to your father and

93

to me. But you must be wise and silent. When you walk with Rose this afternoon your father will meet you and hand you a flat package. Thrust it inside your frock, and say nothing of it to Rose, or to any one, and bring it safe to me."

"Yes, indeed, Uncle Enos," the little girl answered. "Am I to ask Rose to walk with me?"

"Yes, toward the South Meeting House," answered Captain Enos, "about an hour before sunset."

"If I keep silent and bring the package safely, will you forgive me for hiding in the boat?" pleaded Anne.

"Indeed I will, child, and take you for a brave girl as well," he replied.

Anne was joyful at the thought of another word from her father, and Rose was quite ready to go for another walk.

They had just turned into King Street when John Nelson met them. Anne wore the pretty cape Rose had given her and her father slipped the packet into her hand without Rose seeing it. She grasped it tightly, and held it under the cape. "Be a good child, Anne, and do whatever Captain Stoddard may bid thee," her father said, as he bade her goodbye.

CHAPTER FOURTEEN

A CANDY PARTY

THE NEXT MORNING proved warm and pleasant with only a light breeze, but Captain Enos had his sloop ready at an early hour, and when Anne, with Mr. Freeman and Rose, came down to the wharf he was anxious to start at once.

Anne still wore the blue cape, which Mrs. Freeman had insisted on giving her, and the hat was in a round pasteboard box, which Anne carried carefully, and which was put away in the cabin with Aunt Martha's new shawl and the cloth for Anne's new dress.

As the sloop sailed away from the wharf Anne waved her hand to Rose Freeman until she could no longer see her. Captain Enos watched the little girl anxiously; he was half afraid that Anne might be disappointed because she could not stay with her father, but her face was bright and smiling.

"Where is the packet your father handed you?" Captain Enos questioned eagerly, as soon as his sloop was clear of the wharf.

"I have it pinned safe inside my frock," she answered. "Shall I give it to you now, Uncle Enos?"

"Maybe 'tis safer with you, Anne," replied the captain. "It may be that some British boat will overhaul us, and question us.

I'm doing an errand, Anne, for your father. If this boat is taken and I am made a prisoner, you are to say that you want to go to Newburyport. That and no more. Mayhap they'll set you ashore there. Then make your way to Squire Coffin's house as best you may. Give him the packet. Tell him the story, and he'll find a way to reach your father. Do you understand?"

"Yes, Uncle Enos," said Anne very soberly.

"Repeat what I have told you, that I may be sure," said Captain Enos, and Anne obeyed.

"But I do not want to be set ashore in a strange place," she said soberly. "How should I get back to Province Town?"

"You will be taken care of, never fear," responded Captain Enos, "and you'll be doing a good service to the cause of liberty, Anne, if you carry the papers safely. Your Aunt Martha will indeed be proud of you. Remember what I have told you. But I hope to slip in behind Plum Island and make a landing without being seen. The wind is favoring us. You have had a fine visit, Anne?"

"Yes, indeed!" agreed the little girl. "And I have a present for Aunt Martha," she said, as the sloop ran out among the islands. "See, my father gave me this for her," and she held up a gold coin. "Will she not be pleased?"

"But she will be better pleased to have you safe home again," said Captain Enos. "What do you think Amanda Cary will say when she hears of your voyage to Boston and of all the fine things you have seen there? 'Tis not many of the children in Province Town have ever taken such a journey."

"She will think it a better voyage than the one we took to House Point Island," answered Anne. "I have something for Amanda, too. Rose Freeman gave me a package of barley sugar, and I said to myself I would take it home to Amanda."

Captain Enos kept a watchful eye for suspicious-looking craft. But his course lay well inshore, and he was apparently not noticed by any of the vessels. Before noon he was cruising along the Ipswich shore, and made his landing at Newburyport without having been spoken.

"The worst part of the business is before us," he said to Anne, as he made the boat fast. "If I leave the boat here, I may come back and find no trace of her, but leave her I must, or Squire Coffin will wait in vain for the papers."

"But I can carry them," said Anne. "Tell me where to go, and I'll come straight back and say no word of my errand."

" 'Tis the best possible way. Did I not say that you were a wise child!" declared Captain Enos, his face beaming with delight. "Put on your pretty hat and cape, and follow that lane up to the main road. Then ask for Squire Coffin's house of the first person you meet."

In a few moments Anne was ready to start. As she walked up the lane Captain Enos's eyes followed her anxiously. "I can see no danger in it for the child," he said aloud, and then, sailor fashion, set about putting his boat in order.

" 'Twill be a cold night, but the cabin will be snug and warm," he thought. "I'll get out of here before sunset and maybe make Province Town by daybreak."

Anne walked up the pleasant lane. Her feet sank deep in the leaves from the overarching trees, and made a cheerful, crackling sound. She could see the roofs of houses not far away, and as she turned from the lane into a road she met two girls not much larger than herself. They looked at her curiously, and when Anne stopped they smiled in a friendly way.

"Would you please to tell me where I can find Squire Coffin?" Anne asked, feeling very brave and a little important.

"Squire Coffin is my uncle," the larger of the two girls replied. "I'm going there now."

"I have an errand," Anne explained.

"Oh!" responded both the little girls, but Anne could see that they wondered who this strange little girl could be, and what her errand was.

"You may come with us if you want to," Squire Coffin's niece said, and Anne was very glad to walk with these silent little girls, for neither of them spoke again until they stopped in front of a tall, square white house very near the street. As Anne looked up at it she thought that she had never seen so many windows before in one house. "That's Uncle Coffin on the porch," explained his niece.

"Thank you," said Anne, and as the two little girls politely curtseyed she endeavored to imitate them, and with apparent success. Then she went up the stone steps toward the dignified-looking gentleman who stood in the doorway.

She held the packet under her cape, and as she came near him she whispered, as Captain Enos had told her to do, "This is from Boston."

"Great George!" he exclaimed, grabbing the package in what seemed a very rude manner to Anne, and putting it quickly in his pocket, "and how came you by it?"

But Anne remembered her promise to keep quiet, and she also remembered that the squire's niece had made the queer little curtsey on saying goodbye. So Anne bobbed very prettily to the squire, and said "goodbye," and ran down the steps, leaving the squire standing amazed. It was many weeks before he learned the name of the little maid, and that her home was in Province Town.

It was an easy matter to find her way back to the lane. There was an orchard just at the corner of the road, and a man was gathering apples. "Want an apple?" he called.

"Yes, sir," answered Anne, and now, being rather proud of her new accomplishment, she curtseyed very politely.

"Well, well, you are a young lady, miss. Come up to the fence and I'll hand you the apples." Anne obeyed, and the good-natured man gave her two big red-cheeked apples. They seemed very wonderful to the little girl from the sandy shore village, where apples were not often to be seen, and she thanked him delightedly.

Captain Enos was watching for her, and as soon as she was on board he swung the sloop clear of the wharf, ran up his mainsail and headed toward the outer channel. As they looked back at the little wharf they saw a tall man come running down the lane.

"I reckon that's the squire," chuckled Captain Enos.

"Yes, it is," said Anne.

"Well, now for Province Town. I guess we've helped a little bit, Anne. At least you have."

Anne was eating one of the big red apples, and thinking about Squire Coffin's big house and small niece.

"We'll tell Aunt Martha all that's happened," went on Captain Enos, "but do not speak to any one else of it, Anne. 'Twould make trouble for your father and for me if our trip to Newbury-port was known."

"I'll not speak of it," Anne promised.

"It has been a good trip," said Captain Enos. "Mr. Freeman paid me well for the fish. I have a keg of molasses in the cabin, which will be welcome news for Martha."

As they came into harbor at sunrise next morning and Captain Enos dropped anchor and lowered the big mainsail, Anne looked eagerly toward the shore. She could see Jimmie Stark-weather and his father watching them. After Captain Enos had lowered the keg of molasses into the dory, and put in the box that held Anne's hat, and the other packages, he helped Anne over the side of the sloop to a seat in the bow of the dory.

As soon as the boat touched the shore Jimmie and his father ran down to help draw it up on the beach. Jimmie looked at Captain Enos as if he half expected a scolding, but as soon as Captain Enos landed he patted the boy's shoulder kindly, and said:

"The little maid has told me all about it. You were not greatly to blame, Jimmie. And the trip turned out all right."

"I saw my father," said Anne, and then ran away toward home, leaving Captain Enos to tell of the visit to Boston.

Aunt Martha had seen the sloop come to anchor, and was waiting at the door to welcome Anne.

"Uncle Enos and I have a secret with my father," Anne whispered to Mrs. Stoddard, "and we have been to Newburyport." And then the story of the wonderful trip was told, and Anne showed Mrs. Stoddard how she had curtseyed to the squire.

"Well! Well!" exclaimed the good woman in amazement. "It does seem as if you had all sorts of adventures, Anne. To think of Enos undertaking such a thing. I'm proud of you both. 'Twill be a fine story to tell your grandchildren, Anne. How you carried news from Boston patriots to Newburyport. But do not speak of it till we are through with all these troublous days." And again Anne promised to keep silent.

"To think you should run off like that, child," continued Aunt Martha. "When Jimmie Starkweather came up and told me you were gone I could scarce believe him till I had climbed the stairs to the loft and found no trace of you. But I am right glad you wore your shoes and stockings. Where did the blue cape come from?"

By this time they were in the kitchen, and Anne had put down the box that held her hat.

"Mrs. Freeman gave it to me," she replied, "and see! I have a new hat!" and she opened the box and took out the pretty hat.

"I thought thy uncle would take thee straight to Mistress Freeman," said Mrs. Stoddard.

"And we found my father," went on Anne happily, "and he sent thee this," and she drew the gold piece from her pocket and gave it to Mrs. Stoddard.

"Well, well," said Aunt Martha, " 'tis a fine piece of money, and your father is kind to send it. I will use it well."

"And Uncle Enos has fetched you a fine shawl and a keg of molasses," said Anne. "You do not think there was great harm in my hiding in the sloop, Aunt Martha?" The little girl's face was so troubled that Aunt Martha gave her another kiss, and said:

"It has turned out well, but thee must never do so again. Suppose a great storm had come up and swept the sloop from her moorings that night?"

"Rose Freeman looks just like a rose," said Anne, feeling quite sure that Aunt Martha was not displeased; "and she walks so softly that you can hardly hear her, and she speaks softly, too. I am going to walk and speak just as she does."

"That is right," agreed Mrs. Stoddard. "I am sure that she is a well-spoken girl."

When Captain Enos came up the hill toward home Anne had already put her blue cape and hat carefully away, and was sitting near the fire with the white kitten curled up in her lap.

"The Freemans do not eat in their kitchen," said Anne, as they sat down to supper. "They eat in a square room with a shining floor, and where there is a high mantel-shelf with china images."

" 'Tis a fine house," agreed Captain Enos, "well built of brick. 'Twas a great thing for Anne to see it."

" 'Tis not so pleasant a house as this," said Anne. "I could not see the harbor from any window, and the shore is not smooth and sandy like the shores of our harbor."

Captain Enos smiled and nodded.

"That's right, Anne," he said. "Boston houses may do for town people, but we sailorfolk like our own best."

"Yes, indeed!" replied Anne, "and I do not believe a beach plum grows on their shore. And nothing I tasted there was so good as Aunt Martha's meal bread."

The next morning Anne started for school, wearing the new shoes and scarlet stockings and the little plaid shawl. The children were all anxious to hear about what she saw in Boston, and she told them of the soldiers on the Common, and of the shops, and of the houses made of brick and stone, and she showed Amanda how to make the wonderful curtsey. But Elder Haven soon called them to take their seats, and it was not until the noon recess that she found a chance to speak alone with Amanda.

The two little girls sat down on the front doorstep of Elder Haven's house, and Anne told of the wonderful sail to Boston, and had just begun to describe Rose Freeman when the teacher's voice was heard calling them in.

As soon as school closed for the day, Amanda said that she could walk home with Anne and see the new cape and hat, and hear more about Rose Freeman.

"Would you like better to live in Boston than here?" asked Amanda, as they walked along.

Anne looked at her in surprise.

"Why, Amanda!" she said; "of course I wouldn't. It is not seemly there to go out-of-doors without a hat; and Rose Freeman said that she had never been barefooted in her life. She has fine white stockings knit of cotton yarn for summer, and low shiny shoes that she called 'slippers.' "

" 'Twould be hard to wear shoes all the year," agreed Amanda, looking down at her own stout leather shoes, "but I like them well now."

"I brought you a present from Boston," said Anne, just as they reached the Stoddards' door. "Rose Freeman gave it to me, and I saved it for you."

"Well, Amanda," said Mrs. Stoddard, as the two girls came into the kitchen, "are you not glad to have Anne safe home again? 'Twas quite a journey to take."

"She likes Province Town better than Boston," answered Amanda smilingly.

"To be sure she does, and why not?" replied Mrs. Stoddard. "There are few places where there is so much salt water to be seen as here, and no better place for fishing. Now, Anne, I have a little surprise for you. I have asked Mr. and Mrs. Starkweather and their six boys to come up this evening, and your father and mother, Amanda, and you and Amos. The evenings are getting fine and long now and we must begin to be neighborly."

"Then I mustn't stay long now," said Amanda; "it will be pleasant to come up here again in the evening."

Amanda tried on Anne's blue cape and hat, looked admiringly at Mrs. Stoddard's shining gold piece and brown shawl, and then Anne handed her the package of barley sugar.

"I will keep it," said Amanda, gratefully; " 'twould seem ungrateful to eat a present."

Mrs. Stoddard nodded. "Keep it until Sunday, Amanda," she said, "but then it will be well to eat a part of it."

"But can she not taste it now?" asked Anne. "I am sure it is good. It came out of a big glass jar in a shop."

"I see I must tell you two little girls a secret," said Mrs. Stoddard, "but Amanda must not tell Amos."

"No, indeed," said Amanda quickly.

"It is about this evening," said Mrs. Stoddard; "I am going to make a fine dish of molasses candy!"

"Oh, Aunt Martha!" "Oh, Mistress Stoddard!" exclaimed the little girls together.

"It has been years since I tasted any myself," went on Mrs. Stoddard, "but I remember well how it is made; and I do not believe one of you children has ever tasted it."

"My mother has told us about it," said Amanda, "and said that when times were better she would make us some."

"We all need cheering up," said Mrs. Stoddard, "and I am glad I can give you children a treat to remember. Now, Amanda, you see why it will be best not to eat your barley sugar until Sunday."

"I have good times every day since I gave you the white kitten," said Amanda, as she bade Anne goodbye, and started for home.

"We must bring all our chairs into the kitchen tonight,

Anne," said Aunt Martha, as soon as supper was finished, "for even then I doubt if there be seats enough for our company."

"I had best bring in my long bench from the shed," said Captain Enos; " 'twill be just the thing to put a row of Stark-weather boys on."

"The youngest is but two years old," said Mrs. Stoddard; " 'tis like he will find our bed a good resting place."

Mr. and Mrs. Cary with Amos and Amanda were the first to arrive, and as they came in Captain Enos put two big pieces of pitch pine on the fire. In a moment it blazed up making the kitchen as light as day.

The Starkweathers, climbing up the sandy hill, saw the bright light shining through the windows of the little house, and Mrs. Starkweather exclaimed:

"Does it not look cheerful? To think of us all coming to a merrymaking! It was surely a kind thought of Mistress Stoddard's."

"Shall we play games?" asked Daniel, the boy next younger than Jimmie.

"It may be," answered his mother, "and you boys must be quiet and not rough in your play. Remember there is a little girl in the house."

The youngest Starkweather boy, carried carefully by his father, was sound asleep when they reached the Stoddards', and was put comfortably down on Mrs. Stoddard's big bed, while the others gathered around the fire.

"Sit you here, boys," directed Captain Enos, pointing to the long bench, "and you girls can bring your stools beside me. I have a fine game for you to play. Do you see this shining brass button? 'Twas given me in Boston, and came from the coat of a British soldier. Now we will play 'Button' with it," and the captain, with a few whispered words to Jimmie Starkweather, slid the shining button into his hand, and "Button, button! who's got the button?" was soon being laughingly asked from one to another as the brass button went from Jimmie to Amos, passed into Anne's hand and swiftly on to Amanda, and back to Jimmie before Captain Enos could locate it.

"Look!" exclaimed one of the younger Starkweather boys. "Mistress Stoddard is pouring syrup into a kettle!"

103

"Yes, my boy," said Captain Enos laughingly, "and now you will all be glad that I had a good trip to Boston, for I brought home a keg of fine molasses, and now you will have some first-class candy!"

There were many exclamations of surprise and pleasure, even the older members of the party declaring that it would indeed be a fine treat; and Mrs. Starkweather said that it reminded her of the times when she was a little girl like Anne, and her mother made candy for her.

The molasses boiled and bubbled in the big kettle hung over the fire, and Mrs. Stoddard and Mrs. Cary took turns in stirring it. The children brought dippers of cold water for spoonfuls of the hot molasses to be dropped in to see if it had begun to candy; and when Amanda lifted a stringy bit from her tin cup and held it up for Mrs. Stoddard to see, it was decided that it was cooked enough, and the kettle was lifted from the fire and the steaming, fragrant mass turned into carefully buttered pans.

"We must set these out-of-doors to cool," said Mrs. Stoddard; so Jimmie, Amos and Daniel were each entrusted with a pan to carry out on the broad step.

"When it is cool we will all work it," said Mrs. Stoddard; "that means pull and twist it into sticks."

It did not take long for the candy to cool, and then under Mrs. Stoddard's directions each child was given a piece to work into shape. But the candy proved too tempting to work over, and in a few minutes the long bench was filled with a row of boys, each one happily chewing away upon a clumsy piece of molasses candy.

CHAPTER FIFTEEN

A SPRING PICNIC

BEFORE THE SIX weeks of school came to an end Anne could read, and could write well enough to begin a letter to her father, although there seemed no chance of sending it. She thought often of her visit to Newburyport, and wondered if she would ever see Squire Coffin's little niece again. And she remembered William Trull, and his little daughters of whom he had told her. But no news had come to Province Town of how Boston was faring.

A few weeks after Captain Enos's trip to Boston another Province Town fisherman had started out with a cargo of fish, hoping for equal good fortune. But weeks passed and he did not return, and no tidings were heard of him, and his family and neighbors now feared that the British had captured his boat and taken him prisoner.

No word came to Anne from her father, and as the ice formed along the shore and over the brooks, the cold winds came sweeping in from sea with now and then a fall of snow that whitened the marshes and the woods, the little settlement on the end of Cape Cod was entirely shut off from news from Boston, and they knew not what the British were doing.

Captain Enos and the men of the port went fishing in the harbor, and the women and children kept snug at home in the little houses.

Captain Enos had finished the cedar chair for Anne's doll, and Amos had made one as near like it as possible for Amanda's "Lovely Anne." Both the little girls could now knit nearly as smoothly as Mrs. Stoddard herself, and almost every day Amanda came up to Mrs. Stoddard's, for she and Anne were reading *Pilgrim's Progress* together. Now and then Mrs. Stoddard would read several pages aloud of the adventures of Christian, while the two little girls knit. Anne had a warm hood of gray and scarlet yarn which she had knit herself, and mittens to match, so that she could go to church on Sundays, and run down to Mrs. Starkweather's or to see Amanda without being chilled by the cold.

It was a mild day late in February when Jimmie Starkweather brought home a pink blossom from the woods.

"See, mother! The first Mayflower," he exclaimed. "I found it half under the snow. Does it not smell sweet?"

"It does indeed, son," replied Mrs. Starkweather; "bring me your grandmother's pink china cup from the cupboard, fill it with cool water, and we will put the blossom on the table for thy father to see. Spring is indeed close at hand."

On the same day that Jimmie found the arbutus bloom, Captain Enos came in from fishing with news to tell. A Boston schooner outward bound had come near to where he was fishing, and in response to his hail and call of "What news?" had answered that a battle was now expected at any day between the British and Americans.

"If it be so," said Captain Enos, " 'twill not be long before the British ships will be homeward bound, and they'll not stop to trouble us much on their way."

"We must keep a lookout for them," said Captain Starkweather. "I wish we could get more news. 'Tis like enough all will be settled before we know aught of it."

All through March, with its high winds and heavy rains, the people watched the harbor for a sight of the big white-winged ships, knowing that if the English ships were homeward bound it would mean that the Americans had won, and that the colonies would be free from paying the heavy taxes which England had fixed upon them, and that they could go about their work in peace and quiet.

April brought warm, sunny days, and Anne no longer wore the knit hood and mittens, and had once more set her playhouse under the pine trees in order, and now Amanda with her doll often came to play with her.

" 'Tis nearly a year ago since my father was captured by the British," said Anne one day as she and Amanda, followed by the white kitten, went out under the pine trees.

"Anne!" exclaimed Amanda, "I did not know what 'spy' and 'traitor' meant when I called those words at you."

Anne looked at her playmate smilingly. "You would not say them now, Amanda, would you?" she answered.

"Say them now!" repeated Amanda. "Why, Anne, you are my best friend, and your father a soldier. 'Twas but yesterday my father said that there was but one thing that Province Town had to be proud of in this war, and that was John Nelson, your father, because he is the only soldier from the settlement."

Anne's cheeks flushed happily. " 'Twas hard not to have my father," she said, "but he may come back any day now; Uncle Enos says so. And he is to live with us, and help Uncle Enos with the fishing. And then, Amanda, I shall be the happiest little girl in the settlement."

"Tomorrow my mother is going to the marshes to gather young pine tips, and arrowroot, and young spruce tips and the roots of thoroughwort to brew beer with," said Amanda; "Amos and I are to go with her, and if your Aunt Martha be willing you can go with us. She plans to take something to eat and be away till past noon."

"I am sure I may go," replied Anne eagerly, "and we can bring home Mayflowers. There are many all along near the pine trees."

"Yes," said Amanda, "and will it not be fine to eat our dinner out-of-doors? Amos plans to start a fire and cook a fish for us, over it, this time, not under sand as he did when we were on the island."

Mrs. Stoddard gave her consent for Anne to go next day with the Carys. "I will bake you a molasses cake to carry," she said; "if

107

it were a few weeks later you could call it a May party. In England, and I know it is now a custom in many of our towns, all the children gather and put flowers on their heads, and have a Maypole wreathed with flowers, and dance around it. And they choose a little girl for Queen of the May."

"Can we not do that, Aunt Martha, when May is really here?" asked Anne.

"Perhaps," replied Aunt Martha, "if the minister sees no objection, and if we get good news before that time, why, a May Day party would be a pretty thing. The boys could put up the Maypole near the spring, and there will be all sorts of wild things in blossom by that time."

When they started off for the marshes Anne told Amanda what her Aunt Martha had said, and Mrs. Cary and Amos were greatly interested. Amos said that he knew where he could get a fine pole, and Mrs. Cary said that the little girls could gather flowers and fasten them to the pole with vines and strings before it was set up.

"And there must be a big wreath fastened on top of the pole," said Mrs. Cary, "and by rights there should be long bright streamers coming down from the top for each to hold and twist in and out as they dance around it."

"Can we not take long strings and fasten flowers about them?" asked Anne.

"Why, yes, indeed!" replied Mrs. Cary. " 'Twill be better than any bright ribbons. Now we must surely have a May Day party. Near the spring will be the very place."

As they searched for thoroughwort, and picked the tender spruce and pine tips, they all talked of the coming May Day, but Amos soon began to look about for a good place to make his fire. He had brought the fish in a covered basket, and said that he knew he could cook it as well as if he had a kettle to boil it in. He made a fire at a little distance from the woods, and then busied himself in putting up two crotched sticks, one on each side of the fire; a third stick rested across these two, and from it hung the fish, directly over the blaze.

Amos watched his fire very carefully, and kept a brisk blaze until the fish began to grow brown and steam. Then he declared that it was nearly cooked, and so let his fire die down until only a bed of smouldering coals remained.

They all thought the fish tasted as good as if it had been cooked in a pan or kettle, and Mrs. Cary had a fine cake of Indian meal, and with Anne's molasses cake they all said that it was the best dinner any one could have. The April sky was soft and blue, the sun warm, and Amos was sure that in a few days he could go in swimming.

"And it's only the nineteenth of April," said Anne.

Afterward these children always remembered the nineteenth of April, and would say, "That was the day we had our picnic at the marshes," and on that day the minutemen were gathered at Lexington and Earl Percy was urging his tired men to meet them, and the great battle which did so much to settle the fate of the Americans was fought.

But the people at Province Town did not know of this until long afterward. If Anne had known on the day when she was so happy, thinking of the May Day to come, and watching Amos cook the fish over the fire, that her dear father with other brave men was at Cambridge on guard waiting for the British, who were determined to make a stand in their flight from the minutemen, and that on that very day her good friends, the Freemans, were hurrying away toward Watertown to escape the dangers of war which now centered about Boston, she would not have cared so much about the May Day plans.

"It would be well to ask all the grown people as well as the children to the May party," said Mrs. Cary, as the little party made its way toward home that afternoon. "I do not think there has ever been a May Day party before in the town, and it will be good for all of us to try and be cheerful."

Anne and Amanda looked at her wonderingly. The world seemed a very cheerful and happy place to both the little girls, and they could not know how anxious the older people were that the trouble with England might soon come to an end.

CHAPTER SIXTEEN

THE MAY PARTY

"A MAY DAY PARTY, eh?" said Elder Haven, when Anne and Amanda told him of the plan. "Why, I think it an excellent idea. It will surely be a pleasant sight to see the children dance about the Maypole, and I shall like well to come."

After Elder Haven had approved, the parents could find nothing wrong in the idea, and all the children went Maying for arbutus and trailing evergreens to wind about the pole.

Early on the morning of May Day Amos and Jimmie were at the spring with a long smooth pole. The other children soon followed them, and Mrs. Starkweather came to show them how to fasten the wreath at the top and the long strings covered with vines and blossoms which Anne and Amanda, with the help of Mrs. Stoddard and the Starkweather boys, had made ready the day before.

"We used often to dance about a Maypole when I was a girl in Barnstable," said Mrs. Starkweather. "To be sure it is an old English custom, and just now England does not seem our friend, but 'tis a pleasant custom that we do well to follow. I know a little song that we all used to sing as we took hold of the bright streamers."

"I know that song," said Dannie; "you call it 'May Song.'"

"Why, yes," said Mrs. Starkweather, "I'm sure all my boys know it. I've sung them all to sleep by it; and 'tis one I sing about my work, for 'tis a cheerful and a merry lilt."

"It goes this way," said Dannie, and began to sing:

> *"Birds in the tree;*
> *Humming of bees,*
> *Wind singing over the sea;*
> *Happy May Days,*
> *Now do we praise,*
> *As we dance gladly round the May tree."*

As Dannie sang his mother and brothers joined in with him, and the other children listened in delight.

"Can you not sing it when we do 'dance round the May tree,' Aunt Starkweather?" asked Anne; "and if Dannie will sing it over to us a few times I am sure that we can all sing it, and then Elder Haven can hear us."

Dannie liked to sing, and he sang the little verse over and over again until all the children knew it, and until his mother said that they must all run home and make themselves tidy, and then come back, as the dance around the Maypole was to be at two o'clock.

"I do wish that Uncle Enos could see it," said Anne, as she put on her new white pinafore over her plaid dress, and fastened the coral beads around her neck. "I know well he would like to hear the song."

"The boats went out early and may get in in good time," said Aunt Martha.

"Mrs. Starkweather says that there is always a Queen of the May—a little girl whom the other children choose to wear a wreath on her head, and whatever the Queen tells them to do they must do all May Day," said Anne, as she and Mrs. Stoddard walked toward the spring, "but I do think the other children have forgotten all about it."

"What makes the children want to choose one to obey, I wonder," said Mrs. Stoddard, smiling down at Anne.

"It must be because 'tis a little girl whom they all like, and

112

who is always kind and pleasant to the other children," said
Anne. "If 'twas a King of the May we would all want Jimmie
Starkweather; but there are not so many girls as boys."

The other children were all at the spring with bunches and
wreaths of flowers, and Anne was surprised to see that a mound
of sand had been heaped up and covered with pine boughs.

"What is that for?" she asked.

"That's a throne for the Queen," said Dannie Starkweather.

Mrs. Cary and Mrs. Starkweather were talking with the children, and as Anne came near they formed into a little circle
round her, joining hands and singing:

> *"Our May-queen,*
> *Queen of the May,*
> *We're ready to serve you*
> *All this bright day."*

Then Willie Starkweather, who was only four years old, took
Anne's hand and led her to the "throne" and said, "You mutht
thit down, Anne," for Willie lisped, "and I'll put the crown on."

So Anne sat down on the pine-covered sandheap, and Willie
put a wreath of fragrant arbutus on her head.

Captain Enos, hurrying up from the shore, thought it the
prettiest sight he had ever seen. The tall pole, covered with
green vines and bright blossoms, the children forming in a circle
round Anne, and the pleasant May skies over all, seemed to the
sailor to make a picture worth remembering.

Then came the dance round the Maypole and the song. By
this time, the other men had come up from the shore; Elder
Haven was there, and every one in the little settlement had
gathered at the spring. It was a circle of happy faces, and when
the time came for them all to start for their homes, each one said
that Province Town had never seen so pretty a sight.

" 'Tis something we shall like to think about," said Elder
Haven to Jimmie Starkweather, as the two walked toward the
Elder's house.

Anne was sure that it was the happiest day in her life. "I wish
my father could have seen me, Aunt Martha," she said, as they
walked toward home. " 'Twould please him well to know the

children like me. 'Tis only a year since they did scorn me at the spring."

"You must forget about that, Anne," said Aunt Martha. "They chose you for Queen because you have been a pleasant child. You see, it matters not what they said before they knew you."

"Aunt Martha!" exclaimed Anne, suddenly looking up toward the harbor, "see! There are two big ships coming down the bay."

"We are not to be in peace long," said Mrs. Stoddard. "They are coming straight to anchorage."

Every one soon knew that the *Somerset* was back again, and now the English sailors took no trouble to be civil. They laid hands on provisions of all sorts, but nevertheless they brought good news.

William Trull found a chance to tell Captain Enos that the Americans had won the battle at Lexington. "We'll be in harbor here but a day or two," he added; "we must be back to watch the Americans at Charlestown." And, sure enough, the next morning the big ships had sailed away again, taking with them many things that the little settlement could ill spare.

As the summer days lengthened, Anne longed more and more for some news of her father. The battle of Bunker Hill had brought another triumph to the Americans, but the English vessels still cruised about the coast, making the fishermen careful about going far from shore.

"Uncle Enos, could we not go to Boston again and find my father?" Anne would ask, and Captain Enos would grow serious and shake his head, and say it would be too great a risk to undertake. So Anne helped Aunt Martha with the work of the house, played with her doll under the pine trees, and wandered about the shore with Amanda, but always thinking of her absent father, and wishing that she might go and find him.

"I am past nine years old. If I was a boy, I could sail a boat to Boston," she said to Amanda one day, as they went down to the beach to watch the fishing boats come in.

"Yes," agreed Amanda. "I guess that Amos could sail a boat to Boston before he was nine."

"Then he could sail one there now," exclaimed Anne. "Oh,

Amanda, wouldn't Amos sail us to Boston to find my father? Uncle Enos will not; he says 'tis not safe. But surely the English would not hurt two little girls and a boy. Would Amos be afraid?"

"Afraid of what?" Amos had come up beside them, and the sound of his voice made them jump.

"Afraid to sail a boat to Boston," explained Anne.

"That would be easy enough," declared the boy, "and I would like well to get the chance to sail father's *Peggy* to Boston."

"Will you, Amos? And take Amanda and me with you to find my father? I will take all the blame, indeed I will. And if we find him and bring him back, they will all think you a brave boy, Amos."

"They will not let us start," said Amos. "We'd have to put off in the night. But I'll do it. You girls must bring along something to eat, and we'll start at midnight."

"When?" asked Anne.

"Tonight," answered the boy. "Why, 'twill be a greater adventure than any boy of this settlement ever had. If we make Boston, I may be made prisoner by the British," and Amos looked as happy over the prospect as Anne did at the thought of finding her father.

"Mistress Stoddard will not be pleased," cautioned Amanda.

"She did not greatly blame me before," said Anne. "She knows I want much to see my father, and Uncle Enos does not want to go. If we sail safely there and home, it will save Uncle Enos trouble. He will not have to go himself."

"Should we see Rose Freeman?" asked Amanda.

"It may be," said Anne.

"I would like well to go, if we could see her," Amanda said thoughtfully.

Amos was now full of plans for the trip. There would be a favoring tide at midnight, and he was sure they could sail out of the harbor and be well on their way by morning; and, giving the girls many cautions about being on the shore at the right time, he went happily off to look over the sloop *Peggy*, and to wonder what Jimmie Starkweather would say if he knew that he, Amos, was going to sail a boat straight up to Boston!

115

CHAPTER SEVENTEEN

THE SLOOP *PEGGY*

THE SLOOP, *PEGGY,* was becalmed. Anne, Amanda and Amos looked over the smooth stretch of water, but there was not a ripple to be seen. Since sunrise, the boat had not moved. They had made the start at midnight, as they had planned, and had sailed away under a fair wind; but before the sun rose the wind had died away, and the mainsail now swung back and forth and the boat drifted slowly with the current.

None of the children had thought of bringing a jug of fresh water, and the salt fish and corn bread which they had brought along for food made them very thirsty.

"We're off Barnstable now," said Amos. "I've a mind to let the boat drift in nearer shore and anchor, and then row ashore in the tender and get some water."

"How far is Barnstable from Boston?" asked Anne.

"Miles and miles," answered Amos. " 'Tis only about half-way up the cape from Province Town."

"Then we could not walk to Boston from there?"

"No," said Amos; "why should we walk? There'll be a good breeze come sunset. All we need is a good drink of water, and

117

there's a water jug in the cabin. I can take it ashore and fill it at some spring."

As the children talked, the current had carried the boat steadily toward shore, but now it did not move.

"She's stuck on a sandbar," exclaimed Amos, "and the tide's turning. Perhaps I can walk ashore."

It was not long before the boat began to tip to one side, and as the tide went out, they found themselves on a sandbar, a full half mile from shore. The water seemed to flow in little channels, like wide brooks, here and there, between the boat and the land, and Amos wondered if he could either jump or wade those channels. The hot July sun beat down upon them, they were very thirsty and uncomfortable, and Amanda began to wish herself at home.

"We ought not to have started," she said, ready to cry. "I know my mother won't like it, and Mistress Stoddard will not like it, either."

Anne was very quiet. She was thirsty, hot and uncomfortable, and being run aground on a sandbar near a strange shore was a very different thing from her other prosperous voyage with Captain Enos. What if they should never reach Boston at all?

"They will all think that we have run away this time," said Amos, who had stepped over the side of the boat onto the sandbar.

"Oh, no, they won't," said Anne. "I wrote on a smooth chip, 'Amanda and Amos and I have gone to Boston to find my father,' and put it on the kitchen table."

"I believe I could get across those channels some way," declared Amos, "and I am so thirsty that I'm going to try it."

Amanda brought him the small stone jug from the cabin, and telling the girls not even to step out of the boat until he came back, Amos started for the shore. They saw him wade the first channel, run across a long stretch of wet sand, cross the other channel and reach the shore safely.

"Goody!" exclaimed Amanda; "now he will find a spring, fill the jug and hurry back, and we can have a good drink of water," and she turned smilingly to Anne. But Anne was looking very sober. She had been thinking over her other trip, and now remembered what Mrs. Stoddard had said when she returned from Boston.

"Oh, Amanda!" she said, looking ready to cry, "when I ran off before with Uncle Enos, Aunt Martha did tell me that I must never do so again. Now I have disobeyed her, and perhaps she will not want me to live with her any more."

"Then you can live with your father," answered Amanda cheerfully.

"But my father was to live with us," said Anne. "He was to have the big, pleasant loft that looks toward the water, and was to help Uncle Enos with the fishing. Perhaps they will not want either of us since I have been so unruly and disobedient."

Amanda longed to tell Anne that she should have a home with her, but she remembered that the white kitten had to be given away because they could not afford to keep it, and so kept silent.

"I hope Amos will not linger," she said, after a little silence. "He forgets that we are as thirsty as he is."

The little girls watched the shore anxiously, expecting every minute to see Amos hurrying back with a jug full of fresh water, but time passed and he did not come.

"I think the tide has turned," said Amanda. "See, the channels are widening every minute. If Amos does not come soon the water will be too deep. Oh, dear! I am afraid something has befallen him."

"What could befall him?" questioned Anne. " 'Tis a smooth and pleasant shore, with much taller trees than grow about Province Town. He is just playing about and has forgotten us."

Anne was nearly right, for after Amos had found a fine boiling spring and had drunk all he wanted and then filled his jug, he had sat down to rest under a wide-spreading oak tree. The day was hot, he was very tired and sleepy, having been awake all the night before, and without forgetting the *Peggy* or her crew, he dropped gently off to sleep. The tide came in, lifted the *Peggy* from the sandbar and a gentle breeze carried her steadily out from shore, and Amos slept on, knowing nothing of what had happened. The sun was very low in the western sky when he awoke. He sat up, rubbed his eyes, snatched up the jug and ran to the shore, but there was no boat to be seen.

Amos was now thoroughly frightened. He ran up and down the quiet shore, calling the name of his boat and shouting, "Amanda!" "Anne!" at the top of his voice. The shadows of the summer night deepened, a little haze rose over the water, and Amos, crouching down near the water's edge, waited for night to come.

"I know I shall never sleep any more," he whispered to himself, hardly daring to think of what might happen to the little girls. He wished that he had lowered the mainsail before coming ashore.

"I ought to have dropped anchor, anyway," he said aloud, and almost forgot to be hungry in his anxiety.

The shadows grew deeper, night settled down on land and sea and Amos went fast asleep again, with his bare feet almost within reach of the waves that rolled so softly up over the smooth sand.

Anne and Amanda watched the tide come in about the *Peggy*, and soon felt the boat move under them. Then the mainsail filled and swung out, as the breeze came up.

"Try and steer ashore, Amanda," exclaimed Anne.

"I dare not touch the rudder," said Amanda. "Whenever I have been in a boat, my father has told me to sit still; and I do think it is the best thing we can do now, Anne."

"Mayhap the wind will take us home again," said Anne, "and then your father will come back and find Amos."

"More like 'twill take us straight out to sea," said Amanda.

" 'Tis all my fault," said Anne; "I did prevail on you and Amos to come."

"We both liked well to come," answered Amanda stoutly. "Amos should have known better, for he is older. But he likes a risk over well, and now he can play shipwrecked to his heart's desire."

"My eyes are heavy with sleep," said Anne. "Let us say the small prayer that Elder Haven taught us and sleep a little. 'Tis dark and foggy; we can see nothing."

Amanda reached out her sunburned little hand and clasped Anne's, and they repeated aloud the prayer, asking for help and protection, which Elder Haven had taught them; then, curling themselves up in the bottom of the boat, they went fast asleep.

But the *Peggy* did not sail far. The wind died away, and the boat drifted with the tide. When the little girls awoke it was bright sunshine, and a big ship was coming slowly down upon them.

" 'Tis a Britisher!" Amanda exclaimed. "Like as not she's bound for England and will carry us straight off," and Amanda began crying bitterly.

Before Anne could answer there came a hail from the ship, and Anne and Amanda called back, "Sloop *Peggy*! Sloop *Peggy*!" as loudly as they could, as they had heard Province Town captains do in answer to hails from harbor boats.

It was not long before the big vessel was near enough for the sailors to distinguish that there were only two little girls on board the drifting sloop, and a man was ready with a stout boat-hook, which he grappled about the *Peggy*'s" mast, and a big man with reddish hair and blue eyes slid down a rope and swung himself on board the sloop.

"Zounds!" exclaimed the sailor, "if 'tis not the little Province Town maid again! And adrift like this. I'll have to take you to England and let Betsey and Harriet take care of you!"

Before he had finished both Anne and Amanda had begun to cry. They were sure now that they should never see home again, and William Trull had some trouble in convincing them that he did not mean to take them to England.

But the captain had small patience with the delay, and called out that 'twas best to sink the sloop rather than lose a fair wind out of harbor.

"I cannot be leaving two helpless maids adrift," William Trull called back. "They are from the Province Town settlement."

"Take them back to it, if you like, and find your way across the Atlantic as best you may," retorted the English captain angrily. "We can't stand by for such folly."

Poor William Trull looked at the little girls in dismay. To be left stranded on American territory was the last thing he desired.

"Can't you tow our boat down to Province Town?" pleaded Anne. "We won't hurt you."

"Ha! ha!" laughed the captain, and even William Trull joined in the laughter of the crew, while Anne and Amanda wondered why the sailors laughed. "Well," and the captain's voice was more friendly as he leaned over his ship's railing and gazed down at the little girls, "if you won't run us down we'll take you along that far. You can stay on the sloop, Trull, till we get near the tip of the cape. 'Tis plain American children are not easily frighted."

The sloop was now taken in tow, and although the little girls pleaded that a boat be sent to find Amos, William Trull shook his head.

" 'Twill not do," he declared, "to ask it of the captain; and if the boy be a smart boy he'll make his way home, never fear."

It was some comfort to Amanda to declare that Amos was the smartest boy in the settlement; that he could make fire as Indians did, and that he knew many ways of snaring birds and fish.

"Never fear for a boy like that," said the sailor.

Anne was eager to ask him if he knew anything of her father, and William Trull owned that he did.

" 'Twas your father who some way got word to Newburyport and Portsmouth men to be ready to fight," he said. " 'Twas cleverly done, they tell me, but no one has found out how."

"I know," said Anne, "because I helped." Then remembering Captain Stoddard's caution, she put her hand over her mouth. "I must not tell," she said.

The sailor looked at her in astonishment. "Even the children are 'rebels,' " he declared, "and helping when chance comes. 'Tis a great country. I'll not question you, child, but I'll tell my little girls about you, and that you helped to send the English home. Your own father will soon be telling you how the Americans drove the English; but you must keep a kind thought for me."

"Oh, I do wish you would stay and be an American, Mr. William Trull, and bring your little girls to live in Province Town," said Anne.

"Who knows?" said the sailor. "It may be I'll be coming back with my family. I like this country well. Your father will be coming to Province Town soon, never fear," he added, "for now Boston port is open to all, and the fishermen are going in and out as they please."

Amanda had not been much interested in what the sailor had

to say. She was thinking that Amos must be very hungry; and when William Trull climbed aboard the big vessel and the sloop dropped behind near the Province Town shore, she was greatly rejoiced.

It was not long that the *Peggy* was alone. Men on shore had been watching and were quick to recognize the sloop, and a boat was sent out. Amanda recognized that her father was in it, as well as Captain Enos and Jimmie Starkweather, and called out in delight. There was an anxious crowd on the beach, and Mrs. Stoddard and Amanda's mother ran eagerly forward to greet the little girls, and to ask what had become of Amos.

It was soon evident that Jimmie Starkweather and the other boys were inclined to be envious of Amos's good fortune; and when Mr. Cary made his own boat ready to sail for Barnstable to bring Amos home Jimmie was very proud to be selected to accompany him.

"How shall we ever feel safe about thee, child?" said Mrs. Stoddard, as she and Anne walked toward home. "Are you always to be seeking your father without telling us? If you had but waited you would have saved us all this worry, and Amos would now be safe at home."

"But I have news, Aunt Martha," pleaded Anne. "Mr. William Trull told me my father might soon be with us. I will not leave you again, unless, indeed, you no longer want me."

"Of course we want you, Anne. But I have better news than the English sailor gave you. Look! Here comes some one whom you will be glad to see," but before she had finished speaking Anne had sprung forward with an exclamation of delight, for her father was coming down the path to the shore.

"I came down in one of Mr. Freeman's fishing boats," he explained, as, hand in hand, he and Anne walked back to join Mrs. Stoddard. Anne danced along happily, and Mrs. Stoddard smiled as she looked at the little girl.

"And now I hope for peace," declared the good woman. "Anne will not let you go again, John Nelson. You will have to be content to stay in Province Town."

The next day Elder Haven came to see John Nelson to hear more about the great triumphs of the Americans; and when Anne's father told him of Captain Stoddard's trip to Newburyport, with Anne carrying the important message for the New-buryport patriots, the good clergyman held up his hands in wonder. "She is a brave little maid," he said. "It should be put on record that a maid of Province Town helped the Americans to win their just cause against King George. Indeed it should."

"She is a brave child," agreed Captain Enos. "I was sure of it when I heard her defend her father at the spring," and the good captain chuckled at the remembrance of Anne's battle with the Cary children, who were now her staunchest friends.

"Amos is safe home, and proud enough; he is lording it well over his mates," said Elder Haven. "You must not run away again, Anne," he added more gravely, resting a gentle hand on the dark head.

"No, oh, no!" replied Anne, "not unless my father and Aunt Martha and Uncle Enos go with me."

A Little Maid
of Massachusetts Colony

CONTENTS

ONE   AMANDA'S MISTAKE 129

TWO   ANNE DECIDES 137

THREE   A NEW FRIEND 143

FOUR   WITH THE MASHPEES 153

FIVE   AT BREWSTER 161

SIX   AMANDA'S CONSCIENCE 169

SEVEN   THE BLACK-BEARDED MAN 177

EIGHT   THROUGH THE WINDOW 187

NINE   LADY DISAPPEARS 195

TEN   AUNT ANNE ROSE 203

ELEVEN   IN BOSTON 209

TWELVE   A WONDERFUL DAY 215

THIRTEEN   ANNE'S BOOK 223

FOURTEEN   ANNE AND MILLICENT 229

FIFTEEN   AMOS APPEARS 235

SIXTEEN   AN UNEXPECTED VISITOR 241

SEVENTEEN   THE STRANGE SCHOONER 249

EIGHTEEN   A GREAT ADVENTURE 255

NINETEEN   HOMEWARD BOUND 261

CHAPTER ONE

AMANDA'S MISTAKE

"Do you think I might go, Aunt Martha?" There was a pleading note in the little girl's voice as she stood close by Mrs. Stoddard's chair and watched her folding the thin blue paper on which Rose Freeman's letter was written.

"It is a pleasant invitation, surely," replied Mrs. Stoddard, "but the Freemans have ever been good friends to us; and so Rose is to visit their kin in Brewster and then journey back to Boston with her father in his chaise, and she says there will be plenty of room for you. Well! Well! 'Tis a wonderful journey."

Anne moved uneasily. "But, Aunt Martha, do you forget that she asks if Uncle Enos cannot bring me to Brewster?"

"Yes, child, I have read the letter, and I doubt not Enos will set you safe across to Brewster. And your father's vessel will be due in Boston early in September, and he could bring you safely home to Province Town. We'll see what Uncle Enos says about sailing across to Brewster," and Mrs. Stoddard smiled affectionately at Anne's delighted exclamation. It was two years before that Anne Nelson, whose father's boat had been seized by an English ship, had come to live with the Stoddards. Her father had escaped, and, after serving the colonies until after the battle of Lexington, had returned to Province Town, and was now away on a fishing cruise. Anne had visited the Freemans the year before, and now this pleasant invitation for a journey to Boston had been brought by one of the harbor fishermen, the only way letters came to Province Town. It was no wonder Anne was eager for permission to go. It would be a three days' ride from Brewster, and the road would take her through many pleasant towns and villages. There was not a person in the settlement who had taken the journey by land. Uncle Enos declared that Province Town folk who could sail a good boat, with fair winds, to Boston in six hours were too wise to take such a roundabout route as the land offered.

"But it will be a fine ride for Anne," he agreed. "She will learn much by the journey, and Squire Freeman will take good care of her. I'll set her across to Brewster on Tuesday, as Rose says they plan to start early on Wednesday morning. Well, Anne," and he turned toward the happy child, "what do you think the Cary children will say when you tell them that you are to ride to Boston in a fine chaise?"

"I do not know, but I think Amos will say that he would not journey by land; he is all for big ships; but I'm sure Amanda will think it is a wonderful thing, and wish to go with me, and indeed I wish she might. But why do we not have chaises in Province Town?"

"We must have roads first," replied Aunt Martha smilingly; "but Province Town has no need of coaches and roads with good boats in harbor. Now we must see that your clothes are in order, for a week soon goes."

"Anne! Anne!" and before Anne could respond a girl of about her own age came running into the kitchen. "Can you go with me over to the outer beach? May she go, Mrs. Stoddard? See! I have enough luncheon for us both in this basket," and Amanda held up a pretty basket woven of sweet grass.

"May I, Aunt Martha? And oh, Amanda! A wonderful thing is going to happen to me. Isn't it wonderful, Uncle Enos?"

Aunt Martha and Uncle Enos both smiled and nodded, and Amanda looked from one to the other in great surprise.

"Run along with Amanda and tell her all about it," said Mrs. Stoddard, and the two little girls started happily off.

"I can guess," declared Amanda, "for I know that Captain Starkweather brought you a letter from Boston, and I can guess who the letter is from."

Anne shook her head laughingly. "You would guess that it was from my dear father," she answered.

"And is it not?" questioned Amanda in surprise.

"It is from Rose Freeman," announced Anne. "And, oh, Amanda, she asks me to come to Brewster next week, and go with her in her father's chaise to Boston!" And Anne turned, smiling happily, toward Amanda. She had expected Amanda to exclaim with delight over such a wonderful piece of news, but instead of delight Amanda's face expressed an angry surprise. She had stopped short, and stood looking at Anne.

"Rose Freeman!" she exclaimed. "Boston in a chaise! I wonder I play with you at all, Anne Nelson. Why don't you stay in Boston? I shouldn't care if you did!" and throwing the basket of luncheon on the ground Amanda turned and ran back toward home.

Anne looked after her in amazement. "That's the way she used to act before we were friends," she said aloud; "and all that good food thrown down in the sand," for the basket was overturned, and two round ginger cakes, two pieces of corn bread, and two three-cornered tarts had rolled out. Anne knelt down and picked them up carefully, shaking off the sand, and returned them to the basket.

"Her mother cannot afford to have such good things wasted," said Anne; for even the children in Province Town in the days of the Revolution knew how difficult it was to secure supplies. The end of Cape Cod, with its sandy dunes, scant pasturage or tillage, made the people depend on their boats, not only to bring in fish, but all other household necessities. The harbor was unguarded, and its occupation as a rendezvous by English men-of-war had made it very hard for the people to get provisions. So it was no wonder that Anne looked at the ginger cakes and tarts as special delicacies, too precious to lie in the sand.

"I'll go to the outer beach by myself," decided Anne, "but I will not eat my share of the luncheon. I do not see why Amanda should be angry," and the little girl walked on, choosing her way

carefully among the scrubby pine trees or patches of beach-
plum bushes.

Amanda ran swiftly, and in a moment or two was almost back
in the Stoddards' dooryard!

"I mustn't go home," she said to herself; "they would question me, and I would have to tell them all the wonderful news
about Anne. And, oh," she exclaimed aloud, "if I did not throw
down the fine treat my mother put in the basket. I'll go back for
it; Anne Nelson has everything, but she shall not have my tarts."

Amanda made her way back very carefully, hoping to get the
basket and escape without Anne seeing her. But when she
reached the spot where Anne had told the wonderful news neither the basket nor Anne was to be seen.

"She's run off with my basket. She means to eat all that
mother gave me!" Amanda now felt that she had a just grievance
against her playmate. "I'll go home and tell my mother," she
decided, and on the way home a very wicked plan came into the
little girl's mind. She pulled off her gingham sunbonnet and
threw it behind a bunch of plum bushes. She then unbraided her
neat hair and pulled it all about her face. For a moment she
thought of tearing a rent in her stout skirt, but did not. Then she
crawled under a wide-branched pine and lay down. "I must wait
a time, or my mother will think I am too quickly back," she
decided, "and I do not want to get home while Amos is there;"
for Amanda knew well that her brother would not credit the
story which Amanda had resolved to tell: that Anne had pushed
her over in the sand, slapped her, and run off with the basket of
luncheon.

"My mother will go straight to Mistress Stoddard, and
there'll be no journeyings to Brewster to see Rose Freeman, or
riding to Boston in a fine chaise," decided the envious child.

So, while Anne kept on her way to the outer beach, carrying
Amanda's basket very carefully, and expecting every moment
that Amanda would come running after her, and that they would
make friends, and enjoy the goodies together, Amanda was
thinking of all the pleasant things that a journey to Boston
would mean, and resolving to herself that if she could not go
neither should Anne. So envious was the unhappy child that she
tried to remember some unkindness that Anne had shown her,

that she might justify her own wrongdoing. But in spite of herself the thought of Anne recalled only pleasant things. "I don't care," she resolved; "she shan't go to Boston with Rose Freeman, and she has run off with the basket."

"Mercy, child! What has befallen you, and where is Anne?" questioned Mrs. Cary, as Amanda came slowly up to the kitchen door, where her mother sat knitting.

"She's run off with my basket," whimpered Amanda, holding her apron over her face.

"And is Anne Nelson to blame for your coming home in this condition?" questioned Mrs. Cary, a little flush coming into her thin cheeks.

Amanda nodded; some way it seemed very hard to say that Anne had pushed her down and slapped her.

"And run off with my basket," she repeated, "and next week she goes to Brewster, and by carriage to Boston."

"Well, that's no reason why she should turn so upon you," declared Mrs. Cary. "What made trouble between you?"

"I think it was because of this journey," replied Amanda. "She is so set up by it, and she went off with the basket."

"Never mind about the basket, child; but it's a sad thing for Anne to so lose her temper. You did quite right to come home, dear child; now brush your hair neatly, and bathe your face, and then come with me to Mistress Stoddard; though I like not our errand," concluded Mrs. Cary, rolling up the stocking she was knitting.

Amanda looked at her mother pleadingly. "Why must I go to Mistress Stoddard's?" she questioned. "I have run all the way home, and you know she will not blame Anne; it will be me she will question and blame. Oh, dear!" and Amanda, sure that her evil plan would be discovered, began to sob bitterly.

"There, there! I did but think you could tell Mrs. Stoddard of Anne's mischief. You need not go, child. Get you a ginger cake from the stone jar in the cellarway. I'll tell of the way Anne pushed you about, and made off with the basket, and you sit here by the door. There's a sweet breeze coming over the marshes," and, patting Amanda's ruffled locks, Mrs. Cary took down her sunbonnet from its hook behind the door, and prepared to set forth.

"I'll not be long away," she called back, as she passed down the sandy path.

From the pleasant doorway Amanda watched her with a gloomy face. Her plan was going on successfully, but Amanda did not feel happy. She was dreading the time when Amos would return, and his sharp questioning, she knew, would be a very different matter from her mother's acceptance of her story.

"Everybody always thinks that Anne is right," she said aloud.

"Well, isn't she?" said a voice directly behind her, so near that Amanda jumped up in surprise.

"How did you get into the house, Amos Cary!" she exclaimed angrily.

"Phew, Carrot-top! What's the matter?" responded Amos teasingly. "Say, Sis, don't cry," he added. "I won't call you 'Carrot-top' again. You know my hair's exactly the same color as yours, anyway; so it's just like calling myself names."

But Amanda kept on sobbing. "It's Anne," she whimpered. "She—she—she's run off with my basket."

"Anne!" exclaimed the boy in surprise. "Oh, well, she was only fooling. She'll bring it back. You know Anne wouldn't do a mean thing."

"She would, too. She's going to Boston, and to Brewster, with Rose Freeman," said Amanda.

"O-oh! So that's the trouble, is it?" said Amos. "Well, she'll come back, so don't cry," and he stepped past her and ran down toward the beach.

At Mrs. Stoddard's Mrs. Cary was repeating Amanda's story.

"I cannot understand it," said Mrs. Stoddard. "You know well, Mistress Cary, that Anne is a pleasant child, and she and Amanda started out as friendly as need be. Did Amanda say what began the trouble?"

Mrs. Cary shook her head. "No, she is at home crying her heart out about it, poor child."

"I know not what to say," and Mrs. Stoddard's usually smiling face was very grave. "Anne is not home yet, but I will question her. You may be sure, Mistress Cary, that I will not let it pass. Her father leaves her in my care when he is away, and perhaps I am too indulgent, for I love the child."

It was an hour later when Anne came and peered in at the

134

open door. Mrs. Cary had gone home. Mrs. Stoddard looked at the little girl, but not with her usual smile.

"Where is Amanda's basket?" she asked sharply. "Do not stand there; come in." Anne obeyed. "Now, tell me why you pushed Amanda down, and slapped her, and ran off with the basket of food? Mrs. Cary has been here and told me all about it. A nice story indeed for me to hear. But like as not it is my fault for indulging you in everything. But I shall be firm now. Go upstairs and stay until I call you; and as for that visit with Rose Freeman, think no more of it. I shall not let you go. No, indeed, after such a performance as this."

Anne thought to herself that she must be dreaming. "I shall wake up in a minute," she said aloud, but Mrs. Stoddard did not hear her.

"Go right upstairs," she repeated, and Anne, with a puzzled look over her shoulder, went slowly up the narrow stairs.

CHAPTER TWO

———— ❦ ————

ANNE DECIDES

"I DON'T KNOW what to do," Anne whispered to herself, with a little sob, as she looked out of the narrow window in her little room. Captain Stoddard was coming briskly up the path; in a moment he would be directly under the window. "I'll call to him, and if he answers I shall know that I am awake," she decided, and leaning out she called softly: "Uncle Enos! Uncle Enos!"

Captain Stoddard looked up, and answered briskly: "Anne Nelson, ahoy!"

"Uncle Enos, listen!" and Anne leaned out still farther. "I went toward the outer beach with Amanda Cary, and she slapped me and ran off. And when I came home Aunt Martha sent me upstairs. Now what have I done?"

Captain Stoddard chuckled, then he looked very serious indeed, and replied:

"A pretty affair! What have you been doing?"

"Nothing, Uncle Enos; indeed I have done no mischief. Tell Aunt Martha that Amanda slapped me, and that I did not slap back."

Uncle Enos nodded, and made a motion for Anne to be silent, and Anne drew quickly back into the room.

"Uncle Enos will find out," she whispered to the little wooden doll, Martha Stoddard, that her father had made for her when she was a very small girl, and which was still one of her greatest treasures. But the July afternoon faded into the long twilight and no one called to Anne to come down. She began to feel hungry. "I wish I had eaten my share of that luncheon and not given it to Amos to carry home," she thought. For on her way home she had met Amos and had given the lunch basket into his charge, telling him to carry it home to Amanda, but saying nothing of Amanda's anger.

As Anne sat in the loft chamber waiting for the call that did not come, she began to feel that she had been treated very badly. "And Aunt Martha says I shall not visit Rose Freeman, and does not tell me why I shall not go. My father would let me; I know that full well. And I am going; I will walk to Brewster!" Anne's heart grew lighter as she thought of all the joys that a visit to Rose would mean. "I'll start tonight," she decided. "Maybe it will take me a long time, as there are no roads, but I know I can find the way. Oh, I wish it would get dark! I'll take you, Martha Stoddard, but I guess I'll change your name, for Aunt Martha doesn't like me any more," and the little girl began to feel very lonely and unhappy. The room door swung open at that very moment and there stood Mrs. Stoddard with a mug full of creamy milk and a plate of corn bread.

"Here is your supper, Anne. And I hope you are ready to tell me why you pushed Amanda down and ran off with her basket," and Mrs. Stoddard looked at Anne with a puzzled expression in her kind eyes.

"I did not——" began Anne.

"There, there, child. Mrs. Cary told me the whole story. Tell me the truth, and I'll not be hard with you," and Mrs. Stoddard set down the mug and plate on the lightstand and stood waiting.

"I will not say another word!" declared Anne, who felt that even her dear Aunt Martha had turned against her.

"Then you must stay up here until you are a more obedient child," said Mrs. Stoddard, and went slowly out of the room. "I don't see what has possessed the child," she said to Captain Enos on returning to the kitchen.

"She has always been a truthful child, Martha," ventured the captain, "so why not believe her now?"

"I would gladly, Enos; but Mrs. Cary came straight to me as soon as Amanda reached home, and 'twas an hour later when Anne returned, and she has no word of excuse. 'Twill do the child no harm to stay in her room until she can tell me the reason for such behavior. And of course this visit to the Freemans' must be given up. 'Twould not do to let her go after such conduct."

"A pity," responded the captain. " 'Twould have been a fine journey for the little maid."

Anne could hear the murmur of their voices as she drank the milk and ate the corn bread. "I wish I had some bread to take with me," she thought. "I'll take my blue cape, and my shoes and white stockings, for I'm sure I ought to wear them on the chaise," and Anne tiptoed about the room gathering up her clothing. It did not make a very large bundle, even when she decided to take the white muslin dress, and the coral beads. She heard Captain Enos and Aunt Martha go to their chamber, and then, holding Martha Stoddard and the bundle in her arms, crept down the narrow stairway. The outer door stood ajar to admit the cool fragrant air, and in a moment Anne was running along the sandy track that led through the little settlement. It was still early, but there was not a light to be seen in any of the small gray houses. The summer sky was filled with stars, and as Anne ran she could see her shadow stretching ahead of her, "as if I were running right over it all the time," she whispered to Martha Stoddard.

The beautiful harbor seemed like a shining mirror, it lay so calm and still in the shadow of the land. But Anne did not stop to look at stars or sea; she wanted to reach the pines at the end of the village. Then she meant to go on as fast as she could toward Truro. "There will be nice places to rest under the trees, where nobody will ever look for me; perhaps no one will want to look," thought the little girl, with a choky sensation in her throat as she remembered the strange happenings of the afternoon.

The track grew more indistinct toward the end of the settlement, and when Anne reached the woods the shadows were dark, and she was obliged to go carefully in order not to lose her way. The border line between Truro and Province Town was marked by the jawbone of a whale set in the ground by the side of a red oak stump. The path up to this landmark was well known to all the village children; the hill was called Cormorant Hill; and Anne had been there many times with Amanda and Amos and the Starkweather children, and was very sure that from that place she could find her way through Truro to Wellfleet. "I'll not rest until I get to Kexconeoquet," decided Anne. Kexconeoquet was the Indian name for the hill.

About halfway up the slope Anne stopped to rest under a tall pine tree. There was a bed of soft green moss, and as she sat down she gave a little tired sigh. "Maybe it will be morning before I get to the top of the hill," she thought, and put Martha Stoddard carefully down on the moss. "I suppose I might sleep a minute," she said drowsily, arranging her bundle for a pillow and resting her head upon it. And a moment later an inquisitive little squirrel noticed that there was a little girl in a brown gingham dress fast asleep under the pine tree.

Mrs. Stoddard awoke early the next morning, and when she and Captain Enos sat down to their simple breakfast she said:

"I hear no sound of Anne, and I'll let her sleep late this morning; when she wakes she will tell me what happened. I woke up in the night and thought about it, and I feel sure our little maid could not have been all to blame. Amanda is quick to find trouble."

Uncle Enos nodded approvingly. " 'Twill do her no harm to sleep," he agreed, "and do not make up your mind that she must not go for the visit to Brewster and Boston. I can set her across to Brewster come Tuesday. 'Twill give me a chance to get some canvas for a new jib for the sloop."

Captain Enos spoke softly, and tiptoed out of the little kitchen, and Aunt Martha moved quietly about the house until the long summer morning was half over; then she went softly up the stairs, and opened the door to Anne's room. In a moment she realized what had happened: that Anne had run away; and she lost no time in hurrying to the shore, where Captain Enos was salting his yesterday's catch of fish and spreading them on the "flakes"—long low frames—to dry. Captain Starkweather and Amanda's father were near by, busy at the same work, and further along the shore were other groups of men taking care of the "catch" of the previous day. For the dried fish were shipped to many distant places, and curing them was a part of the fisherman's business.

"Anne is gone! She has run away," called Mrs. Stoddard, and in a moment she was telling Captain Enos that she was sure that the little girl had crept out of the house in the night. Captain Starkweather and Mr. Cary listened in amazement.

"But where could she go?" asked Captain Enos. "There's something wrong in this. Anne called to me from her window yesterday that she knew not the reason for her being punished. She has run away from us, Martha, because we have been unfair toward her."

"But where? Stop not to talk, Enos. Is there a boat missing? Like as not Anne has set forth for Boston." And Mrs. Stoddard looked out over the wide harbor as if expecting to see Anne sailing away.

"It may be your little girl is playing about and will soon return," suggested Captain Starkweather.

"Is her doll gone?" questioned Captain Enos; "for if it is not you may be sure that Anne is not far away."

"Indeed, I did not think to look; and you may be right, Captain Starkweather. I'll step back and see," and Mrs. Stoddard's face brightened as she turned toward home, followed by Captain Enos and the two fishermen.

"The doll is gone," she called down from the little chamber, "and Anne's cape and beads, and her shoes and stockings."

In a short time every one in the village knew of Anne's disappearance, and Amanda heard her father say that he feared Anne had started off in one of the little boats. "If she has there is small chance for the child," he said soberly, and Amanda began to whimper.

"She gave me Amanda's basket to bring home yesterday," said Amos; " 'tis in the shed."

"Yes, she ran off with it yesterday, and ate all the lunch herself," explained Mrs. Cary, "and slapped Amanda. Your sister came running home crying as if her heart would break."

"Anne didn't eat the luncheon. 'Twas all in the basket, and I ate it," said Amos. "I don't believe she slapped Amanda, anyway. Or if she did I'll bet Amanda slapped her first."

"Amos!" Mr. Cary's voice was very stern, and the boy said no more.

It was found that a rowboat was missing, and remembering how Anne and the Cary children had once started out to sail to Boston, it was generally believed that Anne had started off in the boat. Nevertheless search parties went across the narrow strip of land to the outer beach and up and down the shore of the harbor and along the edge of the Truro woods. Several boats started off, for it was felt that the best chance of finding her was the hope that the little boat could not have gone very far. "It may have been swept out to sea," Mr. Cary said, and at this Amanda set up such a wail that he instantly added: "But Anne will be found; of course she will."

CHAPTER THREE

A NEW FRIEND

"It's morning!" And Anne sat up and looked about with surprised eyes. Little flecks of sunshine came through the sheltering branches of the tall pine, squirrels ran up and down its trunk, and there were chirpings and calls of birds among the nearby trees. "And I'm not halfway to the top," continued Anne, shaking off the feeling of drowsiness and springing up from the soft moss. She picked up her bundle and Martha Stoddard and started on. " 'Tis about the time that Aunt Martha and Uncle Enos are eating porridge," she thought longingly, and then remembered that on the hillside, not far from the top, there was a spring of cool water, and she hurried on. She could hear the little tinkling sound of the water before she came in sight of the tiny stream which ran down the slope from the bubbling spring; and laying down her doll and the bundle she ran forward, eager for a drink. She knelt down and drank, and then turned to pick up her belongings, but the bundle and doll had disappeared. Anne looked about as if she could not believe her eyes. "They must be here!" she exclaimed aloud, and at that moment Martha Stoddard peered at her astonished owner from behind a tree. The little wooden doll appeared to walk. Then it bowed very low, and vanished. Anne ran to the tree, but Martha was not there; but the doll's head could be seen behind a small bush, almost within Anne's reach; but now Anne stopped, remembering that dolls, even dolls like Martha, could not play hide-and-seek. She felt bewildered, and, although Martha bowed and even tried to dance, Anne did not approach a step nearer. She could see that a small brown hand was keeping a tight grasp on Martha, and as she watched this hand a brown face peered out at her over Martha's head—the brown smiling face of an Indian girl, probably several years older than Anne. After looking at Anne for a few seconds she came out from behind the cluster of bushes. "She's as tall as Rose Freeman," was Anne's first thought.

"Where is my bundle?" she demanded, for although the Indian girl held Martha Stoddard in plain sight the bundle was not visible.

The Indian girl shook her head smilingly, and Anne repeated, "Bundle! Bundle!" and then exclaimed, "Oh, dear, she doesn't know what I say."

The girl now came a step or two nearer, holding out the doll for Anne to take. Her hair was very black and thick, and braided in one heavy plait. There was a band of bright feathers about her head, and she wore a loose tunic of finely dressed deerskin which came to her knees, and was without sleeves. Her arms and feet were bare, and as she stood smiling at Anne she made a very pretty picture.

Anne reached out her hand for the doll, and as she did so the Indian girl grasped it firmly, but in so gentle a manner that Anne did not draw back. The girl drew her along, smiling and saying strange sounding words in her own language, of which Anne could understand but one—"Mashpee." This was the name of a tribe of Cape Cod Indians who owned land, and who were always kind and friendly toward the white settlers; Anne was quite sure that the girl was telling her that she belonged to that nation.

The Indian girl circled around the big tree near the spring, and there lay—spread out on the moss—Anne's pretty blue cape, her white muslin dress, and her shoes and stockings and the bright coral beads. The Indian girl knelt down and picking

144

up the beads fastened them about her own neck; she then threw
the cape over her own shoulders, and picking up the shoes and
stockings, placed them in front of Anne, and put the muslin
dress beside them.

It needed no words to explain this; she had selected what she
wanted from the bundle and Anne could have the things that the
Indian girl did not want.

Anne's face must have expressed what she felt, for the smile
faded from her companion's lips, and the dark eyes grew unfriendly. She snatched the doll from Anne, and turned as if to
run away.

"Nakanit!"

Both the girls gave a little jump, for they had been too much
engrossed in each other to notice that an Indian woman had
come along the path and had stopped a short distance from
them. As she spoke the Indian girl started toward her, and began
to talk rapidly. Anne stood waiting, and wondering what would
happen now, and heartily wished herself safely back in the
Stoddards' snug little house.

As the Indian woman listened Anne could see that she was
angry and when Nakanit, for that was the Indian girl's name, had
finished the woman snatched the cape from the girl's shoulders,
and, pointing to the beads, evidently bade her unfasten them. As
the Indian girl obeyed the woman gave her a sharp slap on the
cheek, and Nakanit, without a look toward Anne, fled into the
forest.

"Here, white child," said the woman, "here are your things.
What are you doing so far from the settlement?"

"I am going to Brewster," replied Anne.

The Indian woman eyed her sharply.

"You have run away from your mother and father," she said
sharply.

"My mother is dead, and my father is at sea," Anne replied,
feeling her face growing red under the sharp eyes of the woman,
and a little ashamed that she did not own that she was running
away from Aunt Martha Stoddard. But she felt that Aunt Martha
had been very unfair toward her.

The Indian woman's face softened. "And you journey alone
to find friends in Brewster?" she asked.

145

"Yes, indeed; I am to go to Rose Freeman, and ride with her and her father in their chaise to Boston, and wait at their house for my father."

The woman nodded. The name of Freeman was known to her, and though a sixty-mile journey seemed a long way for so small a girl as Anne, the woman only wondered at the unkindness of the white women in letting a child go alone.

"Come," she said, and Anne, gathering up her shoes and stockings and the rumpled white dress, followed her.

The woman turned from the path and, as she walked swiftly on, gave several low calls which to Anne sounded like the notes of a bird. The last call was answered, and a moment later Nakanit appeared beside them. For a long time they went on in silence, and at last the woman stopped suddenly.

"Oh!" exclaimed Anne, for directly in front of them was a wigwam, so cunningly built in behind a growth of small spruce trees that unless one knew of its whereabouts it might be easily passed by. The Indian girl laughed at Anne's exclamation, and nodded at her in a friendly manner.

"Go in," said the woman. "Did no woman give you food to eat on your journey?"

Anne shook her head.

"Umph!" grunted the woman, and turned toward Nakanit, evidently telling her to bring Anne something to eat.

The Indian girl opened a basket that stood near the wigwam door and took out some thin cakes made of corn meal, and handed them to Anne. Anne ate them hungrily; they tasted very sweet and good. When she had eaten the last one, she turned toward the woman who sat beside her, and said: "Thank you very much. The cakes were good."

The woman nodded gravely. Anne looked round the wigwam with curious eyes. It was evident that Nakanit and her mother were nearly ready for a journey. The two baskets were near the door, the roll of blankets beside them, well tied up with stout thongs of deerskin, and the little brush wigwam had nothing else in it.

The Indian girl stood with her dark eyes fixed on Anne, and the woman talked rapidly for a few moments, evidently giving the girl information or directions; then she lifted the smaller of the two baskets, and fastened its deerskin strap over Nakanit's shoulders. The roll of blankets and the other basket she carried herself.

"Follow," she said to Anne; "we journey toward Wellfleet and you can go with us."

Anne's face brightened, and she began to feel that her troubles were over. She picked up her own bundle and followed the woman and the Indian girl out through the woods and across a meadow where a few cattle were feeding.

"This must be Truro," Anne thought to herself as she trudged silently on beside her new friends.

It grew very warm and there was no shade, and Anne began to feel tired, but neither Nakanit nor her mother seemed to notice the heat. It was past noon before they made any stop, and as Anne, who was some distance behind her companions, saw the woman turn toward a little wooded hill and begin to lower the basket from her shoulders, she gave a long tired sigh of relief. Nakanit heard and turned toward her, and reached out her free hand to take Anne's bundle. But Anne shook her head, and tightened her hold on it. This seemed to anger the Indian girl, and with a surly word she gave Anne a push, sending her over into a clump of wild rose bushes. As Anne reached out to save herself the thorns scratched her hands and arms and she cried out. The woman turned, and, as she had not seen the push, thought that Anne had stumbled, and began to laugh at her and to mock her cries. This delighted Nakanit, who joined in so loudly that Anne stopped in terrified amazement, and scrambled out as well as she could. Her feet ached, and she could hardly walk, but she went on behind Nakanit into the pleasant shade of the woods. Here her companions set down their baskets, and threw themselves down to rest. Anne looked at them a little fearfully; they had not spoken one word to her since leaving the wigwam.

The woman opened the basket and gave each of the girls some of the corn bread, which they devoured hungrily. "There are berries over there," she said briefly, pointing toward the slope, "and water."

Nakanit was already running toward the slope, but Anne did not move; she was still hungry and very thirsty, but too tired to walk, and as she lay on the soft grass she began to dread the moment when the woman might start on again. It was not long before Nakanit returned. She brought with her a cunningly made basket of oak leaves pinned together with twigs, and heaped full of blueberries. The woman shook her head as Nakanit offered her the berries, and pointed toward Anne. Nakanit obeyed, but somewhat sulkily, for she had meant to help Anne with the bundle, and was still angry at Anne's refusal.

"How good they taste," exclaimed Anne as she helped herself to a handful, and she smiled up gratefully at Nakanit. The Indian girl's face brightened, and she smiled back, and sitting down beside Anne held the basket forward for her to take more. When the berries were finished Nakanit again disappeared.

After several hours' rest the woman started on again, and Anne followed after wondering where Nakanit was. In a short time they came down to a sandy beach.

"Why, look! There's Nakanit!" exclaimed Anne, pointing toward the water, where a bark canoe floated near the shore with Nakanit in it, holding her paddle ready to send the craft to whatever point on the beach her mother might direct.

The woman called, and with a twist of the paddle the girl sent the canoe to the shore. The woman lifted in the baskets, the roll of blankets and Anne's bundle. "Sit there, and be quiet," she said, and Anne stepped in very carefully and sat down on the bottom of the canoe.

It was now late in the afternoon. The water was very calm, and as Nakanit and her mother dipped their paddles and sent the canoe swiftly along, Anne looked back toward the wooded shore and was very glad that she was not plodding along over the fields and hills. It was much cooler on the water, and the little girl wondered if her Aunt Martha missed her at all. "But perhaps she is glad that I ran away," thought Anne, for she was sure that she had not given either Amanda or Mrs. Stoddard any reason to be unkind or to blame her. "Rose Freeman will be glad I came; I know she will," was her comforting thought.

The Indians did not speak save for an occasional word of direction from the woman. The sun had set when they turned the canoe toward the shore. Nakanit pulled the canoe up on the sand beyond reach of the tide, and the woman led the way to a little opening among the trees, and there Anne was surprised to find another wigwam, very much like the one they had left that morning. The woman spread the blankets, gave the girls the corn cakes with strips of dried fish for their supper, and they had water from a nearby brook.

Anne was soon fast asleep, quite forgetful of her strange surroundings and of the friends in Province Town.

Meanwhile those friends had now nearly given up the hope of finding her.

Amanda Cary's jealousy had vanished the moment she heard of Anne's disappearance.

"I do not know what I shall do with the child," Mrs. Cary said anxiously, when Amanda cried herself to sleep on the night after Anne left home, and when, on the next morning, she began sobbing bitterly at the mention of her playmate's name.

"Amanda's ashamed; that's what's the matter with her," declared Amos boldly.

Amanda's sobs stopped, and she looked at her brother with startled eyes. What would become of her, she wondered, if the Stoddards should ever find out that she, Amanda, was the one to blame, that Anne had not deserved any punishment.

"Amos, don't plague your sister," said Mrs. Cary. "You know she loves Anne, even if the girl did slap her. Amanda has a good heart, and she does not hold resentment," and Mrs. Cary looked at Amanda with loving eyes.

At her mother's words Amanda began to cry again. She thought to herself that she could never tell the truth, never. "Everybody will hate me if I do," she thought, and then, remembering Anne and hearing her father say on the second day after her disappearance that there was now little hope of finding the runaway, she felt that she must tell Mrs. Stoddard.

"I'll wager I could find Anne," said Amos as he and Amanda sat on the doorstep. "She's started for Brewster."

"Oh, Amos!" Amanda's voice was full of delight. "I shouldn't wonder if she had."

"But Captain Stoddard says he followed the Truro path and no sign of her; and other people say that wolves would get her if she started to walk."

149

Amanda's face had brightened at Amos's assertion that he knew he could find Anne, and now she asked eagerly:

"What makes you think you could find her, Amos?"

"You won't tell?" and Amos looked at his sister sharply.

"I promise, hope to die, I won't," answered Amanda.

"Well, I'll tell you. I think she started for Truro, and will go by the meadows and over the hill instead of the regular path. I know the way I'd go, and I know I could find her; but father just shakes his head and won't let me try."

"Amos, you go," said Amanda. "Promise you'll go. I'll tell you something if you won't ever tell. It's something awful!"

"I won't tell," said the boy.

"I made Anne run away! Yes, I did. I was angry when she told me about going to Boston again, and going in a chaise, and I pushed her——"

"And then you came home and told mother that yarn!" interrupted Amos; "and mother went and told Mrs. Stoddard, and so Anne got punished and didn't know what for. You're a nice sister to have!" and the boy's face expressed his disgust.

"But, Amos, I didn't s'pose Anne would run away," pleaded Amanda.

"Hmph!" muttered Amos. "Well, she has, and whatever happens to her will be your fault."

"O-ooh—dear," wailed the little girl. "What shall I do?"

"Nothing," answered Amos relentlessly; "only of course now I've got to find her."

"And you won't ever tell about me," pleaded Amanda.

"I'd be ashamed to let anybody know I had a sister like you," answered Amos.

"Amos, you're real good," responded Amanda, somewhat to her brother's surprise. "When will you start?"

"Right off," declared the boy. "I'll put a jug of water and something to eat in my boat, and I'll go round to Truro—Anne must have got that far—and I'll keep on until I find her and tell her how ashamed I am of you."

"And say I'm sorry, Amos; promise to tell her I'm sorry," pleaded Amanda.

"Lots of use being sorry," said the boy. "When they miss me you can tell them just where I've gone and that I'll be home

Saturday night, anyway, or let them hear from me if I don't come."

"I do believe you'll find her, Amos," declared Amanda.

"Sure!" answered the boy.

CHAPTER FOUR

———— 🍎 ————

WITH THE MASHPEES

AMOS WAS so frequently in his boat that no one gave any especial attention when they saw him push off from shore and row steadily in the direction of Truro. He was not missed at home until supper time; then, as the little family gathered around the table, Mrs. Cary said:

" 'Tis time Amos was here. He's not often late for his supper."

"He won't be here for supper," announced Amanda; "he's gone to find Anne!"

"My soul!" exclaimed Mrs. Cary; "gone to find Anne, indeed. What possesses the children of this settlement is more than I can answer. And you, Amanda! Here you are all smiles and twinkles, as if you thought it a great thing for your brother to start off like this."

"He's gone by boat, I vow," said Mr. Cary.

"Yes, he means to row to Truro, and catch up with Anne. And he said to tell you he'd be back, or get you news of him in some way, by Saturday," and Amanda nodded smilingly, as if she were quite sure that her father and mother would be quite satisfied with Amos now that she had given them his message.

"Amos shall have his way in one thing," said Mr. Cary. "As soon as he is back, aye, if he comes Saturday or not, I'll put him aboard the first craft that can get out of harbor, and the farther her port the better. A year on shipboard is what the boy needs."

"You wouldn't send the boy with a strange captain?" Mrs. Cary questioned anxiously.

"Indeed I will. So long as he's on board a ship we shall know where he is," declared Amos's father. "We can do nothing now but wait. Find Anne, indeed! Who knows where to look for the poor child?"

"Amos knows," said Amanda.

But Mr. and Mrs. Cary shook their heads. They did not feel much anxiety as to Amos's safety, for the boys of the settlement were used to depending on themselves, and many boys no older than Amos Cary or Jimmie Starkweather had made a voyage to the West Indies, or to some far southern port; but they were displeased that he should have started off without permission.

Saturday came, but Amos did not appear, but toward evening a Truro man brought Mr. Cary word that Amos had been in Truro, and had started for Brewster that morning.

"He's a sailor, that boy!" declared the Truro man admiringly. "He hoisted that square foot of sailcloth, and went out of harbor at sunrise with a fair wind. He said he had 'business in Brewster,'" and the Truro man laughed good-naturedly. "But he's a smart boy," he added.

Mr. Cary made no answer, but his stern face softened a little at the praise of Amos. Nevertheless he was firmly resolved that Amos should be sent on a long voyage. "The harder master he has the better," thought the father. "I'm too easy with him."

When Amos hoisted his "square foot of sail" and headed for Wellfleet, he saw a canoe some distance ahead of him.

"Two women paddling and one doing nothing," thought the boy. "Wonder where they're bound?" But it was no unusual sight to see Indian canoes in those waters, and Amos did not think much about it. But his course brought him nearer and nearer to the graceful craft, and all at once he noticed that the figure sitting in the canoe was a little white girl. At that very moment Anne turned her face toward him.

"Amos!" she exclaimed, springing to her feet.

There was an angry exclamation from the woman, a yell from Nakanit, and in an instant the girls and woman were in the water. Anne's jump had upset the delicately balanced craft. The baskets bobbed and floated on the water. Anne's bundle was not to be seen, while Anne herself, clutching at the slippery side of the canoe called "Amos! Amos!" in a terrified voice.

But it was no new experience for either the woman or Nakanit. In a moment Anne felt a strong grasp on her shoulder. "Keep quiet," commanded the woman. "Let go the canoe." As Anne obeyed she saw Nakanit close beside her, and, while the woman kept her firm grasp on Anne's shoulder, the girl righted the canoe, and easily and surely regained her place in it. The woman lifted Anne in, and quickly followed her. Amos had brought his boat as near as possible and now rescued the baskets and floating paddles, and handed them to Nakanit.

The woman scowled at Anne, and when the girl bewailed her lost bundle muttered angrily.

"Want to get in my boat, Anne?" asked the boy.

Before Anne could answer the woman with a strong sweep of her paddle had sent the canoe some distance from the boat, while Nakanit called back some word to Amos, evidently of warning not to follow them. But Anne turned her head and called "Amos! Amos!" For the scowling faces of her companions frightened her, and she wished herself safely in Amos's boat.

The breeze had now died away, and Amos was soon left some distance behind. Anne did not dare turn her head to see if he were following the canoe, which was now moving ahead rapidly as the Indians swiftly wielded their paddles.

"Go to Brewster," announced the woman after a little silence.

Anne, huddled up in her wet clothes, frightened and unhappy, nodded her head in answer. Then, remembering that the woman had bidden her to sit still, and that her jump had upset the canoe, she ventured to say: "I'm sorry I jumped."

The woman's scowl disappeared, and she gave a grunt of approval, and then, evidently, repeated Anne's words to Nakanit, for the Indian girl smiled and nodded. Anne began to realize that they were really kind and good-natured, and that she had no reason to be afraid.

"I was surprised to see Amos," she continued.

The woman nodded again, and repeated, "Go to Brewster."

Anne could now hear the sound of the oars, and knew that Amos was rowing toward them. The paddles began to move more swiftly, and the sound of the oars grew more indistinct. Anne realized that Amos could not keep up with the canoe. But she was sure that he would follow them, and it made her feel less uneasy.

"Amos is a good boy," she explained to the woman, but there was no response. "I'd like to tell him that you've been good to me," continued Anne.

At this the woman, with a word to Nakanit, held her paddle motionless, and very soon Amos was close beside them.

"Tell him," commanded the woman.

So Anne told her little story of adventure, and said, "And they are going to take me right to Rose Freeman in Brewster. Nakanit's mother talks English."

Amos listened in amazement. "I told Amanda you'd started for Brewster," he responded, "and I sent word to father that I was going there, so I might as well go. I've got things to eat. Amanda's sorry," he added, looking rather shamed as he spoke his sister's name.

The woman now dipped her paddle again, and the canoe and boat moved forward. Anne began to think about her lost bundle, and to remember how neatly Rose Freeman dressed. "She will be ashamed of me," thought the girl, looking down at her wet and faded skirt and bare feet.

"Say, don't we stop anywhere for dinner?" asked Amos. "It's getting hot work rowing all this time."

The woman looked at the boy sharply, and then turned the canoe toward the shore. They landed on a beach, close by the mouth of a stream of clear water. A little way from the beach they found shade under a branching oak tree.

"I'll build a fire," suggested Amos, "and I'll get some clams; shall I?" and he turned toward the woman.

She nodded, and seemed rather surprised when she saw that the boy understood her own way of getting fire, and when he asked for a basket and soon returned with it well filled with clams, which he roasted in the hot sand under the coals, she evidently began to think well of him. Amos shared his bread and a piece of cold beef which he had brought from home with his companions, and, with a quantity of blueberries that Nakanit had gathered while Amos roasted the clams, they all had enough to eat, and Amos said everything tasted better than if eaten in the house, at which the woman nodded and smiled.

Anne found a chance to whisper to Amos: "Don't tell her I ran away."

"All right, but I fear she knows it," replied the boy.

It was in the early evening when the canoe, closely followed by Amos's rowboat, left Wellfleet harbor behind them and headed for Brewster. The woman had decided that it would be easier to go on than to wait for another day, and Anne and Amos were glad to go on as soon as possible.

At first Amos had wondered why the woman had promised to take Anne to Brewster, and had decided that probably the Indians were bound in that direction when they fell in with Anne. This was really one reason, but it was Anne's mention of the name of Freeman that had made the woman willing to do the girl a service. For the Freemans of Brewster had been good friends to the Mashpee Indians, and the woman felt bound to help any friend of theirs.

She had questioned Amos sharply as to his reason for following Anne, and Amos had told her the truth: that his sister had not treated Anne fairly, so that Anne had been punished, and had run away. "So, of course," added the boy, "I had to come after her and be sure that she was all right."

The woman understood, and evidently thought well of Amos for his undertaking. Anne felt much happier to know that a friend was close at hand, and that Amos on his return home would tell her Aunt Martha Stoddard that she was safely in Brewster. But the lost bundle troubled her a good deal. As she sat in the swiftly moving canoe and watched the steady dip of the paddles she thought that the Indians had been very good to her. "If I had my bundle now I would give Nakanit the cape and the beads; indeed I would," she said to herself.

The midsummer moon shone down upon the beautiful harbor. Every wooded point or sloping field was plainly outlined in the clear water, and there was the pleasant fragrance of pine and bayberry mingled with the soft sea air. It was much pleasanter than journeying in the sun. The woman and Nakanit began to sing, and although neither Anne nor Amos understood the words, they were both sure that the musical notes told of birds flying over moonlit water.

It was midnight when the woman turned the canoe toward shore. It proved to be the mouth of a small inlet up which they went for some distance, Amos keeping close behind.

"Look, Anne!" he exclaimed as the Indians stopped paddling. "There is a campfire. I do believe it's the Mashpee village."

"Sshh," warned the woman in a sharp voice. At the sound of the boy's voice a number of dark figures appeared to spring up from the ground, and the woman called out a word of greeting. A moment later she was talking rapidly to several tall figures who came to meet her, evidently telling Anne's story and that of Amos.

Anne could distinguish the word "Freeman" in the woman's talk.

Amos pulled his boat up on shore, and stood wondering what would happen next. He looked toward the wigwams and the smoldering campfires, and almost forgave Amanda, because his journey was bringing him into the Mashpee village.

One of the Indians gave him a little push, and pointed toward a wigwam. It was evident that the woman was the only one who spoke English.

"Go with him," she said to Amos.

"All right," responded the boy. "Here's your bundle, Anne," he said, holding it out toward her. "I fished it out of the water when you tipped over. Guess it isn't much wet."

Anne was almost too delighted to speak. She hugged the bundle in her arms and followed Nakanit up the path toward the village. This was evidently the squaw's home, and her wigwam had many deerskins, blankets and baskets.

Nakanit led Anne toward the back of the wigwam where lay a pile of spruce boughs over which deerskins were thrown. In a few moments the Indian girl and Anne lay on this rude couch fast asleep.

When Anne awoke the next morning there was no one in the

wigwam. Everything seemed very quiet. Anne's first thought was for her beloved bundle that she had carefully set down beside her bed. It was not there. The little girl slid to her feet, and began looking about the wigwam. There was no trace of it. Anne began to feel very unhappy. It had been hard to make up her mind to give Nakanit her treasured corals and her pretty cape, but it was even harder to bear to have them disappear like this. She threw herself back on the bed and began to cry bitterly. She wished that Rose Freeman had never thought of asking her to come to Brewster, and that she was safe in Province Town with Aunt Martha.

She stopped crying suddenly, for she felt a hand smoothing her hair, and she looked up to find Nakanit sitting beside her, and at her feet rested the bundle. It was plain that the mischievous Indian girl had wished to tease the little white girl, but had relented at the sight of her tears.

"Oh," exclaimed Anne, "I'm so glad!" and she began to unfasten the bundle, spreading out the blue cape and muslin dress, and laying Martha Stoddard down on the deerskins. Then she took up the string of coral beads and turning toward Nakanit fastened them around her neck. "I want to give you these for being good to me," she said. The Indian girl understood the gift if not the words, and was evidently delighted. Hearing a noise at the entrance they looked up to see the woman smiling in at them. She had heard Anne's words, and now came toward the girls. Anne picked up her blue cape and held it out toward the woman. "I wish I had something better to give you," she said.

The woman took it eagerly, and with a grunt of satisfaction, and then, turning to Nakanit, began chattering rapidly. Nakanit ran toward a big basket in the corner and came back with several pairs of soft moccasins. Kneeling before Anne she tried them on her feet until a pair was found that fitted.

"Now go with Nakanit to the lake," said the woman, and Anne followed Nakanit out of the wigwam through the woods to a clear little lake where the girls bathed, braided their hair, and then came back to eat heartily of the simple food the woman gave them.

CHAPTER FIVE

————— ❦ —————

AT BREWSTER

"Look, look, Aunt Hetty. Here are some Indians coming up the path, and I do believe that they have a little white boy and girl with them," and Rose Freeman drew her aunt to the open window that looked down over a smooth green lawn to an elm-shaded village street.

Aunt Hetty's well-starched dress rustled pleasantly as she hurried to join Rose.

"It's old Nakanit and her daughter," she said. "My mother taught her a good deal, and she often comes to see me. Those are surely white children. I wonder what the trouble is. Old Nakanit knows that the Sabbath is not a day for idle visits, and indeed, Rose, it does not become us to be stretching our heads out of the window. There, they are on the porch now. Why, Rose!" For with a quick exclamation the girl had run from the room and when Mrs. Freeman followed she found her with an arm about a little moccasined dark-eyed girl, saying: "Why, it is Anne; it is dear little Anne Nelson."

"I declare!" exclaimed Mrs. Freeman. "And did you fetch the child, Nakanit? Sit down and I will have Hepsibah bring you some cool milk and cake."

161

Nakanit grunted appreciatively, and while the Indians were eating Anne told Rose all the story of her journey.

"I do not know why Aunt Martha shut me up and said that I could not visit you, Rose," said Anne; "if I had been disobedient or careless I do not know it."

Amos listened, looking very flushed and unhappy, for he knew that it was Amanda's story that had caused Anne's punishment and made her a runaway. But he had promised his sister that he would not betray her, and now that Anne had reached Brewster in safety he resolved to keep silent. "But Amanda shall tell Mrs. Stoddard; indeed she shall," the boy said to himself.

The Indians soon rose from the porch steps to depart, and as Anne said goodbye to them she felt that she was parting from friends, and tried to tell them so.

"And you are going home to Province Town, and will tell Aunt Martha that I am safe," she said to Amos. "You were real good to come after me, Amos, and you tell Amanda not to be sorry she slapped me; that it's all right."

Amos wriggled about uneasily at Anne's message. He was almost resolved not to go home at all.

"I reckon I'll stay with the Mashpees a while," he answered. "There's an Indian boy who talks English and he's told me lots of things: how to set traps for foxes and woodchucks, and how to make fish spears, and he can stay under water longer than I can. He's fine. You ought to hear him tell stories. Last night he told me of a tribe of Indians who sent six of their bravest warriors out to sea in a canoe, without food or paddles, so as to prove to other tribes that their braves could not be harmed anywhere. And they were carried by the winds and waves to a wonderful island where there were friendly Indians; and they hunted wild deer, and made bows and arrows, and paddles, and caught wild birds, and when another summer came back they came to Cape Cod with many canoes, and skins, and much deer meat, so that their tribe made them all great chiefs. And this boy who told me is one of the descendants of the very bravest chief, and he wants me to stay and be his brother," and Amos looked as if he would like nothing better than to be adopted into the Mashpee tribe.

"What's the Indian boy's name?" questioned Anne.

"I don't think much of his name," said Amos, a little regretfully. "It's 'Shining Fish.'"

"But you won't stay with the Indians, Amos, will you?" pleaded Anne.

"I s'pose I'll have to go home," agreed Amos. "I wonder what Jimmie Starkweather will say when I tell him about living with Indians," and Amos looked more cheerful at the thought of Jimmie's surprise and envy when he should describe his adventures. "Nothing ever happens to Jimmie," he added, in a satisfied tone.

After Amos and the Indians had started on their way back to the Indian village Rose and Anne followed Mrs. Freeman into the square comfortable house. Mrs. Freeman had heard all about Anne, and now, as she noticed the torn and soiled dress, the untidy hair and moccasin-covered feet, she whispered to Rose: "Take the child right upstairs. I don't want your uncle to see her looking so like a wild child of the woods."

Rose nodded laughingly. Aunt Hetty Freeman was known as one of the best housekeepers in Brewster, and no one had ever seen her looking other than "spick and span," as her husband often admiringly declared. Rose always said that she could tell just what part of the big house Aunt Hetty was in because she could hear her starched skirts rattle; and she realized that Anne's untidy appearance was a real trouble to her kind-hearted aunt.

Anne looked at the broad stairway admiringly, and exclaimed at the sight of a tall clock on the landing. "It's better than Boston, isn't it, Rose?" she said, as Rose took her into the big comfortable room, with its high, curtained bed and chintz curtained windows.

"It's a dear house," answered the older girl, who was too loyal to her home to think any other place quite as good. "You are the bravest child I ever heard of," Rose continued admiringly, drawing Anne down beside her on the broad cushioned window seat. "To think of your starting out to come all the way alone to Brewster through the wilderness!"

"I guess I should have been lost but for the Indians," replied Anne; "but when Aunt Martha said I could not come, that she did not want to hear more of any visit to Brewster or Boston, I had to run away. But now I'm sorry," and Anne began to cry bitterly. Rose, too, looked very unhappy, for she realized that Captain and Mrs. Stoddard would be greatly troubled until they knew of the little girl's safety. And, besides that, she was sure that her father would not be willing to take a runaway child to Boston. But Rose resolved not to worry about it, and not to tell Anne that she feared that she would be sent home to her Aunt Martha, instead of taking the wonderful journey to Boston.

So she comforted her little guest, and told her not to feel bad —that Aunt Martha and Uncle Enos would be only too happy to know that she was safe.

"And see, Anne, what my good mother sent you," and Rose opened a small hair-covered trunk that stood near the tall chest of drawers, and took out a pretty dress of spotted percale, and some white stockings. Then there was a dainty white petticoat, and a set of underwear, all trimmed with a pretty crocheted edge.

"And you can wear your moccasins these hot days," continued Rose, "and you will look very nice indeed."

Anne was soon dressed in the neat clothing, and, with her hair brushed and smoothly braided, she looked like quite a different child from the little girl who had journeyed with Nakanit.

"I am glad to look nice to go to Boston," Anne said soberly, as they went down the stairs.

"Oh, dear!" thought the older girl; "how can I tell the poor child that I am almost sure that father will find a way to send her safely back to Province Town?"

Rose's father and uncle spoke kindly to Anne as she came into the sitting room, and Aunt Hetty's skirts rustled briskly as she moved about the room, and then she went out in the shed and came back with a round, low basket in which lay two black kittens, which she placed in Anne's lap saying: "There, little girls and little kittens always like each other; so you can have Pert and Prim for your own while you stay with us."

"Oh, thank you," said Anne delightedly, for the two little kittens began to purr happily as she smoothed their soft fur.

Rose found an opportunity to tell her father all about Anne's reason for running away.

"She did not know why her Aunt Martha shut her up," pleaded Rose.

But Mr. Freeman shook his head soberly. "We'll have to send her home by the first chance to Province Town," he answered, and Rose went back to her little friend feeling that all her pleasant plans for Anne's visit must come to an end.

"But she shall have a good time here in Brewster," resolved the girl.

"Shall we start for Boston on Tuesday or Thursday?" Anne asked the next morning, as she helped Rose put their pleasant chamber in order.

"Father has not decided," replied Rose, feeling rather cowardly that she did not tell Anne the truth.

"It will be fine to ride in a chaise," went on Anne happily, "and to stop in taverns, and see towns along the way. Your father is indeed good, Rose, to take me."

"We must do up the dishes for Aunt Hetty," said Rose briskly, "and then we can walk down the street, and maybe father will drive us about the town."

While the girls were busy helping Aunt Hetty, Rose's father was on his way to the Mashpee village to see Amos Cary and to give him a letter to take to Captain Stoddard. He found the boy just ready to start. Shining Fish had launched his canoe and was to go part of the way with his new friend, greatly to Amos's delight.

"Anne wasn't to blame." Amos repeated this a number of times so earnestly that Mr. Freeman began to realize that the boy knew more than he was willing to tell, and to blame Amos.

"That Amanda," Amos whispered to himself, as he blushed and stammered and evaded Mr. Freeman's questions.

"I suppose I can trust you with this letter to Captain Stoddard?" said Mr. Freeman.

Amos lifted his head, and his blue eyes did not falter in meeting the stern look of the man.

"I'll give it to him," he replied, and Mr. Freeman felt quite sure that the letter would reach its destination.

When Amos's boat drew near the landing at Province Town, he saw that his father, Amanda, and the Stoddards were all waiting for him. He felt himself to be almost like the chiefs of whom Shining Fish had told him, and quite expected to be praised and made much of; but as he sprang ashore he felt his father's hand on his shoulder.

"March yourself straight to the house, young man. I'll see that you pay for this fool's errand," said Mr. Cary.

Amos wriggled away from his father's grasp. "I've got a letter for Captain Enos. Anne's in Brewster," he announced.

"Thank heaven!" exclaimed Mrs. Stoddard. "And did you find her, Amos? You are a brave boy! Why, Mr. Cary, there's not another boy in the village who thought of Anne's going to Brewster, or man either for that matter," and Mrs. Stoddard patted the boy's shoulder affectionately, while Mr. Cary regarded Amos with puzzled eyes, hardly knowing whether to blame or praise him.

While Captain Enos read the letter Amos briefly told the story of his adventures to the little group, saving all that Shining Fish had told him to relate to Jimmy Starkweather as soon as opportunity should occur.

"Well, go home to your mother," said Mr. Cary in a more gentle voice, and Amanda kept close beside her brother as they turned toward home.

"You've got to tell Mrs. Stoddard," said Amos. "Yes, you have," he went on, almost fiercely, as Amanda began to whimper. "Everybody's blaming Anne, and it's not fair; you've got to tell."

Amanda stopped short and looked at her brother accusingly. "You promised not to tell," she said.

"Well, I haven't," answered the boy, "and I won't. I'm ashamed to, beside the promise. Anne said, when I told her that you said you were sorry, that I was to tell you 'twas all right. She seemed to feel bad because you were sorry."

"Well, Amos Cary, I won't tell Mrs. Stoddard; so now!" declared Amanda angrily. "Anne is all right, and going to Boston in a chaise. You ought to be satisfied. Let them think what they want to, I don't care. And you've got to go to sea. Father's told Captain Nash that he can have you, and the *Sea Gull* sails next week."

"Truly, Amanda! Say, that's great news. I do believe I'm the luckiest boy on the Cape. Are you sure, Amanda?" Amos's eyes were shining, his shoulders had straightened themselves, and, for the moment, he quite forgot everything except the wonderful news.

"Do you want to go?" and Amanda's voice was full of disappointment.

"Want to! Why, the *Sea Gull* is bound for the West Indies her next voyage, and maybe the English will try and catch us," and Amos's voice expressed his delight. "Are you sure, Amanda?" he questioned eagerly, and turned toward his sister in surprise, for Amanda was crying. It seemed to the unhappy child that everything was going wrong. She did not want Amos to go away, and she had hoped that he would persuade his father to let him remain at home, and here he was rejoicing and triumphant. She was in great fear that Anne would tell the Stoddards the truth, and then Amanda hardly knew what might befall her. She wished that she was a boy and could go with Amos in the *Sea Gull*.

"It is indeed good news to know that our little girl is safe in Brewster," said Mrs. Stoddard, as she read Mr. Freeman's letter, "but what shall we do, Enos, about bringing her home? Mr. Freeman truly says that, while Rose is eager to take Anne to Boston, we may feel that it would not be right for her to go. It is indeed a puzzle, is it not? Whatever possessed Anne to turn upon Amanda in such fashion, and then to run off?" And the good woman shook her head dolefully.

"I'll have to sail to Brewster and fetch her home," responded the captain, but his face was very sober. He would have been glad if the Freemans had written that they would take Anne to Boston, for he did not want the child disappointed.

"Well, well, we'll let her see how glad we are to have her safe home, shall we not, Enos? I'll say no more to her about her naughtiness, and I am sure Mrs. Cary will tell Amanda to forgive Anne and be friends again, and all will go on pleasantly." But they both felt sorry that it seemed best for the little girl whom they so dearly loved to have to give up the wonderful journey up the Cape to Boston in the Freemans' fine chaise.

CHAPTER SIX

———— ❦ ————

AMANDA'S CONSCIENCE

AMOS CARY AND Jimmy Starkweather lay on the warm sand in the narrow shadow cast by a fishing dory pulled up on the beach. No chief returning from far-off islands could have been more a hero than was Amos among the boys and girls of the settlement. They followed him about, and listened eagerly to all that he had to tell them of the Indians. Then, too, he was to go in the *Sea Gull* with Captain Nash, the swiftest schooner and the smartest captain sailing out of the harbor, and Jimmie Starkweather felt that Amos was having greater good fortune than any boy could hope for.

"Maybe the *Sea Gull* can't get out of port," said Jimmie, digging his bare toes in the soft sand. "The English ships keep a sharp outlook for a schooner loaded down with salt fish. I'll bet Captain Nash won't get beyond Chatham."

"Pooh!" responded Amos scornfully. "We can sail right away from their old tubs. But 'twill be great if they do follow us."

" 'Twould be just your good fortune," said Jimmie. "I do wish my father would let me go with you, Amos. Who knows what adventures you may have!"

For a few moments the two boys did not speak; they lay looking out over the beautiful harbor, and their minds were full of vague hopes of adventure. Jimmie was the first to break the silence.

169

"You won't see Shining Fish again, will you, Amos?"

"No; did I show you what he gave me?" And Amos pulled out a stout deerskin thong from inside his flannel blouse. The claw of a bird was fastened to the thong. "See! It's a hawk's claw," exclaimed Amos. "And as long as I wear it no enemy can touch me. I gave Shining Fish my jackknife," continued Amos. "You'd like him, Jimmie; he knew stories about chiefs and warriors, and he had killed a fox with his bow and arrow. He told me about a chief of their tribe who lived long ago and was the strongest man that ever lived. He used to go on long journeys, way beyond Cape Cod, with his band of warriors, and once he met an unfriendly tribe, and they laughed when the braves told how strong their chief was. 'Can he conquer a wild bull?' one of them asked, and the brave answered, 'Aye, or two wild bulls.'

"So the unfriendly Indians laughed louder, and were glad, for they thought they could destroy the chief even without a battle. Well, they arranged that this brave chief was to go alone into a fenced-in place and meet two wild bulls, and if he conquered them the unfriendly tribe would own him the strongest chief in the world, and would be subject to him. It was great, Jimmie, to hear Shining Fish tell it. He said the great chief marched into the place where the bulls were, and they came dashing toward him, and their hoofs rang upon the ground, and their nostrils sent out sheets of flame, but the chief never flinched a step, and the bulls stopped short and trembled. Then the chief sprang upon the nearest, and seized him by the horns, and they wrestled until the bull fell to its knees tired out. Then he grabbed at the other, and threw it, and all the Indians began to wonder how any chief could be so strong."

"S'pose it's true?" questioned Jimmie.

"Sure!" answered Amos. "What's Captain Stoddard doing to his boat?" he continued. Captain Enos was evidently not bound out on a fishing trip, for he was making his boat as tidy as possible.

"He's going to sail over to Brewster to fetch Anne back," answered Jimmie.

"But Anne is going to Boston with Rose Freeman," said Amos.

Jimmie shook his head. "No, the Freemans won't take her

because she ran away," he explained, and looked up in amazement, for Amos had sprung to his feet and was racing along the beach toward Captain Stoddard's boat as fast as his feet would carry him.

Jimmie laughed. "I'll bet Amos wants to go to Brewster," he decided.

Amos did not want to go to Brewster. But he had instantly resolved that Anne must not be stopped from going to Boston. Even as he ran he could see that there was no time to spare in reaching Captain Enos, for he was already pushing off from shore.

"Captain Enos! Captain Enos!" he called frantically, and the captain looked toward him. "Wait a minute! Wait!" yelled the boy, and the captain waited, saying good-humoredly:

"Never saw such a boy as that one. He can't bear to see a boat put off unless he's in it."

"Captain Enos, you mustn't bring Anne back," said Amos as he ran out into the shallow water and grasped the side of the boat. "It wouldn't be fair; it wasn't her fault," he added.

"Whose fault was it?" asked the captain.

"Wait!" commanded Amos, remembering his promise to his sister. "Wait just ten minutes, Captain Enos, before you start. I'll be back," and away went Amos up the beach and along the sandy path to the house.

"Amos is going to come out first rate, I can see that plain enough," said Captain Enos, watching the boy's flying figure, and he was not surprised when he saw Amos coming back with Amanda held fast by the hand.

The boy and girl stopped at the edge of the water.

"Tell him, Amanda," commanded Amos.

"It's my fault," whimpered Amanda. "I got my mother to tell Mrs. Stoddard that Anne slapped me and ran off with the luncheon. And she didn't. I slapped her."

"Clear as mud," muttered the captain; then in a louder tone, "Amos, you're going to make a good American sailor, and we're all going to be proud of you. And I guess Amanda's going to do better after this," and he pushed off from shore.

"But you won't go to Brewster now!" called both the children.

171

"I'll have to. Must go and tell the Freemans that we're willing for Anne to go to Boston, and to tell Anne that her Aunt Martha knows the truth. You just run up and tell Mrs. Stoddard all about it, Amanda," he answered; and, having sent his boat into deep water, the captain drew in his oars and began hoisting the big mainsail.

For a few moments the boy and girl stood watching him. Then, with a long sigh, Amanda turned to go toward the Stoddard house. Amos began to feel a little sorry for her.

"Say, Amanda, I'll go tell her," he called.

"You mind your own business, Amos Cary," and Amanda turned toward him angrily. "I'll tell Mrs. Stoddard myself, and then I'll go home and tell my mother. I'll tell everybody, and when everybody hates and despises me I reckon you'll be satisfied," and without waiting for any response she went on up the path.

Amos turned and went back to the shade of the boat, but Jimmie Starkweather was no longer there. He wished more than ever that he was back with Shining Fish. Then he remembered that in another week he would be on board the *Sea Gull*. He watched Captain Stoddard's sloop until it was only a white blur against the distant shore, and then went up the beach toward home.

Captain Enos had a favoring wind and a light heart, for he was glad to know that their little maid had not been to blame. "She ran away because she had not been fairly treated. 'Tis what older people sometimes do," he said to himself. " 'Twas the very reason that sent our fathers out of England to America. I'll not fetch Anne back, for she called to me from the window and would have told me all the story had I been willing to listen," and then because his mind was at ease the captain began to sing an old song that he had learned as a boy. He had a musical voice, and the words drifted back pleasantly:

> "*A fit and fa-vor-able wind*
> *To further us provide;*
> *And let it wait on us behind,*
> *Or lackey by our side;*
> *From sudden gusts, from storms, from sands,*

And from the raging wave;
From shallows, rocks, and pirates' hands,
Men, goods, and vessel save."

In Brewster time was going very smoothly with Anne. The Freemans were kind and pleasant people, and the big house was filled with many things of interest to a little girl. First of all there was Hepsibah, a black woman whom Captain Freeman had brought, with her brother Josephus, from Cuba when they were small children. They had grown up in the Freeman household, and were valued friends as well as servants. Anne liked to hear Hepsibah laugh, and the woman's skirts were as stiffly starched as those of Mrs. Freeman herself, who had taught Hepsibah, and trained her to become an excellent housekeeper.

On the high mantelpiece in the dining room were great branches of white coral, brought from the South Seas; on each side of the front door were huge pink shells. And in the funny little corner cupboard were delicately tinted pink cups and saucers, and the mahogany table was always set with a tall shining silver teapot, and a little fat pitcher and bowls of silver, and the plates were covered with red flowers and figures of queer people with sunshades. Rose told her that these plates came all the way from China, a country on the other side of the earth.

"When does your father say we shall start for Boston?" Anne asked, as the two girls walked down the shady pleasant street that led to the wharves. Anne was not a dull child, and she noticed that no word had been said of Boston, and began to wonder if Mr. Freeman blamed her for running away. "Perhaps your father thinks I am a wicked girl to have run away," she added before Rose could answer.

"Oh, Anne, no indeed; nobody would think you wicked," Rose answered promptly. "But father sent a letter to Captain Enos by Amos, and he expects that the captain will get word to us today or tomorrow——"

"To say whether I may go or not?" interrupted Anne. "Oh, Rose!" and there was a pleading note in the little girl's voice, "I do want to go so much, and I do wonder and wonder why Amanda should have slapped me, and why Aunt Martha should have punished me. I do wish I could hear Aunt Martha say again that I was a good child, as she used often to do."

Rose clasped the little girl's hand affectionately. "I believe that Amanda was jealous because you were to have this visit," said Rose, "and who knows, perhaps by this time she is as sorry as can be, and has told Mrs. Stoddard all about it. Perhaps word may come this very night that your Aunt Martha thinks you are a good child, and forgives you for running away."

As the girls walked along they met a party of men carrying rifles, and hurrying toward Brewster Common.

"They are going to the training field," explained Rose, at Anne's surprised exclamation, "and may have to march to Boston tomorrow. Father is anxious to get home."

The wharves at Brewster were much larger and better cared for than the Province Town landing places; but there were few boats to be seen. Far out a sloop, coming briskly on before a favoring wind, attracted the girls' attention.

"Rose, that's the *Morning Star*, Uncle Enos's sloop. I know it is," declared Anne. "And he will never let any one else sail her, so it's Uncle Enos! Let's hurry! He's coming straight for this very wharf."

The big sloop swung round, the mainsail came rattling down, and Captain Enos ran his craft skillfully up beside the long wharf just as Anne, closely followed by Rose, came running down the pier.

"Uncle Enos! Uncle Enos!" exclaimed Anne joyfully. "I'm so glad you've come," and she clasped both hands around his brawny arm as he stepped on the wharf. "And here is Rose," she continued as the elder girl stepped forward to speak to the captain.

"Growing more like a rose every day," declared Captain Enos, as he shook hands with Rose. "And here is our little maid all ready to start on the great journey, eh?" and he looked kindly down into Anne's smiling face. "And what would you girls say if I told you that I had sailed over here to take Anne back to Province Town?"

"Oh, Uncle Enos!"

"Oh, Captain Stoddard!" exclaimed the girls fearfully.

"Wouldn't like it, eh? Well," said the captain, "then we won't have it that way, and Anne may go with you."

"Oh, Uncle Enos!"

"Oh, Captain Stoddard!" The exclamations were the same, but the words were in such joyous tones that Captain Enos began to laugh heartily, as did Rose and Anne, so that it was a very merry party that went gaily up the street toward Mr. Freeman's house, where Captain Enos was warmly welcomed.

After supper he and Anne had a long talk together about Amanda and Amos. "Amanda's had a hard time, I reckon," declared the captain, "and if I know aught of her parents she will remember this all her life, and will not be so ready to bear false witness against her neighbor."

"I did not so much mind Amanda's slapping me," replied Anne soberly, "but I thought when Aunt Martha shut me up that 'twas because she no longer loved me."

"Tut, tut, and so you walked off into the wilderness. A very wrong thing to do, Anne," and Captain Enos's voice was very grave. "Your running away has made a sad talk in the settlement, and some of the people are ready to say that we have not treated you well, or you would not have fled from us."

Anne began to realize, for the first time, that she had acted very selfishly. Thinking of nothing but her wish to go to Boston with Rose she had made her best friends anxious and unhappy.

They were sitting on the broad sofa in the quiet sitting room, and Anne leaned against Uncle Enos and said quickly: "I ought to go straight back to Province Town!" She said it in such a sharp voice that Uncle Enos looked at her wonderingly, and saw that tears were very near falling.

"No, Anne," he answered kindly. "I want you to go with the Freemans, and have a pleasant visit. Your father's ship will be in Boston in a few weeks, and he will rejoice to find you there and will bring you safely back to Province Town."

CHAPTER SEVEN

———— 🍎 ————

THE BLACK-BEARDED MAN

ANNE AND ROSE Freeman stood at the gate all ready to enter the comfortable chaise with its broad seat and big wheels. The big brown horse was apparently eager to start, but Josephus held him firmly until the girls and Mr. Freeman were seated, and then handed the reins to Mr. Freeman.

"Goodbye, goodbye," called the girls, leaning out beyond the hood of the chaise to wave to Aunt Hetty and Captain Freeman and Uncle Enos, who had stayed to see the travelers start on the ride to Boston.

"A horse is useful," remarked Uncle Enos, thoughtfully, as he watched them drive away, "but there's not one in Province Town settlement as yet. We have little need of one, with so many good boats."

The summer morning was clear and bright, and not too warm. They had made an early start, and the heavy dew still lingered on the trees and flowers.

"How far shall we go today, father?" asked Rose.

"We will pass the night in Sandwich, if all goes well," replied Mr. Freeman. "Your aunt has put us up a fine luncheon, and we will give Lady a rest toward noon and enjoy it."

177

The sandy roads made it rather slow traveling, but Anne was as happy as a bird. They got many glimpses of the sea, and now and then some wild creature would run across the road, or peer at them from the shelter of the woods. Once or twice a partridge, with her brood of little ones, fled before them, and there was a great deal for them to see and enjoy. Anne felt very happy to know that Aunt Martha and Uncle Enos had forgiven her for running away, and that they were glad for her to go to Boston. She did not cherish any ill-will against Amanda, and thought herself a very fortunate little girl to be sitting beside Rose Freeman and riding along the pleasant road in such a grand chaise.

Mr. Freeman told them that there was something very wonderful to be seen in Suet, a little village that they would pass through on their way to Sandwich. "Captain Sears is an old friend of mine," said Mr. Freeman, "and we will make him a call and he will be glad to show us how salt is made."

"Can he make salt?" questioned Anne.

"Yes, and a good thing for the colony it is; for salt is hard to get, with English frigates taking all the cargoes afloat," answered Mr. Freeman; "and Cape Cod is the very place to make it, for there is plenty of salt water." Then he told them how Captain Sears had first made long shallow troughs and filled them with the sea water, and the sun dried up the water, leaving the salt in the bottom of the vats. "And now," continued Mr. Freeman, "I hear he has had big kettles made, and with huge fires under them boils the water away and gets good salt in that fashion. We'll stop and have a look, if time allows."

Just before noon the sky began to grow dark, and there was a distant rumble of thunder. They were driving through a lonely stretch of country; there was no house in sight, and Mr. Freeman began to watch the sky with anxious eyes. He knew that, on the bare sandy plain over which they were now traveling, the wind would sweep with great force, sufficient perhaps to overturn the chaise. Rose and Anne grew very quiet as they heard the thunder and watched the threatening sky.

"We'll soon reach the Yarmouth woods," said Mr. Freeman encouragingly, "and if the storm comes may be able to find some sort of shelter, but I fear it will prevent our reaching the salt works."

Rose and Anne both thought to themselves that troughs and kettles filled with salt water would not be very much of a sight, and were very glad when the sandy plain was behind them and they were once more in the shelter of the woods, which broke the force of the wind. It was now raining in torrents.

"One good thing about this is that the rain will beat the sand down and make the traveling better," said Mr. Freeman.

The road was a mere lane, and they all began to feel a little uncomfortable and discouraged as the thunder deepened and came peal after peal, followed by shooting darts of lightning. The big horse was going at a good pace, but, all at once, Lady made a quick turn, and before Mr. Freeman could stop her had swung into an even more narrow track, half hidden by underbrush from the main road. In a few moments they saw a long low shingled house nearly hidden by closely growing trees.

"Well done, Lady!" exclaimed Mr. Freeman laughingly, as Lady stopped directly in front of the door.

Mr. Freeman handed the reins to Rose and sprang out, and rapped on the door, but no answer came.

"I don't believe there is any one here," he declared. "Stay in the chaise a moment, and I'll find out." As he spoke he gave the door a little push when, much to his surprise, it swung open and Mr. Freeman found himself face to face with a tall, black-bearded man who regarded him with a scowling countenance.

"What do you want?" he asked gruffly.

At that moment a peal of thunder heavier than any preceding it made Rose and Anne shrink more closely together in the corner of the chaise. "He looks like a pirate," whispered Rose fearfully.

"We want shelter until this storm is over," Mr. Freeman replied. "May I drive my horse into that shed?"

The man grunted an unwilling assent, and Mr. Freeman sprang back into the chaise and drove Lady under a rough shelter in the rear of the house.

"Don't go in the house, will you, father?" whispered Rose; for the man had opened a back door leading into the shed and was regarding his undesired guests with suspicious eyes.

"How did you happen to come here?" he asked gruffly. "This road don't lead nowheres."

"My horse turned in from the main road very suddenly," explained Mr. Freeman. "We had no plan except to get on to Sandwich as fast as possible."

"Going far?" questioned the man.

"We are on our way to Boston," answered Mr. Freeman.

"Guess the English are going to give the Yankees a lesson even if they couldn't hold Boston!" said the man with a smile, as if he would be glad to know his words would come true.

"I think not, sir," answered Mr. Freeman sharply; "and a Cape Cod man ought to be the last to say such a thing."

"You're not a Tory, then?" exclaimed the man eagerly. "Get right out of that chaise and come in. These your girls? Let me help you out, missy," and he came toward the carriage.

"Get out, Anne," said Mr. Freeman in a low tone, and in a moment the two girls were following the black-bearded man into a low dark kitchen.

"You folks looked so dressed up I thought like as not you were Tories," declared the man, as if wishing to explain his rude reception. "Now take seats, and I'll put your horse where it can have a bit of fodder."

Mr. Freeman followed the man back to the shed, and Anne and Rose looked at each other, and then glanced about the low dark room.

"I don't believe he's a pirate," whispered Anne. "Anyway, I'm glad to be in out of this dreadful storm."

"So am I," answered Rose, "but it is a funny house. What do you suppose made Lady turn in at that place? This man may not be a pirate, but there is something odd about him. This whole place is queer. I almost wish we had stayed in the chaise."

Under the two windows that faced toward the woods ran a long box-like seat, and in one corner of the room stood a shoe-maker's bench, with its rows of awls, needles threaded with waxed thread, hammers, sharp knives, tiny wooden pegs, and bits of leather; a worn boot lay on the floor as if the man had started up from his work at Mr. Freeman's rap.

"What's that, Rose?" questioned Anne, pointing to a piece of iron that could be seen extending from beneath an old blanket which lay under the bench.

"It's a rifle!" answered Rose. "Look, Anne! Quick, before he comes back. I believe there are a lot of guns there."

Anne knelt down to lift the blanket. Rose was close beside her, leaning over to see what the blanket might conceal, when the kitchen door swung open and the man entered. As he looked at the two girls his face darkened again, and he came quickly forward.

"Aha!" he muttered. "It's just as I thought. Pretty clever of the old Tory to bring these girls along to peek about and find out all they can," but the girls did not hear him until he stood beside them, and then his scowl was gone and he spoke pleasantly: "A good many rifles for one man, but they are not all mine. I'm storing them for friends."

"Where's father?" asked Rose, a little anxiously.

"He's giving the pretty horse a rub down," answered the man. "Now there's a better room for young ladies than this old kitchen," he continued. "Just come this way," and he opened a door into a long dark passage, into which the girls followed him.

"Right in here," said the man, opening a door at the further end of the hall, and holding it ajar for the girls to pass in.

"It's all dark!" exclaimed Anne, who had been the first to enter. Rose was close behind her and as Rose crossed the threshold the heavy door swung to behind them. They heard bolts shot and then all was quiet.

Rose sprang against the door with all her strength, but instantly realized that it was useless to try to open it. "Father! Father!" she screamed, and Anne, hardly knowing what she said, called also "Father!"

"It's dark as pitch," whispered Anne, clutching at Rose's dress. "There can't be a window in this room, or we'd see light somewhere."

The two girls clung together, not knowing what next might befall them.

"There may be some other door," said Rose after they had screamed themselves hoarse. "We must not be frightened, Anne, for father is sure to look for us. Let's go round the room and try and find a door. We can feel along the wall." So the two girls began to grope their way from the door.

"These inside walls are brick!" exclaimed Rose, as her hands left the wooden framework of the door. "Oh, Anne, I do believe it is a sort of prison all walled inside." Just then their feet struck against something hard and round which rolled before them with a little rumble of sound. Rose leaned down. "They're cannonballs," she whispered. "Oh, Anne! There's a whole pile of them. Don't go another step; we'll fall over them. I do believe the man is a pirate, or else a Tory." For in those troublous times the Americans felt that a Tory was a dangerous enemy to their country.

As the girls groped about the room they came to a heavy iron chest, and sat down, realizing that all they could do was to wait until Mr. Freeman should discover them.

"Don't be afraid, Anne," said Rose, putting her arm about her little companion, and felt surprised when Anne answered in a hopeful voice:

"Rose, look! Right up on that wall there's a window. I can see little edges of light."

"So there is, but it's too high to do us any good; we can't reach it," answered Rose.

"Well, I'm glad it's there," said Anne.

Now and then they heard the far-off roar of the thunder, but at last it seemed to die away, and little edges of light showed clearly around the shuttered window on the further wall. The girls watched it, and, their eyes becoming used to the shadowy room, they could now distinguish the pile of cannonballs in the opposite corner, and behind them a small cannon and a keg. They could see, too, the outlines of the doorway.

"How long do you think we shall have to stay here?" whispered Anne, as the dreary fearful moments dragged by.

"I don't know, dear," answered the elder girl, "but we mustn't be afraid."

The hours went by and the little edge of light around the high shuttered window began to fade a little, and the girls knew that the long summer day was fading to twilight, and that it had been about noon when they came to the house. A great fear now took possession of Rose's thoughts, the fear for her father's safety. She was sure that unless some harm had befallen him he would have found them before this time.

"Rose!" Anne's sharp whisper interrupted her thoughts. "If

182

I could get up to that window I could get out and go after help. The window isn't so very high; it isn't as if we were upstairs."

At that very moment the big door swung open, and the man entered. He had a candle in one hand and carried an armful of rough gray blankets which he dropped on the floor beside the girls, and instantly, without a word, departed, and the girls heard the bolts shot on the outside.

"Those blankets are for us to sleep on. Oh, Anne, what has he done to my dear father?" Rose began to cry bitterly.

"Rose, he's coming back!" warned Anne, but the girl could no longer restrain her sobs and their jailer entered, this time carrying the big lunch basket which Aunt Hetty had put under the seat when they drove off so happily from Brewster.

"Here's your own grub," said the man roughly. "Your father'll have to put up with what I give him."

"You—you—won't kill my father, will you?" sobbed Rose.

"Oh, no, no!" answered the man, and then apparently regretting his more friendly tone added, "But I reckon I ought to, coming here a-peekin' an' a-pryin' into what don't concern him," and he set the basket down on the iron chest with such a thud that it fairly bounced.

"Oh, he wasn't. I was the one who peeked at the guns," said Anne.

"Oho! Peekin' at the guns! Well, I've got you now where you can't peek much," came the gruff answer.

"Won't you leave the candle?" asked Rose.

"I guess not," he answered with a little laugh, and pointed toward the keg. "Look at that keg! Well, it's full of powder, and powder's too sca'se an article these days to leave a candle in the same room with it."

"But we can't see to eat," pleaded Anne. "We'll be real careful; we won't go near the corner."

For a moment the man hesitated; then he set the candle down on the chest beside the basket.

"All right," he said. "I'll leave it; 'twon't burn more than an hour." He looked down at Rose's tear-stained face, and added, "Ain't no cause to cry about your father; he's had a good supper, and I ain't goin' to hurt him."

"Oh, thank you!" and Rose looked up at him gratefully.

183

The door had hardly swung to before Anne whispered, "Rose, Rose, I must get out of that window some way. You know I must. It's too small for you, but I'm sure I could get through."

"Let's eat something before you think about that," suggested Rose, who began to feel more hopeful now that she knew her father was safe, and opened the big basket. The man had brought them a pitcher of cool water, and the girls ate and drank heartily.

"Aunt Hetty would be surprised if she knew where we were eating these lovely doughnuts," said Anne, holding up the delicately browned twisted cruller.

"Anne, if we could push this chest under the window I could stand on it and try to open the window and if I can open it, then I will lift you up and you can crawl through," said Rose, biting into a chicken sandwich.

Anne nodded, watching the candle with anxious eyes, remembering that their jailer had said that it would burn but an hour.

"Now, Anne," said Rose, after they had satisfied their hunger, and closed the basket, "we must try to push the chest."

To their surprise it moved very easily, and they soon had it directly under the window. Rose was on top of it in an instant, and Anne held the candle as high as she could reach so that Rose could examine the fastening.

"Why, Anne, it pushes right out," said Rose. "It's only hooked down. Look!" and she pushed the heavy square outward. "But it doesn't go very far out," she added. "I wonder if you can crawl through. I do believe this shutter is shingled on the outside, so that nobody could tell there was a window. Oh, Anne! Isn't this a dreadful place!" Rose peered cautiously out of the open space. "Blow out the candle," she said quickly, drawing back into the room. "He might be outside and see the light."

Anne instantly obeyed.

"Now, Anne, dear," said Rose, "if you can get out what are you going to do?"

"I'll run back to the road as fast as I can go and get some people to come back here and rescue you," said Anne.

"Yes, but you had best go on; you know there are no houses

for a long way on the road we came, and we must be nearer the Suet settlement than any other. You won't be afraid, Anne!"

"No, Rose," declared the little girl, "and if I think of you shut up here, even if I am afraid, I shall keep on until I find somebody and bring him to help you."

"That's splendid, Anne!" answered Rose. "Now step here beside me, and I'll lift you up."

CHAPTER EIGHT

—— ❦ ——

THROUGH THE WINDOW

"HOLD TIGHT, ANNE," whispered Rose.

Anne had succeeded in squeezing through the narrow window space, and Rose, leaning out as far as possible, kept a firm grasp on the little girl's hands.

"I'm going to let go now," whispered Rose; "try to drop easily, Anne," and in an instant Anne's feet touched the soft earth.

Rose watched her jump up and a moment later vanish in the thick growth of trees. Then she hooked the window securely, and sat down again on the iron chest. Her arms and shoulders felt lame and sore from holding Anne, but after a moment she forgot the ache and her thoughts turned to her father, and to brave little Anne traveling off through the darkness of the summer's night to bring help to her friends.

The house was so closely surrounded by woods that Anne had to move very carefully. The storm was over, but it was very dark in the shadow of the trees. For a few moments she wandered about, not quite knowing if she were moving in the right direction, but at last she found herself in the rough path up which Lady had made her way from the main road. Once or

187

twice she stumbled and nearly fell over stumps of trees, but at last she reached the junction, and now the moonlight enabled her to see the white line of the sandy road stretching far ahead.

"I can run now," she whispered to herself, and sped away, her moccasin-covered feet making no sound as she ran. All at once Anne stopped suddenly, for coming down the road toward her were a number of dark figures. They were so near that she could hear the sound of their voices. Anne turned quickly to the roadside and crouched behind a bunch of low-growing shrubs. As the men came nearer one of them said:

" 'Twas about here I saw something run into the woods."

"A fox, maybe," answered one of his companions.

"Maybe, and maybe not. It's not the time to take chances of a spy being about with those guns stored at Bill Mains'. I'm going to have a look around here and make sure," and the man turned straight toward the place where Anne crouched, fairly trembling with fear, for she had heard the man speak of the guns, and was quite sure that these men were Tories, as she supposed Bill Mains to be. She moved unconsciously, and the rustling betrayed her whereabouts, and the man took hold of her shoulder and drew her out into the road.

"Look at this! A little girl! Where's your father?" he demanded, drawing Anne toward his three companions, who were evidently too surprised to speak. "Where's your father?" he repeated, giving Anne a little shake.

"He—he's at sea," half sobbed Anne, hardly daring to lift her head, and wondering what dreadful fate would befall her if these men should discover that she had just escaped from Bill Mains' house, and that she knew all about the guns hidden there.

"Don't be rough with the little maid, Dan," said one of the men; "it's early in the evening yet, and no harm in a child being on the road. Like as not she hid there from fear of us. Do you live near here, little one?"

Anne now ventured to look up, but in the dusk could only see that the man who spoke so kindly was bareheaded, while the others wore slouch hats which shaded their faces.

"No, sir," she answered.

"There's no house for miles," declared the man who had

discovered Anne, "and there's some older person about, you may be sure."

As he spoke Anne said to herself that she would not let them know how she came there. "If I do perhaps they will kill Mr. Freeman," thought the frightened child. So when they questioned her she would not answer, and the men now had some reason to believe that Anne had older companions who might indeed be spies upon those who sympathized with the Americans.

"Is it safe to go to Mains' house?" questioned one of the men, and there was a little talk among them over the matter, but they decided to go on; and, holding Anne fast by the hand, the man who had drawn her out from her hiding place led the way, and Anne had not been away from the shingled house but an hour or two before she found herself again at the front door.

In response to a low whistle the door opened and the men filed into the room. Bill Mains, holding a candle in his hand, stood in the little passageway and as he saw Anne he nearly let the candle fall, and exclaimed in amazement:

"Where did you find that child? I had her double locked up in the brick room."

"Are you sure of it?" asked the man who kept so tight a grasp on Anne's arm that the mark of his fingers showed for several days after.

"Of course I'm sure; locked two of them up there before the thunderstorm, and have their father tied up in the kitchen. Tory spies they are."

At the sound of the hated words Anne exclaimed: "Indeed we are not Tory spies. We are not either of those things. Mr. Freeman is a patriot, and his son is with Washington. How dare you say we are Tories and treat us so!" and the little girl quite forgot her fear, and, as the hold on her arm loosened, she took a step away from the man and said: "We were going to Boston, and going to stop at Suet to see Captain Sears, and that man," and she pointed at Bill Mains, "shut us up because Rose and I peeked under a blanket at some guns."

As Anne stopped speaking the men looked at one another in surprise. At last the bareheaded man began to laugh, and the

189

others joined in; all but Bill Mains, who looked somewhat ashamed.

"You've been a bit too cautious, I reckon, Bill," said the man who had found Anne. "Mr. Freeman of Boston is known as a loyal man. Did he not tell you who he was?"

"I gave him no chance after I found this little maid looking at the guns I had covered with blankets," confessed Mains. "I told him I'd gag him if he said one word, and I reckon he thought he had fallen into the hands of a rank Tory. Who are you, little maid?" and he turned kindly toward Anne.

"I am John Nelson's daughter, who is at sea on the *Yankee Hero*, and I live with Uncle Enos and Aunt Martha Stoddard in Province Town, but now I am going with Rose Freeman for a visit in Boston," explained Anne, who could hardly realize that these men were now kindly disposed toward her, and that Bill Mains was sadly ashamed to have so ill treated his unexpected guests. "You must let Rose right out of that dark room," she added hastily.

"I should say so. You shall open the door yourself, little maid," answered Mains. "You boys go on to the kitchen and get Mr. Freeman's pardon for me if you can," and he turned and led Anne toward the room where Rose was locked in.

When Rose saw Anne standing in the doorway she exclaimed: "Oh, Anne, has he brought you back!" in such an unhappy voice that Bill Mains felt very uncomfortable.

"It's all right, Rose. You are to come right out where your father is. There are some nice men out there," declared Anne, clasping her hands about Rose's arm.

"Oh! then you found help," and there was a world of relief in Rose's voice as Anne led her out of the room, which Mr. Mains did not forget to lock carefully behind them.

"He thought we were Tory spies; that's why he locked us up," Anne explained, in a tone that almost seemed to praise Mr. Mains for such precaution.

"Tory spies, indeed!" said Rose, sending a scornful glance in his direction. "He should have known better. Where is my father?"

"Right this way, miss," replied Mr. Mains humbly, and the girls followed him to the kitchen where they found Mr. Freeman surrounded by the four men who had brought Anne back to the house.

Rose's father was as ready to pardon the mistake as Bill Mains was eager to have him.

"It's worth a little trouble to find we have such good men ready to defend our cause," he declared, "but I am afraid my girls here are pretty tired, and if you can give them a room without cannon and powder, I'm sure they will sleep well," as indeed they did in a neat little chamber into which Mr. Mains conducted them, bringing in the little trunk which had been strapped on the back of the chaise.

Mr. Freeman had believed that he was in the hands of the Tories, so that he did not greatly blame his host for being doubtful regarding him.

"It will delay us a little on our journey, but it is no great matter," he said pleasantly in response to Mains' repeated apologies. Then Mains explained that this house had been built of brick, and then boarded over and covered with shingles, as a storehouse for supplies for the American army. The four men had just returned from carrying powder to a couple of Yankee boats at Plymouth. These boats were among the many privateers that cruised about during the Revolution, harassing English vessels, and often capturing rich prizes, and helping the American cause. They stayed late in the evening talking with Mr. Freeman, and listening with interest to what he could tell them of affairs in Boston; and when they started off on their way toward Brewster they promised to let his brother know of the mistake, which seemed to them a very good joke on their friend Mains.

Mr. Mains was up at an early hour the next morning, and Mr. Freeman declared the breakfast to be the best that he had ever tasted. There was broiled partridge, hot corn bread, a big dish of freshly picked blueberries, and plenty of good milk; and Anne and Rose thought that nothing could be better, and even decided that Mr. Mains did not look like a pirate after all. "For I don't believe pirates wear brown gingham aprons, do you, Rose?" said Anne, watching Mr. Mains awkwardly tying his apron strings.

Lady had been well cared for, and was rested and ready for

the journey when Mr. Mains led her up to the door for the girls to enter the chaise.

"I'm mighty sorry," he repeated as he helped the girls in, "sorry, I mean, to have locked you folks up; but real glad to know you," and he waved them a smiling goodbye, as Mr. Freeman carefully guided Lady along the rough way to the main road.

"Well, Anne, I guess you'll remember this journey all your life," said Rose, as they reached the highway and Lady trotted briskly along as if glad to find her feet on good sand again. "Just think, father," she continued, "of all that has happened to her since she left Province Town, and she's not in Boston yet."

"Things happened when I went to Boston before," said Anne, remembering her brief visit to Newburyport, when she had safely carried a paper of importance to loyal Americans.

"I think all will go smoothly now," said Mr. Freeman, "but it was a very brave thing for a little girl to start off alone for help, as you did last night, Anne," and he looked kindly down at the little girl beside him. "Had we indeed been held prisoners by Tories you might have secured help for us, as you thought to do."

"But she really did help us, father," said Rose; "it was Anne who made them understand who we really were. I do believe we might be shut up still if Anne had not found a way to help us. Your father will be proud of you, Anne, when I tell him the story."

It made Anne very happy to have Mr. Freeman and Rose praise her, and she quite forgave the man who had pulled her from behind the bushes, and whose finger marks she could still feel on her arm.

"I hope it won't rain today," said Mr. Freeman. "We ought to get to Sandwich by noon, and after Lady has rested, we'll go on as far as we can. Lady seems as anxious to get to Boston as we do," for the big horse was traveling at a rapid pace, and going as if she enjoyed it.

"You shall go and see Faneuil Hall when you are in Boston, Anne," promised Rose, "and Mr. Hancock's fine house. It has terraces and stone steps, and the English officers would well like to take up their quarters there."

"They seem well satisfied with Vardy for a landlord at the

'Royal Exchange,' " answered Mr. Freeman smilingly. "Look, there is a wasp's nest as big as a bucket," and Mr. Freeman pointed his whip toward a huge gray ball hanging from the branch of a partly decayed tree near the road.

"It's a beauty," said Rose, leaning out to see the wonderful ball of gray paper which swung from the branch above them.

Mr. Freeman turned Lady to the further side of the road and said, "If the wasps have deserted their house, as they sometimes do at this season, I'd like to get it to take home to the children. I never saw so large a nest. I can soon find out," he concluded.

The brown horse stood quietly while Mr. Freeman and the girls got out of the chaise.

"Stay here a moment," said Mr. Freeman, and he walked back toward the tree and threw a small round stone at the nest. It hit the mark, but no angry wasps appeared. Another stone touched it more forcibly, and, when the third failed to bring a single wasp from the nest, Mr. Freeman declared that he knew it was vacant, and cutting a branch from a slender birch tree with his pocketknife, which he speedily made into a smooth pole, he managed to secure the nest without damaging it and brought it proudly back to show to Rose and Anne, neither of whom had ever seen one before.

"It's just like paper," said Anne admiringly, touching it carefully.

"That's just what it is," said Mr. Freeman. "I expect men learned from wasps how to make paper. For wasps go to work in a very businesslike way. They chew up dead and crumbling wood and spread it out smoothly, and when it dries and hardens there is a sheet of paper, all ready to be used as one of the layers for this dry warm nest. Men make paper by grinding up wood or linen rags."

"You can put the nest in our lunchbasket, father," said Rose. "Frederick and Millicent will think it the most wonderful thing they have ever seen."

Frederick and Millicent were Rose's younger brother and sister. Frederick was about Anne's age, but little Millicent was only six years old.

Lady turned her head as if to ask why they were lingering so far from a good stable; and Rose and Anne stopped a moment before getting in the chaise to rub her soft nose and tell her that she would soon be in Sandwich and should have a good feed of oats for her dinner.

CHAPTER NINE

LADY DISAPPEARS

"WE SHALL REACH the tavern in good season for dinner," said Mr. Freeman, as they drove into the village of Sandwich.

It seemed a very wonderful thing to the little maid from Province Town to drive up to the inn, with its big painted sign swinging from a post near the road, and she took hold of Rose's hand as if half afraid.

Rose looked down at her little friend with a smiling face.

"Why, Anne," she said laughingly, "you were not a bit afraid to start off through the woods alone, or to journey with Indians, and here you are trembling because you are going into this little tavern for dinner."

Anne managed to smile, but she kept a tight clasp on Rose's hand. It was not that she was frightened, but as she stepped from the chaise she had heard one of the loiterers about the door exclaim, "Look at the child, bareheaded and wearing moccasins," and her quick glance had comprehended the exchange of smiles; and Anne now felt uncomfortable and realized that she was not suitably dressed to travel in the high chaise. She looked at Rose, with her pretty dress of blue dimity, and white hat with its broad ribbon, her neat shoes and stockings, and realized that

195

there was a great contrast in their appearance. Anne was very silent all through the meal and ate but little. Even Mr. Freeman began to notice that she was very silent and grave, and thought to himself that the little girl might be homesick.

"We can drive to Plymouth this afternoon," he said, as they finished their dinner. "It is only about twenty miles, and we can get there early in the evening."

Anne knew all about Plymouth. From the hill in Province Town she had looked across the water to Plymouth, and Uncle Enos had told her that many years ago a band of Pilgrims from England had landed at Province Town, and then sailed on and settled in Plymouth. Uncle Enos had wondered at it, and had shook his head over a people who would willingly settle in any other place than Province Town.

The road now followed the shore very closely, and Rose was interested in watching the boats, and the many flocks of wild sea-birds circling about in the summer air. But Anne leaned back in the corner of the chaise silent and troubled. The more she thought about her lack of all the things that Rose had the more unhappy she became. "They will all be ashamed of me when I get to Boston," she thought, "and I have no money to buy things, and it will be three weeks or more before my dear father will reach Boston. Oh, dear!" And Anne, for the moment, wished herself back on the Province Town sands where a bare-headed, moccasin-shod little girl could be as happy as the day was long.

The sun had set, and it was in the cool of the early evening when they drove through Plymouth's main street. They were all tired and quite ready for bed. It seemed a very large town to Anne, with its meetinghouses and stores, but she was glad that it was nearly dark and hoped that no one would notice that she had no hat or sunbonnet.

"If I had not run away Aunt Martha would have seen to it that I had things like other girls," and she said to herself that "always, always, after this I'll tell Aunt Martha before I do things."

"Tomorrow night we'll be in Boston, Anne! Think of that," said Rose happily, when the landlady had shown them to the comfortable chamber that they were to occupy for the night. "Father says we'll start by sunrise, and give Lady a rest at

Scituate. Just think of all I shall have to tell when I get home. And then we'll go to the shops the very next day. Oh, Anne! I can't keep the secret another minute," and Rose came to the window where Anne stood looking out, and putting her arm over the younger girl's shoulder whispered in her ear: "Captain Stoddard gave me two golden guineas to spend for you, Anne. He said your father left them to buy clothes for you. I planned not to tell you until we were really in the shops and ready to purchase, but I thought it too good news to keep longer," and Rose smiled down at her little friend.

"Two guineas to buy clothes!" Anne's voice sounded as if such good fortune was almost beyond belief.

"And I can have a hat, and shoes and stockings, since my own were left behind in the wigwam?" she said questioningly.

"Indeed you can. And mother will go with us, and I doubt not you will have a pretty dress and slippers as well as shoes, and many fine things, for two guineas is a large sum to spend."

"Perhaps I shall not need to spend it all for clothes," said Anne; "then I can buy a present for Aunt Martha and Uncle Enos, and perhaps something for Amanda."

"Amanda!" echoed Rose. "Well, Anne, I would not take her home a gift; she does not deserve one from you."

Anne was silent, but she was excusing Amanda in her thoughts. As Amos so often said of Jimmie Starkweather that "nothing ever happens to Jimmie," so did Anne think of Amanda. She somehow felt sorry for Amanda, and had quite forgiven the ugly slaps her playmate had given her.

It took Anne a good while to go to sleep that night. Blue dimity dresses and shining slippers danced before her wakeful eyes, and a white ribbon to tie back her hair. Already she was trying to decide what her present to Amanda should be; and it seemed to her that she had just gone to sleep when Rose was shaking her gently and saying: "Time to get up."

The travelers were all in the best of spirits that morning: Rose, happy to be so near home, Anne delighted at the prospect of having dresses like the girls who lived in Boston, and Mr. Freeman had had the best of news from Plymouth friends, who declared that news from Philadelphia had been received stating that the Congress there was agreed upon declaring the independence of America.

" 'Tis what Mr. Samuel Adams has worked so hard for," Mr. Freeman told the girls; "and when the Congress has fully determined upon the form of the declaration word will be sent posthaste to Boston; and I trust, too, that Mr. Adams may be spared for a visit to his family. He has been absent from Boston for a year past."

Mr. Freeman had asked the landlord to furnish them with a luncheon, as he did not know if there would be a suitable place to procure food in Scituate; and with a bag of oats for Lady fastened on top of the little trunk, and a basket of luncheon under the seat of the chaise, the travelers could choose just when and where to stop.

"We'll keep a sharp outlook for a good clear stream of water," said Mr. Freeman.

"And I hope we can stop near the shore," said Rose; "I'd like to go in wading."

Anne thought that it would not make much difference where they stopped. The fragrant summer air, the pleasant shadow of the trees along the road, and the hope of soon being in Boston so filled her thoughts that where or what she ate seemed of little consequence.

Several hours after leaving Plymouth they found themselves on a pleasant stretch of road bordering the water.

"There is the very beach for wading!" exclaimed Rose happily, and even as she spoke they heard the splash of falling water and just before them was a rough bridge of logs over a rapid stream of clear water. Lady nearly stopped, and gave a little whinny as if asking for a drink.

"Just the place!" declared Mr. Freeman; "and here's a good piece of greensward in the shade for Lady," and he turned into a little grassy field beyond the bridge where a big beech tree stood, making a grateful circle of shade.

"Lady must have a couple of hours' rest," said Mr. Freeman, "so you girls can go down to the beach or do whatever you like until you are ready for luncheon."

The girls took off their shoes and stockings and ran down to the water's edge, and were soon wading about enjoying the cool water. After a little while they tired of wading and went up on the dry warm sand. Patches of bayberry bushes grew near the shore, and their fragrant leaves and small gray berries at once attracted Rose's attention. She had never before seen this shrub, a species of myrtle, and Anne was delighted to find something that she could tell the elder girl.

"It's bayberry, Rose. Just rub the leaves between your fingers and see how sweet it smells," she said. "Aunt Martha makes candles of these little green berries, and likes them better than tallow candles. When you snuff them out they make all the room smell just like this," and Anne held the bruised leaves up for Rose to smell.

"I don't see how candles could be made of these little berries," said Rose.

"And Aunt Martha makes a fine salve from them, too," continued Anne. "When she makes the candles I gather the berries, quarts and quarts, and she boils them in a kettle, and then skims off the top, and boils it again, and then turns it into the molds."

"Come to luncheon, girls!" called Mr. Freeman, and they ran back to the grassy field and the shade of the beech tree. On one side Lady was nibbling her oats happily. The lunch basket stood open; Mr. Freeman handed Rose a small tin drinking cup, and the girls ran down to the brook for a drink of the clear water.

"Cape Cod twists about Massachusetts Bay like a long arm, doesn't it, father?" said Rose, as they all seated themselves around the lunch basket.

Mr. Freeman laughed at Rose's description of the Cape, but nodded his head in agreement.

"I believe it does, my dear," he answered. "Province Town is the hand curved in, and Truro the wrist; Chatham must be the elbow, and now we are getting pretty well up to the shoulder."

After luncheon they all went back to the shore, and picked up many tiny shells. Some of these were clear white, and others a delicate pink. Mr. Freeman told them that the Indian women pricked tiny holes, with a small sharp-pointed awl, in these shells and strung them like beads, and Rose and Anne thought it would be a fine plan to carry a quantity of shells to Boston and string them into necklaces.

The time went swiftly, and when Mr. Freeman said that Lady

had now had a good rest and would be quite ready to start on, the girls reluctantly left the beach and walked slowly toward the chaise.

"I wonder where father and Lady are?" said Rose, and as she spoke Mr. Freeman came running across the little green field.

"Lady is gone! Stolen, I'm afraid," he called out.

The girls looked at him in amazement.

"She was securely fastened, and even if she got loose would not have gone far," he continued, "and there is no trace of her." Mr. Freeman's face was very anxious, and Rose exclaimed:

"But who could take Lady, father? We have not seen a person since we left Plymouth."

"Some strolling person," answered Mr. Freeman; "perhaps some frightened Tory from one of the loyal settlements on his way toward a place of safety."

Anne stood silent, holding up the skirt of her dress filled with the pretty shells.

"And shall we have to walk to Boston?" asked Rose.

"And leave this good chaise? I think not; though I hardly know how we can remain here," said Mr. Freeman.

For an hour or more they searched the nearby woods and up and down the road, but there was no trace to be found of Lady, nor did they find anything to tell them of how she had vanished.

"Your mother told me that it was no time for a visit so far from home," said Mr. Freeman, "and if Lady is indeed stolen I shall have good reason to wish that I had stayed at home. I hardly dare send you girls along the road alone, but if I leave this chaise it may disappear as Lady has done."

"Where could we go, father?"

"We are not far from Scituate, and any of the settlers who have a horse would come back and get the chaise," he answered. "I do not know of any harm that could befall you if you keep in the highway."

"Of course we must go," Rose decided quickly, and Anne looked at her friend admiringly, thinking, as she so often did, that she would like to be exactly like Rose Freeman.

In the excitement of discovering that Lady had disappeared Rose had dropped all the pretty shells she had gathered, but Anne was holding her skirt tightly clasped.

"Put your shells in the lunch basket, Anne," said Mr. Free-man; "I'll pick up those you have dropped, Rose. We shall reach Boston some time, and you will be glad of these to remind you of an adventurous journey," and his smile made the girls ready to start off with better courage.

"Stop at the first house on the road," directed Mr. Freeman; "tell them who you are, and what has befallen us, and ask them to come to my assistance, and for permission to stay at the house until I come for you."

"Yes, father," replied Rose, and then she and Anne started down the road. They kept in the shade for some distance, then the road ran up a long sandy hill where the sun came down fully upon them, and before they reached the summit they were very warm and tired.

"There's a house!" exclaimed Anne, as they stopped to rest on the top of the hill.

"Thank goodness!" exclaimed Rose. "And it's a farmhouse. See the big barns. There are sure to be horses there."

The girls quite forgot the heat, and ran down the sandy hill and hurried along the road, which now was a smoother and better one than any over which they had traveled, and in a short time were near the comfortable farmhouse. A woman was stand-ing in the doorway watching them.

"Where in the world did you girls come from," she called out, as they opened the gate, "in all this heat? Come right in. I should think your folks must be crazy to let you walk in the sun. Was that your father who went galloping by on a brown horse just now?"

As soon as the woman finished speaking Rose told her their story.

"Then that man had stolen your horse! A Tory, I'll wager; and like enough a spy," said the woman; "and my menfolks all away. There are two horses in the pasture; if you girls can catch one of 'em and ride it back to where your father's waiting, why, you're welcome."

Anne and Rose looked at each other almost in dismay. Nei-ther of them had ever been on the back of a horse, and to go into a pasture and catch a strange horse seemed to them very much like facing a wild beast.

"We'll try," said Rose, with a little smile.

"I thought you would," said the woman approvingly. "I'd go myself, but I've got bread in the oven, and I must see to it."

The woman led the way to a shed and filling a shallow pan with oats from a big bin, handed it to Rose, saying: "You go right through those bars—leave 'em down; I'll put 'em up for you— and shake these oats and call 'Range, Range,' and the old horse will be sure to come, and the colt will follow."

Rose took the pan, and Anne pulled back the heavy bars, and they went a few steps beyond the fence into the pasture and began to call "Range! Range!"

In a moment there was the thud, thud of hoofs and two black horses came dashing down the pasture. Their long manes and tails gave them a terrifying look to the two girls, who, nevertheless, stood their ground, Rose holding out the pan as the woman had bidden her.

"Oh, Rose! They'll run right over us!" exclaimed Anne, watching the horses rushing toward them so swiftly.

CHAPTER TEN

AUNT ANNE ROSE

BUT THE HORSES came to a sudden stop a few feet from where the girls stood. Then one turned and rushed away, kicking up his heels as if to say: "I'm not to be caught!"

Rose kept on calling "Range! Range!" and shaking the pan, and the other horse stepped forward and stuck his nose into the dish.

"Grab hold of his mane, Anne. Quick! and hold on tight!" said Rose; "the woman is coming now with the bridle."

Anne obeyed, holding fast to the black mane until Mrs. Pierce came running from the barn, bringing a blanket and a bridle.

"I'm glad you caught Range," she said; "he's used to a saddle, and the colt is wild as a deer." While she talked she was strapping the blanket securely on the horse's back, and now slipped the bit into his mouth.

"The little girl better go," she continued, nodding toward Anne. "You just climb that fence, and I'll lead Range alongside and you can get on his back nicely. Sit boy fashion; it's safer. No sense as I can see in a girl jest hanging on to one side of anything," and almost before she knew it Anne found herself on the back of the black horse.

Mrs. Pierce, who had told the girls her name on the way to the pasture, led Range out into the road and headed him in the right direction.

"If he don't go fast enough kick your heels against his sides and call to him," directed the woman, handing the reins to Anne, and giving the horse a sharp slap that sent him off at a good pace.

It seemed to Anne as if she were going up into the air, or over the horse's head. But somehow she managed to keep on Range's back, though she did not dare to give a backward look.

"Range will bring your pa back in no time, don't you worry," said Mrs. Pierce, giving Rose a kindly pat on the shoulder; then exclaiming, "The bread!" she ran back to the house, leaving Rose looking down the road, and wondering, a little fearfully, if Anne would reach the big beech tree without being thrown into the road.

Then she looked the other way, in the direction of Boston, and wondered what would befall Lady.

"Come in, my dear, out of this hot sun," Mrs. Pierce called from the doorway, and Rose went slowly up the path and entered the big square room at the right of the small square entry.

"You sit right down and I'll bring you a drink," and Mrs. Pierce drew forward a comfortable rocking chair for her young guest, and was soon back with a cup of milk and a square of fresh gingerbread.

"I should admire to have a girl just like you," declared Mrs. Pierce, taking the empty cup. "I can see that you've a real good disposition, and a girl would be a sight of company to me."

Then Rose told her about her own mother, and had begun to tell her Anne Nelson's little history, when Mrs. Pierce again exclaimed: "My bread!" and hurried off to the kitchen.

Rose went to the open window and looked out, wondering how long it would be before her father would reach the farmhouse, and it seemed a long time to wait in spite of the friendly kindness of Mrs. Pierce.

The black horse went along at an easy pace, and after a little

Anne ceased to be afraid, held the bridle-reins more easily, and even ventured to look about a little.

"Things keep happening," she thought. "I hope nothing has carried off Mr. Freeman and the chaise!"

Mr. Freeman was standing in the roadway, and as he saw Range with Anne on his back coming rapidly toward him he gave an exclamation of surprise. At a word the horse stopped, and Mr. Freeman lifted Anne from his back.

"A man went by Mrs. Pierce's with Lady before we got there," said Anne, after she had told him of the farmhouse, of Mrs. Pierce, and of catching Range.

While she talked Mr. Freeman was harnessing Range into the chaise, and they were soon on the way to the farm.

Rose and Mrs. Pierce were at the gate to meet them.

"Oh, father! Can't you go after Lady?" asked Rose.

Mr. Freeman looked at Mrs. Pierce questioningly. "If Mrs. Pierce will lend me a horse I'll go at once," he replied; "there are a good many houses along the way now, and I might get some trace of the thief."

"You go right along. Take the colt; he's as fast as any horse hereabouts, and maybe you can overtake the fellow," replied Mrs. Pierce.

Mr. Freeman captured the colt, and, telling Rose not to worry if he did not return until night, started off, the colt going at a pace that made the girls exclaim in admiration.

"I'm real sorry you folks should be so set back in your journey, but it's real pleasant for me to have company," said Mrs. Pierce, with a smiling look at her young visitors. "It's days and weeks sometimes without my seeing any one but my husband and the boys. Now we'll sit down here and you tell me all about your journey."

"It's just like a story!" declared Mrs. Pierce, when they had finished. "And now you are going to Boston, and you will see the streets and shops, and churches." She gave a little sigh as she finished, and Anne and Rose wished that it was possible for Mrs. Pierce to go to Boston with them.

"I don't suppose you could mark out a little plan of Boston, could you?" she said to Rose. "I like to imagine things to myself when I'm here alone, and if I knew how the streets went, and where you lived, why, I could say to myself, 'Today Rose and Anne are going up King Street toward the State House, and up Longacre Street to the Common,' and it would seem almost as if I saw you when I looked at the plan.''

"Yes, I think I could," said Rose, and Mrs. Pierce brought a sheet of paper and a red crayon from a big desk in the corner and laid them on the table.

Mrs. Pierce and Anne watched Rose mark out the Common and the Mall. "The Mall is where the fine people walk in the afternoon," she said. "Mr. Hancock's mansion is right here, on Beacon Hill, where you get a fine view across the Charles River to Charlestown."

Then she marked Copp's Hill. "This is where the British had their guns when the great battle was fought at Bunker Hill," she said.

Mrs. Pierce listened eagerly. "I can 'most see it all!" she exclaimed. "Now show me where your house is," and Rose made a little square for her home.

"We are nearer the harbor than many houses are," she explained, "for my father owns a wharf, and it is convenient to be where he can see boats and vessels coming in."

The girls had been so interested, Rose in drawing and explaining, and Anne in listening, that time passed very rapidly, and when Rose finished Mrs. Pierce opened the door of a queer little cupboard beside the chimney and took out a small square box.

"My! Is that a gold box!" exclaimed Anne admiringly, for the box shone and glittered in the light.

"If it was I wouldn't keep it these days, when our poor soldiers need food and clothes," replied Mrs. Pierce. "It is brass, one my grandfather brought from France." As she spoke she lifted the cover and took out two little cases of brown leather, and handed one to Rose and the other to Anne. "Open the little clasps," she said.

The girls obeyed, and as the little cases opened they exclaimed admiringly, for each case held a pair of scissors, a silver thimble, a tiny emery ball and a needle book.

"My uncle brought me those when I was about your age," Mrs. Pierce said to Anne. "I never quite made out why he brought two until this very day, but I see now," and she smiled happily at her little visitors. "I see now, because I can give one to each of you girls!"

After the girls had thanked her, and tried on the thimbles, and declared that the cases were almost too nice to use, Mrs. Pierce left them for a few moments.

"Rose," exclaimed Anne, "wouldn't it be splendid if Mrs. Pierce would let us make believe that she was our aunt?"

"Perhaps she will; she told me that she hadn't any brothers or sisters, or anybody except her husband and two sons," said Rose. "We might ask her if she would be willing for us, when we talk about her to each other, to call her 'Aunt Anne Rose'!"

"If your father only gets Lady back we'll be real glad the man took her; shan't we, Rose?" said Anne thoughtfully.

"Because we found Aunt Anne Rose? Why, yes, I suppose we shall," replied Rose. "But isn't it funny she should have our names! You ask her, Anne, if she is willing for us to call her aunt."

"There!" exclaimed Mrs. Pierce, when Anne ran into the kitchen and asked the question, "if I wasn't wishing for that very thing. I count it as a real blessing that some one went off with your horse! I do indeed. And if Rose's father don't find Lady he can borrow our colt for the rest of the journey."

It was late in the afternoon before Mr. Freeman returned, but he did not bring Lady, nor had he any news of her.

Mr. Pierce and his sons returned home at nightfall, and made the travelers feel that they were as pleased as Aunt Anne Rose to have their guests remain for the night.

CHAPTER ELEVEN

———— ❧ ————

IN BOSTON

Mr. Freeman looked a little puzzled when he heard the girls calling Mrs. Pierce "Aunt Anne Rose," and when Mrs. Pierce told him that was really her name he thought, as the girls had, that it was almost like discovering a relative. Mr. Pierce had insisted that they should borrow the black colt for the remainder of their journey, and they were ready to start at an early hour the next morning.

Rose was tying the ribbons to her pretty hat, while Anne watched her a little wistfully, wishing that she had a hat—almost any kind of a hat, she thought—so that she might not look like "a little wild girl," as she had overheard some one call her at the Sandwich tavern. Just then she felt something placed gently on her head and saw two broad brown ribbons falling each side of her face.

"Oh!" she exclaimed, looking up in wonder.

Mrs. Pierce stood beside her. "There!" she exclaimed. "What kind of a milliner do you think I should make for the fine ladies in Boston?" and she lifted the hat from Anne's head, holding it up for the girls to see.

It was a round flat hat, plaited of straw. It had no trimming save a pretty bow and strings of brown ribbon, but Anne thought it was a beautiful hat.

"It's one I plaited last year," continued Mrs. Pierce, putting the hat back on Anne's head, and tying the brown ribbon under her chin. "I did it evenings, just to keep busy. I do wish I had a prettier ribbon for it."

"Is it for me?" asked Anne, almost afraid that it was almost too much good fortune to expect.

"Of course it is. 'Twill serve to remind you of your Aunt Anne," and the friendly woman smiled down at Anne's happy face.

"We will write you a letter, Aunt Anne Rose," said Rose, as they walked down the path to where the chaise awaited them, "and you will come and visit my mother in Boston, will you not?"

"Mr. Pierce has already promised that they will both come," said Mr. Freeman.

"And, Anne," and Mrs. Pierce patted the little hand she was holding so closely, "you tell your father that you have found another aunt, and that he must let you come and stay with me for a long long visit."

Then goodbyes were said, and they were again started on their journey.

"No stops this time—except to ask for news of Lady—until I reach my own house," declared Mr. Freeman. " 'Tis a good cool morning and we ought to get home by midday."

"Perhaps we shall find Lady," suggested Rose. But Mr. Freeman shook his head.

"I'm afraid it will be a long time before we get any news of her," he said soberly. "I only hope the thief will not abuse her." The brown horse had always been petted and made much of, and neither Mr. Freeman nor Rose could bear to think of her in the hands of people who would not be kind to her.

Every now and then Anne would take off the plaited straw hat and look at it with admiring eyes. "I shall not have to buy a hat now, Rose," she said.

"But you will want a prettier one than that," responded her friend.

"A prettier hat!" Anne's tone seemed to say that she could

not imagine a prettier hat, and she shook her head. "I sha'n't ever want any other hat," she declared. "I mean to keep this always because Aunt Anne Rose gave it to me."

The black colt sped along as if it was nothing but play to pull the big chaise. The girls told Mr. Freeman of all that Aunt Anne Rose had said about the big farm, and of her own loneliness when her husband and sons were away. Rose noticed that, although her father listened, his glance traveled sharply over the pastures as they went along; and that now and then he leaned out for a clearer view of some horse feeding near the road, and she realized that he was keeping an outlook for Lady.

But there was no sign of the pretty brown horse, and Mr. Freeman's inquiries at houses and in villages along the way did not give him any news of Lady. There was so much for Anne to see and think about that she hardly realized what a serious loss had befallen her good friends. But as they drove down Longacre Street, past Boston Common, and turned into the street where the Freemans' house stood, she saw that Rose and Mr. Freeman both looked very downcast.

"What will mother say?" Rose half whispered, as if to herself.

Mrs. Freeman was at the door to welcome them.

"And here is our little maid from Province Town," she said, putting her arm about Anne. "You are indeed welcome, dear child; and it is a fine time for a little girl to visit Boston."

Mr. Freeman had expected his wife to ask what had become of Lady, and was surprised that she did not. He led the colt toward the stable, which stood in a paved yard back of the house, and Frederick ran ahead to open the stable door.

"Upon my soul!" exclaimed Mr. Freeman, for there in her own comfortable stall was Lady, munching her noonday meal as if everything was just as usual.

"The man got here last night with Lady," explained Frederick; "he was in a great hurry to get a boat, and he told me—for mother was at a neighbor's—that you'd be coming on today. Was he taking a message to American troops? Mother said that must be his business; that you'd lend Lady for no other reason," and the boy looked at his father questioningly.

"I hope that may have been his errand," said Mr. Freeman, "but I fear he was on other business. The Tories are more anxious than Americans for boats just now," and he told the boy how Lady had been stolen. "But who ever it was must have known me and where I live," he concluded; " 'tis not every thief who leaves the horse in its owner's stable."

"But your name is on the little brass plate on Lady's bridle," Frederick reminded him, "so 'twould be easy if the man were honest."

Mr. Freeman cautioned them not to tell any one but Rose's mother of their discovery of the shingled house in the woods where Bill Mains had the hidden stores.

"No one knows just whom to trust these days," he said, "and if such news was known to those who sympathize with the English they'd soon be after his guns and powder."

"I think we will have a sewing bee," Mrs. Freeman said, when Rose had told her the story of Anne's flight from Province Town, and that the little girl had no clothing, but had two golden guineas to spend. "You and Anne will have to be busy with your needles for a part of each day until she has proper clothes. And early tomorrow morning we will walk up to Mistress Mason's shop on Cornhill and get her some shoes."

The little room that opened from Rose's chamber had a broad window which looked toward the harbor. There were white curtains at this window, tied back with crocheted bands of white cotton. The floor was painted a soft grayish brown, and there were strips of rag carpet spread beside the white covered bed, and in front of the mahogany bureau. There was a looking-glass hung over this bureau. By standing on tiptoe Anne could see herself in it. In one corner of the room was a washstand with a blue china bowl and pitcher. Near the window was a low table and a rocking chair.

It was a very neat and pleasant room, and to Anne it seemed beautiful. That it opened directly into the big square chamber where Rose slept made her feel very much at home. She wished that Aunt Martha Stoddard could see it, and she went to the window and looked off across the blue waters of the harbor wishing that she could see Aunt Martha and tell her all the wonderful things that had befallen her.

It was decided that Anne was to have a pair of slippers with straps fastening around the instep, and a pair of shoes for everyday wear. Mrs. Freeman had a good store of white stockings which Rose had outgrown and from these a number were selected for Anne. When she was dressed ready to go to the shops with Mrs. Freeman and Rose the latter exclaimed:

"Mother, mayn't I open the parlor shutters so that Anne can see herself in the long mirror?"

"Why, yes; but be very careful to close them that the sun may not strike on the carpet," replied Mrs. Freeman, a little reluctantly; for the Freemans' parlor was a very grand room and opened only when company was asked to tea, or when some distinguished person came to call.

Rose turned the brass knob, pushed open the white-paneled door and tiptoed into the shadowy room. "Come in, Anne!" she called, and Anne followed. She had not seen this room when she had visited the Freemans with Uncle Enos two years before.

"Oh!" she exclaimed, half fearfully, as her feet sank into the soft carpet. Then she stood quite still until Rose had opened the paneled inside shutters at one of the large windows. She looked about her in wonder. Directly opposite the door was a fireplace with a high white mantel, and over the mantel was the portrait of a very old lady who seemed to be smiling straight at Anne.

"Come in," Rose repeated, with a little laugh of pleasure at Anne's evident admiration, and she led her little visitor toward the front of the room where a long mirror, from ceiling to floor, was fastened against the wall between the two windows. "Look at yourself, Anne. You can see the room afterward," she said, and Anne looked into the mirror and smiled, for she saw a little dark-eyed girl with smoothly braided hair, wearing a hat of plaited straw with a brown ribbon, and a dress of brown linen with a pretty frill at the neck. She looked down admiringly at her white stockings and new shoes, and then twisted her head in the hope of seeing the back of this neat little girl. She quite forgot the soft carpet, and the shining tables and cushioned chairs.

"I do wish Amanda could see me," she said; "she'd be real glad I had these fine things."

CHAPTER TWELVE

A WONDERFUL DAY

ANNE HELD ROSE's hand very tightly as they walked along. It seemed to the little girl that all the people of the town were out walking up and down the streets. Now and then there would be a clatter of hoofs over the cobblestone pavements and Anne would look up to see a man go by on horseback. And Mrs. Freeman told her to notice a fine coach drawn by two horses that stood in front of the very shop they were about to enter.

"If I spend a guinea for clothes will it not be enough?" Anne questioned, as Mrs. Freeman asked a smiling clerk to show them blue dimity.

"Why, yes, Anne; I think we can manage very nicely with a guinea," responded Mrs. Freeman, who meant to supply Anne with many needful things from her own stores. "Do you wish to save one?"

Anne shook her head. "No," she responded, "but I want to buy a grand present for Aunt Martha and Uncle Enos, and something for Amanda Cary. I should like to take Amos and the Starkweather children something, but I fear there will not be enough money."

Mrs. Freeman smiled at Anne's thought for her playmates.

215

"You can perhaps make something for some of your little friends. Would not the Starkweather children like a little work-bag or a hemstitched handkerchief?" she asked.

The thought of the Starkweather boys with workbags and hemstitched handkerchiefs seemed very funny to Anne, and she gave a little laugh, saying, "But they are all boys."

"Oh, well, then we will make some fine candy just before you go home, and you and Rose can make some pretty boxes to put it in. So there's your present for the Starkweather boys. And you'll have a whole guinea to buy gifts for Mrs. Stoddard and the captain, and for Amanda. I suppose Amanda is your dearest friend, isn't she?" and Mrs. Freeman looked down into Anne's happy smiling face, quite sure that Mrs. Stoddard must be very glad that she had taken the little girl into her own home.

"Best friend, indeed!" exclaimed Rose, before Anne could answer. "Why, mother! Had it not been for that Amanda, Anne never would have run away."

"But Anne wants to take her a present," said Mrs. Freeman.

A little flush crept into Anne's brown cheeks. "I guess Amanda didn't mean to," she said.

The clerk was waiting patiently, and Mrs. Freeman now begged his pardon for so long delaying her purchases, and ordered enough dimity for Anne's dress. It was a light blue with a tiny white sprig, and Anne thought it the prettiest pattern that any one could imagine.

"I have plenty of nainsook in the house for your underwear, so we will not purchase that," said Mrs. Freeman, "but we will buy some good white cotton yarn so that I can take up some stockings for you. It will make work for you at odd times." For in those days children were taught that useful occupation brought as much pleasure as play, and every girl had "pieced a quilt" before she was ten years of age, worked a sampler, and usually knit all her own stockings and mittens.

"Can't Anne have some thread gloves like mine?" Rose asked, and Anne drew a quick breath of delight. "White thread gloves," she thought to herself, would be more than she could hope for, but Mrs. Freeman seemed to think it a very reasonable request, and told Rose to go with Anne to a shop on Queen Street and select a pair of gloves.

"I must go home now," she added, "for it is Saturday, and I have much to do. After you have purchased the gloves you girls can walk up to the Common if you wish; but be sure and be home in good season for dinner."

The girls both promised, and Mrs. Freeman left them, with a word of caution to be careful in crossing Longacre Street, where there were always many teams, carriages and horsemen going back and forth.

"You are almost a young lady, aren't you, Rose?" Anne said admiringly, as she looked up at her friend.

"I suppose so," Rose replied laughingly. "See, my skirts come to my ankles, and Aunt Hetty said I must twist my braids around my head now. And I think it does become me better," and Rose put up her white-gloved hand to be quite sure that the braids were smoothly fastened.

The girls walked along the Mall, and a little way toward the Charles River. Rose met several girls of her own age who greeted Anne pleasantly. One of them asked Rose if she knew that a messenger had reached Boston with a copy of the Declaration of Independence. "It is to be read from the balcony of the State House on Tuesday," said Rose's friend. " 'Twill be a great day, and 'tis well you have reached Boston in time for it."

When Anne and Rose reached the Freeman house little Millicent was at the door waiting for them. She had a big doll in her arms and told Anne that its name was "Hetty," because Aunt Hetty Freeman had made it and sent it to her. Frederick had hung the wasp's nest in his own room, and declared that there was not another boy in Boston who possessed one. Several of his friends had already seen it, and Frederick was quite sure that he was a very fortunate boy to have it for his own.

On Sunday morning Anne was awakened by the sound of the bells of Christ Church, which was not far distant from the Freemans' house. She lay listening to the musical notes, and wondering if those could really be church bells.

"They sound like far-off voices singing," she thought to herself. And when Mrs. Freeman, at breakfast time, told her that there were eight bells, and that they came all the way from Gloucester, England, in 1745, and were the first ring of bells in

North America, they seemed even more wonderful to the little girl.

"William Shirley was Governor of Massachusetts at that time," said Mr. Freeman, "and when the bells reached Boston it was found that there was no money in the church treasury to raise them to the church belfry, and just then Boston had the good news that the colonial forces under General Pepperell had captured Louisburg. Well, every bell in Boston was ringing with triumph, and it did not take long to start a subscription and get money enough to put those fine bells where they could be heard. They were made by good English bell-makers, and there are none better," concluded Mr. Freeman. Anne thought to herself that she would be sure to remember about these wonderful bells so that she could tell Amanda.

On the morning of the 18th of July people began to gather in King Street and the vicinity of the State House, so that long before one o'clock, the time advertised when the Declaration of Independence was to be read, there was a crowd. Mr. and Mrs. Freeman with Millicent, Frederick, Rose and Anne had a very good place where they could see the little balcony where Colonel Crafts was to stand.

"Look, father! There are some of the British officers!" said Frederick.

The crowd near where the Freemans were standing stood courteously back to make way for several British officers in full military dress. They secured a place where they could hear well, and Mr. Freeman and several gentlemen exchanged smiles of satisfaction to see these officers present. When the clock struck one, Colonel Crafts, surrounded by a number of gentlemen, appeared on the balcony, and in a clear voice read the declaration announcing to the world that the American colonies were no longer subject to Britain.

What a chorus of shouts and huzzas filled the air! Frederick's cap went so high that it lodged on the State House balcony, but no one seemed to notice it, and Frederick could not recover his property until late that afternoon. There sounded the measured boom of cannon, and thirteen volleys of musketry. A military band played, and the people dispersed, quietly, and as if they had taken part in a great ceremony, as indeed they had.

"Now you girls will have to settle down; dresses do not make themselves," said Mrs. Freeman; "nor do stockings grow on trees. Your father's ship will be coming into harbor before you know it, Anne; and you must have your clothing in order, and Rose has agreed to help you. So tomorrow we must begin in earnest."

"I have a chance to send the black colt to Mr. Pierce tomorrow," said Mr. Freeman, "and I have bought a good side-saddle for Mrs. Pierce, that they may know we do not forget their great kindness."

"That is the very thing, father!" exclaimed Rose. "Now Aunt Anne Rose can ride to the village and see her friends whenever she wishes. She will not be so lonely."

"I thought of that," said Mr. Freeman.

"You girls must make up a little package for the colt to carry to your new aunt," suggested Mrs. Freeman.

Anne had her golden guinea and several shillings besides in a pretty knit purse that Rose had given her, and she was very happy to think that, out of her very own money, she could buy something for Aunt Anne Rose.

"I know what she'd like," said Anne. "I told her about the fine book that my Aunt Martha keeps in the chest. 'Tis called *Pilgrim's Progress.* And Aunt Anne Rose said that if she had a book to read at times 'twould be as good as company."

"You girls shall step into Mistress Mason's and select a suitable book," said Mrs. Freeman. "You can write her name in it and put 'From Anne and Rose to Aunt Anne Rose'; no doubt 'twill please her. And this evening we will make some sweets to send her. We wish her to be very sure that we do not lack in gratitude."

Mistress Mason's shop in Cornhill seemed a very wonderful place to Anne, with its shelves filled with bright pewter, tall brass candlesticks, and large and small boxes. On a lower shelf at the back of the small room was a row of books. On a narrow counter stood boots, shoes, and slippers. Above this counter, fastened to a stout cord, were hung a number of dolls dressed in the latest fashion. Each one of these dolls had a small white card fastened to its sleeve.

When the girls entered they did not at first see anyone in the shop, but in a moment Anne noticed that a very tiny old lady was standing behind the further counter.

"Why, she isn't any bigger than I am!" thought the little girl.

"Good afternoon, Mistress Mason," said Rose; "this is my friend, little Anne Nelson, from Province Town."

"Not so very little, as I view it. Fully as large as I am myself. I should call her large; that is, large for a girl," responded the little white-haired woman, who was rather sensitive in regard to her size. "I see you wear good shoes," she continued, peering over the low counter and pointing a tiny finger toward Anne's feet. "I know my own shoes when I see 'em," and she laughed pleasantly. "My brother makes every shoe I sell; makes 'em right back here in his own shop, as Miss Rose Freeman well knows."

"Yes, indeed," answered Rose, "and Mistress Mason makes dolls, Anne—all those fine ones near the door."

"All but the ones with china heads; I make only bodies for the heads. The china heads come from France and cost me dear. But they are good bodies, as you can see, my dears; with joints where joints should be, and with feet and hands of soft kid. 'Tis some work, I do assure you, young ladies, to stitch fingers and toes as fingers and toes should be stitched," and Mistress Mason looked very serious indeed. "And as for making dolls with kid-covered heads, and then painting their faces and giving a good expression to eyes and mouths, I do feel that it's almost beyond me. I do indeed!"

The little old lady trotted briskly across the shop and unfastening several dolls from the line held them toward her visitors. "Now here is Lady Melissa Melvina," and Anne saw that on each of the white cards was written the name belonging to the doll on whose sleeve the card was pinned. "Lady Melissa Melvina is all kid," went on Mistress Mason, "head, body, feet and fingers; and every stitch she wears is of the best. She's worth twenty shillings. But——!" and Mistress Mason made an impressive pause and shook her head. "Could I get that amount? No. So, though 'tis far too little, you may have her for ten shillings six," and she smiled as if she were really bestowing a gift upon them.

"We did not come to buy a doll, Mistress Mason, although I'm sure Anne would like greatly to have so fine a doll as this; but we want to purchase a book," said Rose.

The little old woman was evidently disappointed. "A book, indeed," she responded. "I know not what is coming to people. Everybody, even the very children, are asking for books. We can hardly keep our shelf neatly filled, and I have half a mind not to keep them. Many a person who should buy a stout pair of shoes puts the money in books," and she shook her head as if not understanding such folly.

" 'Tis for a present," responded Rose, as if to excuse their purchase, "to a lady who lives in the country and is much alone."

"I see; well, maybe such folk find company in reading," said the shopkeeper. "Here is a book may please her," and she took up a thin volume and opened it. " 'Tis a book of verse, but 'tis well thought of. I see but little sense in verse myself; but, for verse, this reads well:

> " 'Great conquerors greater glory gain
> By foes in triumph led than slain,' "

she read, and went on to a second couplet:

> " 'Ay me! What perils do environ
> The man that meddles with cold iron.'

And I declare here is what I've always said of poetry. 'Tis as true as I make good dolls:

> " 'Those that write in rhyme still make
> The one verse for the other's sake.' "

"I think Aunt Anne Rose would like *Pilgrim's Progress,*" Anne ventured, a little timidly, to suggest.

"Maybe. I have a fine copy. Not too large, and easy to read. 'Twill cost five shillings," and Mistress Mason put back the book of verse and took from the shelf a small square book that she handed to Rose.

The girls looked it over carefully. "But it is not like Aunt Martha's book," said Anne; " 'tis not so large, nor has it such fine pictures. These pictures are little and black."

"It tells the same story," Rose assured her, "and I know it

would please Aunt Anne Rose. It will cost us two and six, sixty-two cents, apiece."

They decided to purchase it, and Mistress Mason wrapped it up in a neat package for them, and said that she hoped they would step in again. She followed them to the door, and Rose and Anne both bowed very politely as they wished her good day.

CHAPTER THIRTEEN

———— ❦ ————

ANNE'S BOOK

"Rose," said Anne, as soon as they left the little shop, "I know what I shall buy for Aunt Martha; I shall buy her one of those fine pewter dishes."

"So you can! It will be sure to please her," replied Rose, looking kindly down at her little friend. "You are always thinking of giving people things, aren't you, Anne? My Grandmother Freeman, who lived in Wellfleet, used to say that it was a sign that a child would grow up prosperous and happy if it had the spirit to give instead of to take."

When the girls went up the brick walk to the Freeman house they saw Frederick and a number of small boys in the yard. Frederick was standing on a box with a paper in his hand, from which he was reading, and he and his companions were so interested that they did not notice the girls.

"He's playing that he's Colonel Crafts reading the Declaration," Rose whispered to Anne, as they opened the front door, and entered the house. "Fred has made believe everything that has happened here in Boston for the last two years."

"It's warm weather for candy-making," said Mrs. Freeman, as the family gathered at the supper table in the cool pleasant dining room, "but Caroline is going to see her mother this evening, so you children can have the kitchen, and you will not have another opportunity for a long time to send Aunt Anne Rose any remembrance."

The children all declared that it was not too warm for candy-making, and as soon as Caroline, a young woman who helped Mrs. Freeman and Rose with the household work, gave them permission Rose, Anne, Millicent and Frederick went into the kitchen. Rose opened a deep drawer in a chest which stood in one corner of the room.

"Look, Anne," she said, and Anne peered in, exclaiming:

"Why, it's filled with little boxes!"

"Yes," said Rose, picking up one shaped like a heart; "stormy days, and sometimes in winter evenings, when I do not feel like knitting or sewing, I make boxes out of heavy paper or cardboard, and cover them with any bits of pretty paper or cloth that I can get. Frederick helps me. He can make even better ones than I can, and Millicent helps too," and she smiled down at the little sister who stood close beside Anne.

"Let's send Aunt Anne Rose the heart-shaped box," said Anne.

"And fill it with heart-shaped taffy," added Frederick, running toward a shelf filled with pans and kettles of various shapes and sizes, and taking down a box. "See, we have little shapes for candy," and he opened the box and took out some tiny heart-shaped pans, and dishes shaped in rounds and stars and crescents.

"My!" exclaimed Anne, "and can you make the candies in these?"

"No!" and Frederick's voice was a little scornful. "We have to boil it in a kettle, of course; then we grease the inside of these little pans with butter and turn the candy into them, and when it cools we tip them out, and there they are. Fine as any you can buy, aren't they, Rose?"

"Yes, indeed, and Frederick knows just how to take them out without breaking the candy. He is more careful than I am," said Rose, who lost no opportunity of praising her little brother and sister, and who never seemed to see any fault in them.

"Molasses taffy is the best," declared Frederick, "but you can make some sugared raisins, can't you, Rose?"

"We'll have to be very careful in putting the candy in the boxes so that it will not melt," said Rose.

Before it was time to pack the candy Mrs. Freeman came into the kitchen and untied a bundle to show the children what it contained.

"It's lovely, mother!" exclaimed Rose, lifting up a little fleecy shoulder cape of lavender wool. "Why, it's the one you knit for yourself!" and she looked at her mother questioningly.

"It seemed all I had that was pretty enough to send Mrs. Pierce," replied Mrs. Freeman.

"But she lives way off in that lonesome place where she never sees pretty things. She'd be pleased with anything," said Rose, who almost wished that her mother would keep the pretty shawl.

"That's why I want to send this to her," responded Mrs. Freeman. "If she had all sorts of nice things I wouldn't do it; I'd just send her a cake with my love."

"Send the cake, too," said Mr. Freeman, who had followed his wife. "Send the cake with my love."

"Why, so I will," said Mrs. Freeman. "Caroline made two excellent loaves of spice cake this very day and we can well spare one of them. But you children must trot off to bed. It's been a very exciting day."

Little Millicent was quite ready for bed, but neither Anne nor Rose was sleepy, and Rose followed her little friend into her room.

"See how clear the night is, Anne," she said, looking out of the window toward the harbor. "The water looks like a mirror."

Anne came and stood beside her. Her thoughts traveled across the smooth waters to the little house in Province Town. "I shouldn't wonder if Aunt Martha were looking out at the water and thinking about me," she said, drawing a little nearer to the tall girl beside her. "I wish she knew how good everybody is to me."

Rose put her arm about the little girl. "She expects everybody to be good to you, Anne," she responded; "but I have thought of something that you can do for Mrs. Stoddard that I am sure will please her, and will be something that she will always like to keep."

"What is it, Rose?" and Anne's voice was very eager.

"Let's sit down here on the window seat, and I'll tell you. You have learned to write, haven't you, Anne?"

"Not very well," confessed the little girl.

"All the better, for what I want you to do will teach you to write as neatly as possible. I want you to write a book."

"A book!" Anne's voice expressed so much surprise and even terror that Rose laughed aloud, but answered:

"Why, yes, and you must call it 'Anne Nelson's Book,' and you must begin it by telling what Amanda Cary did to you, and how you believed that Mrs. Stoddard would be glad if you went away. And then you can write all your journey, about the Indians, the house in the woods, Aunt Anne Rose, and all that you see and do in Boston."

"I haven't any paper," said Anne, as if that settled the question.

"I have a fine blank book, every page ruled, that will be just the thing," responded Rose, "and I will help you write it. I can draw a little, and I have a box of watercolors. I will make little pictures here and there so that Mrs. Stoddard can see the places."

"Oh, Rose! That will be fine. Shall we begin the book tomorrow?"

Anne was soon in bed, but there were so many wonderful things to think of that she lay long awake.

The Freeman household rose at an early hour. After breakfast Mrs. Freeman said: "Now, Anne, we will make believe that you are my own little girl, and I will tell you what to do to help me, just as I do Rose. You see," she added with a little laugh, "that I am like Frederick. I like to play that all sorts of pleasant things are really true."

Anne smiled back. "I like to make believe, too," she said.

"Then we'll begin right now. You can help Rose put the chambers in order, and dust the dining room. After that Rose can show you the attic, if you want to see where the children play on stormy days, or you may do whatever you please."

"The attic will be the very place for Anne to write her book," said Rose, and told her mother of their plan.

It was a very happy morning for Anne. Rose tied a big white apron around her neck, gave her a duster of soft cloth, and showed her just how to make a bed neatly, and put a room in order. Then, when the work was finished, the girls went up the narrow stairs to the attic, a long unfinished room running the whole length of the house with windows at each end. Under one of these windows stood a broad low table. Rose had brought up the blank book, a number of pens, made from goose quills, and a bottle of ink. She put them on the table and drew up a high-backed wooden chair for Anne. "I'll sit in this rocking chair at the end of the table with my knitting," said Rose.

Anne looked about the attic, and thought that the Freeman children had everything in the world. There was a big wooden rocking horse, purchased for Frederick, but now belonging to Millicent. There were boxes of blocks, a row of dolls beside a trunk, a company of tin soldiers, and on a tiny table was spread out a little china tea set. It was rather hard for Anne to turn away from all these treasures and sit down at the table. She had never seen so many toys in all her life, and she thought she would like to bring her own wooden doll, Martha Stoddard, that her father had made for her years ago, up to the attic to visit with these beautiful dolls of china, wax, and kid. But Rose had opened the book and stood beside the table waiting for Anne to sit down.

"How shall I begin?" questioned the little girl anxiously.

"Why, I'd begin just as if I were writing a letter," said Rose.

So Anne dipped the quill in the ink, and, with her head on one side, and her lips set very firmly together, carefully wrote: "My dear Aunt Martha."

Rose looked over her shoulder. "That is written very neatly, Anne," she said.

"Don't you want to make a picture now, Rose?" said the little girl hopefully.

Rose laughed at Anne's pleading look, but drew the book toward her end of the table, and taking a pencil from her box of drawing materials made a little sketch, directly under Anne's written words, of a little girl at a table writing, and pushed the book back toward Anne.

"Now I will knit while you write," she said.

So Anne again dipped the quill into the ink, and wrote: "This is a picture of me beginning to write a book. Rose made it." The attic was very quiet, the sound of Anne's pen, and of Rose's knitting needles could be heard, and for a little time there was no other sound; then came a clatter of stout shoes on the stairway, and little Millicent appeared.

"See, I found this in Anne's room!" she exclaimed.

Anne looked around, and saw Millicent holding up her beloved Martha Stoddard. With a quick exclamation she sprang up and ran toward her. "That's my doll," she exclaimed, and would have taken it, but Millicent held it tightly exclaiming:

"I want it!"

Anne stood looking at the child not knowing what to do. This doll was the dearest of her possessions. She had given her beautiful coral beads to the Indian girl, and now Millicent had taken possession of her doll. She tried to remember that she was a big girl now, ten years old, and that dolls were for babies like six-year-old Millicent. But Martha Stoddard was something more than a plaything to Anne; she could not part with it. But how could she take it away from the little girl?

"I want it," repeated Millicent, looking up at Anne with a pretty smile, as if quite sure that Anne would be glad to give it to her. Anne put her hands over her face and began to cry.

CHAPTER FOURTEEN

ANNE AND MILLICENT

ANNE HAD SPRUNG up from her seat so quickly that she did not think of her book, pen, or ink. Her arm had given the book a careless push, sending it against and overturning the ink bottle, and she had dropped the pen on the white paper, where it made a long ugly blot.

Rose had been quick to seize the bottle before it rolled to the floor, and was now using a big dusting cloth to wipe up the ink. Her attention was so taken with this that she did not really know what was happening, when the sound of Millicent crying made her look quickly around.

"What is the matter?" she asked, turning toward the little girls.

Anne, with her hands over her face, was evidently crying; and Millicent, grasping the wooden doll with both hands, was making as much noise as she possibly could in a series of half-angry little sobs.

"Millicent, stop this minute," said Rose, going toward them, "and you, too, Anne, and tell me what you are crying about," and, quite forgetting the inky cloth in her hand, Rose took hold of Anne's arm.

Anne looked up, the tears streaming down her cheeks.

"There, there," said Rose, wiping Anne's face, and leaving it almost blacker than the cloth. "Oh, what have I done!" exclaimed Rose, while Millicent's sobs ceased for a moment to be followed by a shriek of terror to see Anne's face turn black so suddenly. "Stop, Millicent," said Rose. "Come downstairs, Anne, and I'll wash the ink off. And tell me what the matter is."

"Rose! Rose!" called Mrs. Freeman from the floor below. "What is the matter?"

"I've got ink on Anne's face and Millicent is frightened," Rose called back, drawing Anne toward the stairs. Millicent stopped crying, and finding that no one took the wooden doll from her, trotted across the attic and introduced the newcomer as "Lady Washington" to the other dolls, sat down on the floor beside them and began to play happily.

Anne followed Rose down the stairs and into the sink room, where Rose began to scour her face vigorously.

"I don't mean to hurt you, Anne," she said laughingly, "and I'm awfully sorry I wiped your face with that dreadful inky cloth, but I have to rub hard to get it off."

"It's my—fault," Anne managed to say. "I was crying."

"There isn't any blame in crying, if you have anything to cry about," said Rose.

"Millicent wanted my doll," said Anne.

Rose did not speak for a moment. She was very fond of Anne Nelson, and thought her a very generous and thoughtful child, and could not understand why she should cry because little Millicent had taken what Rose called to herself "an old wooden doll."

"Well," she said, "Millicent won't hurt your doll."

"But she wants to keep it," said Anne, as Rose gave her face a vigorous wiping with a rough towel.

Rose made no answer. She thought it rather selfish of Anne, when they had all done so much for her, that she should be unwilling for Millicent to keep the doll.

Anne was not a dull child, and Rose's silence made her realize that she had acted selfishly; still, she could not feel that wanting to keep Martha Stoddard was wrong.

"There! You are quite rid of ink now," said Rose, "and there

230

is an hour before dinner. Do you want to write some more in your book?"

"No," said Anne. It seemed to her that she should never want to write in the book again. She wished that she and Martha Stoddard were safe back with Aunt Martha in Province Town.

"Well, I have some errands to do for mother, so I'll run along," said Rose pleasantly, and left Anne alone in the little square room called the "sink room," because of two sinks near the one window which overlooked the green yard at the back of the house. There was a door opening into the yard, and Anne looked out feeling more unhappy than she had since the night when Aunt Martha had sent her upstairs.

Frederick was in the yard. He was setting what looked to Anne like wooden bottles in a straight row at the further end of the square of greensward. Then he ran across to the open door where Anne was standing.

"Want to play bowls?" he asked.

"I don't know how," replied Anne.

"I'll show you; it's easy," replied the boy, picking up a big wooden ball and balancing it on one hand. "Come on out and try," he urged, and Anne stepped out into the yard. "Watch me!" said Frederick.

He stepped back a little, sent a keen glance toward the wooden "bottles," as if measuring the distance, then holding the ball in one hand and leaning a little sideways, swung it back and forth for a few times and then sent it rolling across the grass. It struck one of the "bottles," and that in falling sent over two more.

"Oh, I can do that!" exclaimed Anne.

"All right, try. I'll set up the pins for you," said Frederick.

Anne thought to herself that it was funny to call those wooden objects "pins."

"You'd better take a smaller ball," said Frederick, selecting one from a number lying near the door; and he handed her a ball that Anne thought was about the size of a pint dipper.

Frederick told her how to hold it, how to stand, and how to get the right motion to send it in a straight line.

"It's all in your eye, looking straight, and getting the right swing," he said.

Anne's first ball did not go half the proper distance, but she kept on trying, and before dinner time could send a ball nearly as well as Frederick himself.

"It's fun," she declared. Her face was flushed with the exercise, and her eyes shining with pleasure. For the moment she had forgotten all about the wooden doll. She and Frederick stopped in the sink room to wash their hands before going in to dinner.

"Anne plays a good game of bowls," said Frederick, as they took their places at the table.

"I want to bowl," exclaimed little Millicent.

"You can, any time you want to," said Frederick, with his pleasant smile. "I'll show you after dinner when Rose and Anne are sewing."

Anne thought to herself that the family all wanted Millicent to do everything she wanted to, and she remembered Martha, and wondered what Millicent had done with her beloved doll, but did not dare ask. They were all pleasant and kind to Anne, but she felt as if Rose did not look at her quite as kindly as usual.

"I have your blue dimity all basted, my dear," Mrs. Freeman said to Anne, as they left the dining room, "and you can sit with me and stitch up the seams this afternoon. Rose is to help Caroline with some cooking."

Anne felt rather glad of this, for she dreaded having Rose say something about the happening of the morning. Mrs. Freeman led the way to her pleasant chamber. A little rush-bottomed rocking chair stood near one of the windows.

"You may sit in the little chair, Anne; that is where Rose always sits. Now let's see if this will fit your thimble finger," and Mrs. Freeman held out a little shining steel thimble, and fitted it on Anne's finger. "It's just right," she said. "That is a little present for you, Anne; to go with the work-case that Mrs. Pierce gave you."

"Thank you," said Anne in a very low voice, looking at the pretty thimble, and wondering if Rose had told her mother about her trying to take the wooden doll from Millicent. "I'll always keep it," she said, looking up into the friendly face.

"Here is your work, my dear. Now set your stitches right along the basting, and set them evenly and as small as possible," and Mrs. Freeman handed Anne the strips of dimity. "But about your thimble, Anne," she continued. "I shall be better pleased if some time, when you perhaps have a thimble of silver, or have outgrown this one, you will give it to some other child who is learning to sew and has no thimble. We mustn't plan to keep gifts always, even if we do prize them. Sometimes it is best to pass them on."

Anne was quite sure that Mrs. Freeman meant that she ought to give the wooden doll to Millicent.

"I gave my coral beads, that Mistress Starkweather gave me, to the Indian girl," she said, wishing in some way to prove that she was not selfish.

"That was quite right, and I am sure that Mrs. Starkweather will tell you so," responded Mrs. Freeman.

Anne stitched away, setting her stitches very carefully. But she felt unhappy. She had quite forgotten the pleasant game with Frederick, the book that she was to write for Aunt Martha, and even the delightful fact that she was sewing on the pretty dimity dress, and had a new thimble of shining steel. All that she could think of was that she was sure that Mrs. Freeman and Rose believed her to be a selfish and ungrateful girl. "They think I want to keep everything," she said to herself. The July day grew very warm. Mrs. Freeman leaned back in her comfortable chair, closed her eyes, and indulged in a little nap. Anne's dark head began to nod, the pretty dimity slipped from her fingers to the floor, and the new thimble fell off and rolled under the table. Anne had gone fast asleep.

Rose, looking in at the chamber door, smiled to herself, tiptoed gently in and picked up the dimity dress and carried it to her own room, where Millicent was having her afternoon nap on her sister's bed.

"I'll stitch up these seams while Anne's asleep," thought the kind-hearted girl, "and I'll tell her that we have a family of fairies living in this house who do things for people. I wonder if Anne ever heard of fairies?"

Mrs. Freeman was the first to wake, and, noticing that Anne's work had vanished, smiled to herself, quite sure that Rose had taken it. It was some time later when Rose brought it back and laid the thin goods on Anne's lap.

233

"Oh," exclaimed Anne, waking suddenly, "I dreamed of Martha Stoddard," and then, noticing the smile fade from Rose's face, Anne wished that she had not spoken, for she felt that Rose would be sure that she was still blaming little Millicent, who entered the room that very moment holding the wooden doll.

"Where did you get the wooden doll, dear?" Mrs. Freeman asked.

"Anne gave it to me," replied Millicent.

"O-oh!" Anne exclaimed impulsively, only to be sorry the next moment that she had not kept silent, for Mrs. Freeman looked up questioningly.

"Didn't you give the doll to Millicent, Anne?" she asked.

Millicent looked as if she wondered why Anne had said "Oh!" and Rose looked at her wonderingly. She could not understand why Anne should not want Millicent to have the doll, and Rose began to think that Anne was indeed selfish and ungrateful, and Anne knew what her friend was thinking, and tried hard not to cry.

"You let me have it, Anne, didn't you?" Millicent said confidently, and Anne, feeling as if she was parting from her dearest friend, managed to say: "Yes."

Mrs. Freeman's face brightened. "What is the doll's name?" she asked.

"I called her Martha Stoddard," Anne replied.

"I've named her over," said Millicent. "I've named her Anne Rose, and I like her best of all my dolls."

"Have you thanked Anne for giving you her doll?" asked Mrs. Freeman.

"I'm going to give her one of mine back," declared Millicent. "I'm going to give her Miss Fillosee Follosee."

Anne wanted to cry out that she didn't want any other doll, that she wanted her own dear Martha Stoddard, but she kept silent.

CHAPTER FIFTEEN

AMOS APPEARS

ANNE PICKED UP her thimble and said: "I'm sorry I went to sleep. I sewed only a little."

"Let me see," and Mrs. Freeman picked up the dress, and looked at the neatly stitched seams. "These seams are all stitched," she said smilingly.

Anne looked at them in surprise. "Did you do them?" she asked.

Mrs. Freeman shook her head. "No," she replied; "you see, I went to sleep, and awoke only a few moments since."

Anne hardly knew what to make of this, for she was quite sure that she had waked when Rose entered the room.

"P'raps it's fairies!" said little Millicent hopefully. "Don't you know about fairies, Anne?" And Millicent came close to Anne and laid the beloved "Martha" in her lap. "I'll tell you," she went on, in response to Anne's puzzled look. "Fairies are little, oh, littler than my thumb. I've never seen one, but Caroline's grandmother saw one, and real good children may see them some time."

"But how could anything so small sew?" questioned Anne.

"Fairies can do anything!" declared Millicent. "Caroline

knows all about them. Let's go out in the yard where she is sitting with her sewing and get her to tell us a fairy story."

"Run along," said Mrs. Freeman. "You see you need not stay in to sew, since the seams are stitched."

Anne actually forgot Martha Stoddard, so that when she jumped up to follow Millicent the wooden doll fell to the floor without either Anne or Millicent heeding it.

Rose smiled as she picked it up. "Fairies are useful little people sometimes," she said to her mother.

The days went very rapidly. Every morning Anne helped Rose with the household work, and sewed on the garments Mrs. Freeman basted for her. Every day, too, she wrote in the book for Aunt Martha. Rose made tiny sketches on many pages: of a wasp's nest, of Anne riding Range, of Aunt Anne Rose; and here and there were little landscapes. Anne had made up her mind to let Millicent keep the wooden doll, but she sometimes wished that she had left Martha Stoddard safe at home in Province Town.

Beside the work there were games of bowls on the green back of the house, and pleasant walks about the town. Rose and Anne had made several visits to Mistress Mason, and Anne had already purchased a fine pewter pitcher to take home to Aunt Martha, and was knitting a warm scarf for Uncle Enos. She had not spent all of her money, and planned to buy a wonderful blue silk sash, which Mistress Mason had shown the girls on one of their visits, as a gift for Amanda. She had sent a letter to Aunt Martha Stoddard by a Province Town fisherman known to the Freemans, and the time was near when the *Yankee Hero,* of which Anne's father was first mate, was due in Boston.

"Like as not your father's vessel will bring a fine prize into harbor," Frederick said one morning as he and Anne were teaching Millicent to bowl, "unless some English frigate has captured her," he added.

All up and down the coast English vessels were on the alert to seize American ships; but the American vessels were also on the outlook and had captured many of the enemy's ships.

"They'll not capture the *Yankee Hero,*" declared Anne. "She's sailed by Province Town sailors," and Anne gave her head a little toss, as if to say that Province Town sailors were the best in the world, as she indeed thought they were.

Frederick laughed pleasantly. "You think a good deal of that old sand heap," he replied.

Anne held a ball ready to roll, but at Frederick's remark she dropped it, and stood looking at him angrily.

"It's your turn!" he reminded her, looking at her in surprise.

"It's not an old sand heap. It's the loveliest place in the world. You can see twice as much salt water there as you can in Boston," she declared.

"So you can," agreed Frederick, "but it's a sand heap just the same. A good place to catch cod, though."

"Want to see my workshop?" the boy asked when they were all tired of bowling. "Father's given me some fine pieces of wood, and I'm making a sled for Millicent to play with next winter."

Frederick's workshop was a corner of the carriage house, where the fine chaise stood, and he had a workbench there well supplied with tools, and spent many happy hours over his work.

"I'm going to have a shipyard and build ships," he told Anne. "See this little model!" and he held up a tiny wooden ship, fully rigged, with a little American flag fastened at the top of the mainmast. "Rose made that flag," he said proudly. "See, there's a star for each colony, thirteen of 'em."

Almost every day Anne and Rose walked to the wharves with Mr. Freeman to hear if there was any news of the *Yankee Hero*. It was the very last day of July whn Mr. Freeman said, as they walked down the wharf, "There's a Province Town schooner in harbor, Anne—the *Sea Gull*. She came for a new mainsail and will probably sail when the tide serves. There's a boat from her now, headed for my wharf."

Anne did not know that Amos Cary was on board the *Sea Gull*, but she was eager to see anyone who came from the place Frederick had called "the old sand heap," and watched the boat from the schooner as it came swiftly toward the Freeman wharf.

"Oh!" she exclaimed suddenly, and ran further out on the pier, quickly followed by Rose. "It looks just like Amos Cary's head. Do you suppose it is?" she asked turning to Rose.

"If it is, Amos is probably with it," Rose answered laughingly. "I suppose Amos is Amanda's brother, who came to Brewster with you. Is it that red-headed boy sitting in the bow?"

"Yes, yes!" answered Anne, fairly jumping up and down in her excitement.

Amos was now near enough to recognize Anne, and took off his cap and waved it gaily. The boat drew up to the wharf, but Amos did not jump out as Anne expected.

"I can't," he explained. "Father told Captain Nash not to let me set foot on shore," and Amos grinned as if he was delighted at what his father thought would be discipline. "I'm going to be on the *Sea Gull* for months; maybe a whole year! Isn't that fine?"

"Jump out, Amos," said Captain Nash.

"But father said I wasn't to step foot on shore," responded the surprised boy.

"Unless I told you to," added the captain, and Amos scrambled up onto the wharf a little disappointed at the permission. "Mr. Freeman has invited you to dinner," added the captain, "but you must be here at the wharf at two sharp."

"Yes, indeed, sir," Amos answered promptly, looking back almost reluctantly toward the boat.

"Born for a sailor," the captain said to Mr. Freeman, as Amos walked with Anne and Rose toward the Freemans' house. He answered Anne's questions about Aunt Martha, Uncle Enos, Amanda and the Starkweathers, and listened to her account of the wonderful journey to Boston.

"Wasn't it great to be shut up in that dark room!" he exclaimed, when Anne told him of Bill Mains' mistake. "Wish I'd been there. But maybe the *Sea Gull* will run afoul of a pirate ship before long," he concluded hopefully.

When Anne introduced him to Mrs. Freeman Amos took off his cap and bowed very politely, as he had noticed Captain Nash do. Frederick and he became friends instantly, and Amos was taken out to the workshop to see the model ship which had the American flag fastened to its mainmast, and he listened to Frederick's plans for building ships approvingly.

"Maybe I'll sail one of your vessels for you," he said. "I'm going to learn navigation. I'm not planning to be on shore much after this, I can tell you."

Frederick listened enviously; he thought Amos was a very fortunate boy to be going for a year's voyage on the *Sea Gull*.

CHAPTER SIXTEEN

———— 🦃 ————

AN UNEXPECTED VISITOR

"I'll bring you some coral beads, Anne," Amos promised as he said goodbye, and started back for the wharf. Frederick went with him, and listened admiringly to Amos's plans of all he meant to see and do. Frederick began to think that it would be better to go to sea than to build ships. He watched the *Sea Gull*'s sails as they caught the wind, and his eyes followed the little vessel until it looked not unlike the white-winged bird whose name it bore.

As he entered the yard Rose came down the path to meet him. She had a small package in her hand.

"I want you to do something for me, Fred," she said, "and I don't want anyone, especially Anne and Millicent, to know anything about it."

This sounded interesting to Frederick, and he looked up hopefully. Perhaps there was some message to be carried from Boston to the American troops in New York, and that he, Frederick Freeman, had been selected to carry it. Probably it was wrapped up in that package which Rose held so carefully. Why, it would be a greater adventure than any Amos Cary would encounter on the *Sea Gull*.

"Is it in that package, Rose?" he asked eagerly.

"How did you guess?" and Rose looked at her small brother in surprise.

"Come on out to the carriage house, and tell me when you want me to start," and Frederick grasped Rose's arm and hurried her along. "When do you want me to start?" he asked.

"Why, right away," answered Rose in rather a puzzled tone.

The brother and sister entered the carriage house, and Frederick led the way to the corner where his workbench stood, and they sat down.

"Nobody will hear us here," said Frederick in a mysterious whisper, looking sharply about the room.

"Oh, Fred! I do believe that you are making believe that you are a Tory spy in danger of capture," laughed Rose.

"Indeed I'm not! I wouldn't make believe be a spy," responded the boy scornfully. "I'm a loyal messenger, ready to carry news to General Washington!"

"Here is the message," and Rose handed her brother the package.

Frederick took it with shining eyes, and held it closely.

"Oh, Rose, is it truly? And where am I to take it?" he asked.

"Why, Fred, you 'pretend' splendidly," said his sister. "I suppose you'd really like to be messenger for Washington, but that isn't it, you know. Just unroll that package and tell me how good a doll you can make."

"Make a doll!" Fred flung the little bundle to the floor and looked ready to cry. "I suppose you think it's funny to make me believe I could do something to help Washington, when you really just had an old wooden doll to show me."

"Now, Fred," and Rose put her hand on her brother's shoulder, "own up that I didn't say a word to make you imagine such a thing. You know I didn't! I asked you if you would do something for me, and not let anyone know."

"Well, I might have known nothing interesting would happen to me," said Frederick. "Nothing ever does," and he regarded poor Martha Stoddard with scornful eyes.

"I want you to make a wooden doll as nearly like this one as you can," said Rose. "Millicent has taken possession of this one, and it's the only doll Anne has, and I'm sure that she doesn't want Millicent to have it. I thought if you could make one just like it that Millicent would like the new one better, and then Anne could have her own."

"All right," but Fred's voice was a little surly.

"And as for nothing happening to you, Fred, you ought to be thankful that nothing does happen, and that we are all safe and well. Suppose the British had won the battles at Concord and Lexington and Bunker Hill," and Rose looked at her small brother more sternly than ever before. "I could tell you of something very pleasant that is going to happen to you," she concluded.

"What is it, Rose?" and Fred was again eager and hopeful.

But Rose shook her head. "You just wait and see. Make the wooden doll. I'll tell you when the doll is finished," and she picked Martha up from the floor where Frederick had dropped her.

"Can't I keep her for a pattern?" asked Frederick.

"Yes. Anne and Millicent are making paper dolls, and they won't miss her for a little while, but bring her in before supper time."

"All right," and Frederick nodded cheerfully. He was already looking over his stock of wood for suitable pieces for the new doll, and wondering what the pleasant surprise would be.

Millicent could cut out very queer little dolls, and she and Anne were quite happy together under the big horse-chestnut tree until Anne said: "Where is my wooden doll, Millicent?"

"It's mine; my Anne Rose," said little Millicent placidly. "I don't know where she is. I guess she's lost," and Millicent carefully folded a piece of paper to cut another doll.

"Lost!" Anne repeated.

"Yes," agreed Millicent, indifferently. "I guess she is; p'raps she isn't, though."

Anne remembered Caroline's story of elves, and was quite sure that her head was filled with them, for she felt as if she wanted to shake Millicent, and at the thought that her dear Martha was really lost Anne began to cry.

Millicent put down the scissors and paper, and looked at Anne with startled eyes, and then she began to cry. Rose came running out from the carriage house.

"What is the matter, dear?" and she kneeled down beside her little sister. But Millicent sobbed on.

"Tell me, Anne," and she turned toward her little visitor.

"Millicent has lost Martha Stoddard," Anne managed to reply, wiping her eyes, and feeling very much ashamed that Rose should have seen her cry.

"Nonsense! The doll isn't lost. I saw it a minute ago. Come, Millicent; I'll go with you and Anne for a little walk toward King's Chapel," and Rose held out a hand to each of the girls.

"Rose," exclaimed Anne suddenly, "I know that you think I'm selfish about Martha Stoddard, but Rose, listen!" and Anne looked up pleadingly into her friend's face. "When I was a little girl, not as large as Millicent, and my mother had died, and my father and I were all alone, he made me that wooden doll! I never had anything else to play with until I went to live with Aunt Martha. It isn't just a doll, Rose; it's—why, it's most like a real person," and Anne's voice sounded as if it was hard work to keep back the tears.

"You ought to have told me before," replied Rose kindly. "You see, Millicent is too little to understand, and we all love her and don't like to make her unhappy. Martha is all right, and you shall have her safely back, dear," and Rose's voice was even more kind and friendly than usual as she told Anne of the new doll that Fred was making for Millicent.

"A new doll!" exclaimed Millicent happily, and could hardly wait for the time when Fred would finish it.

"So there goes my great secret!" laughed Rose. Anne was looking quite her happy self again, and Millicent was skipping along quite forgetting that she had ever wanted the wooden doll from Province Town.

"I don't believe I like secrets anyway," continued Rose. "Let's go back to the carriage house and watch Fred make the new doll, and I'll bring out the clothes I have made to dress it."

Frederick looked up from his work in surprise when the girls entered the carriage house. "Thought it was a secret!" he exclaimed.

"No more secrets in this family," declared Rose.

"Glad to hear it. Now I can know what's going to happen to me," responded Fred.

"Of course you can. Father has to go to Salem next week and he is going to take you with him."

"Nothing will happen in driving to Salem in the morning and back at night," said Frederick, a little scornfully.

"Wait and see!" And Rose nodded so hopefully that Frederick wondered to himself if she had really told him all she knew about his father's plans.

While the children were in the carriage house they heard the clatter of horses' hoofs on the driveway.

"Look!" exclaimed Frederick. "There's a man and a woman riding into our yard. Why, the woman is riding that black colt that brought you home."

But Rose and Anne had not waited for the end of Frederick's exclamation. Looking out they had seen the pretty black colt, and on its back a slight figure in a brown dress sitting very straight indeed, and wearing a hat of plaited straw with a brown ribbon—a hat exactly like the one Anne was so proud of.

There was a chorus of "Aunt Anne Rose! Aunt Anne Rose!" in which Millicent and Frederick joined, as the children ran out to welcome the unexpected visitors.

"I am here, too!" said Mr. Pierce laughingly.

The visitors were warmly welcomed by Mr. and Mrs. Freeman.

"I couldn't be satisfied, after this fine saddle came, until I had taken a journey," declared Aunt Anne Rose, with a happy little laugh. "And my boys were sure that they could keep house without us, so Silas and I started off. Having nieces to visit I felt as if I must come."

"Anne Rose has never been in Boston before, and she thinks it must be as large as London itself," said Mr. Pierce.

"There are indeed many places to see," said Mrs. Freeman, "and it will be a great pleasure for us to show them to Mrs. Pierce."

"There is Mistress Mason's shop," suggested Anne.

"And Governor Hancock's fine house," added Rose.

"And the wharves and shipyards," said Frederick.

As they talked the little party moved toward the house. Rose ran to the kitchen to help Caroline prepare an early supper, and

Mrs. Freeman sent Anne to show the visitors to the big spare chamber.

"I wear my fine hat every day," said Anne, as she and Aunt Anne Rose went up the stairs together.

"I really think that we must take Anne back to Scituate with us," said Mr. Pierce. "What do you say, Anne?"

"My father's ship may come any day now," answered the little girl, "and then we must go home to Province Town."

It seemed to Anne as if Mrs. Pierce's face grew very grave, and she wondered to herself if Aunt Anne Rose would really like to have her live with them.

"Your cheeks are just as red, and your eyes shine; you look just like a girl, Aunt Anne Rose," she said admiringly, as Mrs. Pierce took off her hat and brushed her pretty black hair, that waved back from her face.

"It's because I'm on a visit," declared Mrs. Pierce, "and a visit to Boston. I've always wanted to come, and here I am! Everybody looks young and pretty when she is happy, Anne. But I'm not young. I'm past forty, and I never was pretty," and the dark-eyed little woman smiled radiantly, as if everything in life was planned just right.

The Pierces declared that they could stay only two days, so that evening many plans were made that they should fill the time with as much pleasure as possible. Mr. Pierce had some business to attend to with various merchants, and Anne and Rose were eager to show Mrs. Pierce the shops, the fine houses and churches; and directly after breakfast the next morning Mrs. Freeman sent them all off. Millicent was quite happy to stay with Frederick and watch him finish the wooden doll, while Rose and Anne, with Aunt Anne Rose between them, started off to visit Mistress Mason's shop, where Mrs. Pierce insisted on buying the largest of the fine dolls as a present for little Millicent, a pink silk sash for Anne and a lace collar for Rose.

"I want you girls to think often of your new aunt," she said. "And I am hoping that when Anne's father comes he will decide to bring her to visit us. I have written a letter to him, Anne, and I will give it to you. You must hand it to him, and tell him that you would like to come."

"Yes, ma'am," answered the little girl, but not very eagerly.

For Anne was now counting the hours until the *Yankee Hero* should reach Boston harbor, and when she and her dear father could sail off to Province Town and tell Aunt Martha all about the wonderful visit, and give Amanda the blue silk sash. She almost wished that Aunt Anne Rose had not told her about the letter.

CHAPTER SEVENTEEN

———— 🍎 ————

THE STRANGE SCHOONER

ON THE MORNING when Mr. and Mrs. Pierce started for home, Rose and Anne went to Mistress Mason's shop on an errand. As they walked along the street Rose exclaimed suddenly: "Anne, look! There is one of father's best friends!" And Anne looked up to see a gentleman, wearing a cocked hat and red cloak, coming toward them. He was very erect and his wig was tied with a narrow ribbon.

"Good morning, Mistress Rose," he said, and Anne thought to herself that his voice was very kind and pleasant.

"Good morning, Mr. Adams," Rose responded. "This is Anne Nelson from Province Town."

The friendly smile now rested on Anne. "Let me see; was there not a little maid from Province Town who helped the cause of Liberty by carrying a message to Newburyport?" he asked, clasping her hand.

Anne looked up at him and smiled. "I went with Uncle Enos," she answered.

"So you did! And now you are a visitor in Boston, as I am myself, for my family are now living in Dedham," he responded pleasantly, and, with a friendly message for Mr. Freeman, he bade the girls goodbye, and walked on.

"That is Mr. Samuel Adams," explained Rose. "He came from Philadelphia but a few days ago. He signed the Declaration of Independence, Anne. And father says had it not been for Samuel Adams 'twould have been years before Congress would have come to so great a decision."

"And to think he knew of me!" said Anne.

"He knows of everybody who helped even a little bit toward American independence," said Rose. "Mr. Adams goes back to Philadelphia in September. 'Twill be a fine thing to write in your book, Anne, that you have spoken to him," said Rose, "and very likely your father will be pleased to have you go and stay with Mrs. Pierce. It's so much nearer Boston than Province Town, and the Pierces have such a pleasant house."

"It's not so pleasant as my Aunt Martha's," declared Anne loyally.

It seemed to Rose that it would be a very fortunate thing for her little friend to live with Aunt Anne Rose, and she could not understand Anne's eagerness to return to Province Town.

"May we not walk down to the wharf, Rose?" Anne asked eagerly. "Your father may have news of the ship."

But Mr. Freeman only shook his head, a little soberly, Anne thought, and the day passed without any sight or news of the *Yankee Hero*.

Anne was not very happy that day. She wondered what would happen to her father if the English had captured his ship, and wished with all her heart that she was with Aunt Martha Stoddard. That night she dreamed of a fairy hid beneath her pillow, and that it whispered to her, "There is your father! Right beside the bed," and when she awoke the next morning Anne said to herself, "I feel happy, but I don't know why," and then decided that a good fairy had visited her. But when she went downstairs, there in the front hall stood a dark man smiling as Anne exclaimed, "My father!"

For the *Yankee Hero* had arrived in the early evening of the previous night, and John Nelson had lost no time in making his way to Mr. Freeman's house, hoping for news of Anne. And he had tiptoed into her room for a look at his little daughter, just as the fairy whispered.

There was so much for Anne to tell him! John Nelson looked very grave when he heard of Anne's running away in the night.

"But Uncle Enos and Aunt Martha know that I believed they no longer wanted me," pleaded Anne. "And, oh, father, Aunt Martha said I was not to go to Brewster and journey to Boston with the Freemans to see you."

Anne had not known that her father could be so stern.

"You might never have been heard from, Anne, starting off like that. I do not know if Mistress Stoddard will be willing to again take charge of you," he said.

But after Rose had told him the story of their journey, of Anne's courage when they believed themselves prisoners in the house in the woods, and had said that it was really Amanda Cary's fault more than Anne's that she had run away, Mr. Nelson was quite ready to forgive her.

"I am glad indeed that my little girl has a good friend in Mrs. Pierce," said Mr. Nelson, after he had read Aunt Anne Rose's letter, "but I think we must go to Province Town at the first opportunity."

Anne now felt that there was nothing to wish for. With her dear father safe on shore, and the prospect of soon sailing away to Province Town she was quite happy.

"You must make Rose a fine present, Anne," he said one day as they came down King Street.

"I heard her say once that she hoped some day to have a gold ring," replied Anne.

"You shall give her one," said Mr. Nelson.

"I'll give it to her when I say goodbye," said Anne as they walked toward home.

"That may be tomorrow," responded Mr. Nelson, "for Mr. Freeman says that not a boat from Truro, Wellfleet or Province Town has come into Boston for a week, so if the wind favors, 'tis like tomorrow will give us a chance for a passage."

Rose was on the porch, and as she watched Anne come up the path thought to herself that she would be very lonely without the little maid from Province Town.

"Captain Starkweather from Province Town is at father's

wharf," she said, "and I had half a mind to tell him not to take any passengers back to Province Town, for father says he will start back when the tide serves very early tomorrow morning."

Mr. Nelson hurried away to the wharves, and Anne and Rose went up to the attic for Anne's book. "For I suppose we must pack up your things tonight," Rose said. "Your father has bought you a fine portmanteau. It's in your room now."

Anne picked up the book, and was eager to hurry to her room to see the new bag, but Rose detained her a moment.

"Why, Anne," she exclaimed, "you have left out the most important thing."

"What did I leave out?" questioned Anne.

"Why, about Amanda!" replied Rose. "You started this on purpose for Mistress Stoddard, so that she could know all about your running away."

"Oh," said Anne, in a tone of relief, "then I haven't forgotten anything. You see, Rose, Amanda told Aunt Martha all about it, so it's all right."

Rose looked at her little friend for a moment as if she were going to scold her, then she began to smile, and leaning down kissed the little girl's cheek.

"You know how to be a friend, Anne," she said, "and I'm sure Amanda will never do another hateful thing to you."

"Captain Starkweather says he'll take me to Province Town to see his boys some time," Frederick announced as the family gathered at the supper table, "and Anne's father tells me that if I go to Salem tomorrow I'll see ships that go to all parts of the world."

"That is true, my son," replied his father. "There's a ship now in Salem just arrived from Cadiz with a load of salt, and another with tea and silks from China. 'Twas great good fortune that they reached harbor safely. They would have been a fine prize for some British ship."

The Freemans all went down to the wharf with Anne the next morning. The fine portmanteau, filled with Anne's new clothing and with her gifts for the Province Town friends, was placed carefully in the little cabin. Captain Starkweather had already hoisted the sloop's mainsail, and gave Anne a warm welcome as her father helped her on board.

"Goodbye, goodbye, dear Rose," Anne called back.

As the sloop swung off from the wharf and the little girl looked back toward the friends who had been so kind to her there was a little mist in her eyes.

"It's good luck indeed to have this favoring wind," said Captain Starkweather, as the boat moved swiftly down the harbor. "I doubt not Amanda Cary is on the beach already hoping we may have sailed at midnight," and the Captain nodded smilingly toward Anne. "What are you watching so sharply, John?" he asked, for Mr. Nelson, shading his eyes with one hand, was watching a small schooner.

"Why, I'm wondering a bit about that schooner," he replied. "Her sails were hoisted and her anchor up when we left the wharf, and she's kept the same course. She couldn't be after us right in Boston harbor, but I don't like her keeping so close."

" 'Tis hard work to know friends from foes on land or sea these days," said Captain Starkweather a little anxiously. For several fishermen had recently been captured by English vessels, the men taken to England, and their boats kept by the captors.

"Hoist the jib, John," directed the captain. "We'll sail away from that craft; I don't like her company."

Up went the jib, but the sloop did not increase the distance from the schooner. Both boats had now left Boston harbor well behind them. The sloop could not hope for any help now if the schooner really meant to capture it.

"There are guns on that schooner," exclaimed John Nelson. "Go into the cabin, Anne, and don't come out until I tell you to. Remember, stay in the cabin," and almost before she realized what had happened Anne found herself in the sloop's cabin, and the little door shut. A moment later she heard the bang! bang! of a gun, and felt the boat swing heavily to one side.

CHAPTER EIGHTEEN

———— 🍎 ————

A GREAT ADVENTURE

ANNE'S FIRST IMPULSE was to open the cabin door, but she had learned one lesson by her runaway journey—to obey and wait. It was very hard for the little girl to keep quiet, for she could hear her father's voice, and that of Captain Starkweather, and loud commands in strange voices, and the sloop seemed to be moving this way and that as if it had lost its pilot.

"We are captured by that English boat; I know we are," Anne whispered to herself.

And that was really what had happened. The English schooner had sent a shot through Captain Starkweather's fine new mainsail, followed by a command to lay to, and before Mr. Nelson had had time to fasten the door of the cabin, the schooner was abreast of the sloop and in a few moments the Province Town boat was taken in tow by the English schooner, and Mr. Nelson and Captain Starkweather found themselves prisoners.

"Leave 'em on deck, but make sure they can't move hands or feet," Anne heard a rough voice command, and there was the sound of scuffling feet, and gradually the noise ceased; and all that Anne could hear was a faint murmur of voices, and the ripple of the water against the side of the boat. These sounds gradually ceased, and the frightened child realized that the wind had died away, and that the boats were becalmed. She peered out of the little cabin window and saw that the English boat was very near. The tide sent the sloop close to the schooner, and now Anne could hear voices very plainly.

"Pull in that tow line, and make fast to the sloop," she heard the same gruff voice command, and in a few moments the sloop lay beside the schooner.

"I could get on board just as easy," Anne thought, and wondered if her father would tell the English that his little daughter was in the sloop's cabin.

Poor John Nelson, lying on the schooner's deck, tied hand and foot, feared every moment that his conquerors would discover that there was another passenger on board the boat. "They would not harm my little maid," he assured himself, "but there is food and water in the sloop's cabin, and Anne is best off there."

Both he and Captain Starkweather hoped that some American vessel might come to their rescue. But now that the wind had died away there was no chance of that for the present.

"A midsummer calm. May be stuck here for twenty-four hours," Anne heard a grumbling voice declare.

The long summer day dragged by. Anne opened the lunch basket, but had little appetite. At sunset there was a ripple of wind and the two boats, side by side, moved a short distance.

Anne, shut up in the tiny cabin, had come to a great resolve. "Father told me to stay here, but if I could creep aboard the schooner and untie the cords, then father and Captain Starkweather could get free," she thought. And the more she thought of it, the more sure she was that she could do it.

The twilight deepened, and now Anne ventured to push open the cabin door a little way. The sailors were in the forecastle, but Anne could see a dark figure in the stern of the schooner. She ventured out and softly closed the cabin door. Now, on her hands and knees, the little girl crept across the little space toward the side of the schooner. It looked like a black wall, but not very high above her, and there were ropes; and Anne was used to boats. Grasping a rope she drew herself up, hand over hand, until she could reach the deck rail. Now she gave a swift glance toward the dark figure at the stern. "I do believe he's asleep," she thought, and Anne now pulled herself to the top of the rail and dropped noiselessly to the deck of the schooner. For a few moments she cowered in the shadow, and then looked anxiously about. Near the cabin she could see two black shadows, and knew that they were her father and Captain Starkweather.

Keeping close in the shadow Anne crept along the deck. But, noiseless as her progress had been, Anne had been seen the moment her little figure reached the top of the deck rail. John Nelson's keen eyes, staring into the summer night, had recognized his little daughter, and instantly realized that Anne meant to help them. He held his breath for fear that some sharp ear had caught a sound, and then whispered to his companion, "Don't move, or call out, captain; Anne is on deck and will help us."

The little girl was now close beside her father. "Feet first, Anne," he whispered, and Anne's eager fingers pulled and worked at the tough knots so securely tied until they loosened, and John Nelson could move his feet. Her father did not dare even whisper again. He longed to tell her to hurry, but dared not speak. Anne was now tugging and twisting at the rope which held her father's wrists, and managed to loosen it so that he could work his hands free. Then they both began to loosen Captain Starkweather's cords, and in a few minutes he too was free. The same thought was running through the minds of both men: If a girl like Anne had such courage, why couldn't two sailors make a prize of this good English boat?

"Go back to the sloop's cabin, Anne. We'll follow," whispered her father. And Anne obeyed. She was not afraid now. How easy it had been, she thought happily, as she slid down the rope to the sloop's deck, and found herself again in the little cabin.

The dark figure, dozing at the schooner's helm, did not see the two creeping men who so suddenly were upon him. A twisted scarf over his mouth, and no sound to warn his mates, his hands and feet bound with the very cords that had secured his prisoners, he was left a captive. Then John Nelson and Captain Starkweather sped toward the forecastle; the open hatchway was closed so quickly that the men below hardly realized what had happened, and it was securely fastened before they could help themselves.

"The breeze is coming," declared Captain Starkweather. "Shall we put back to Boston, John? We'll not know what to do with this craft in Province Town."

"A good night's work this, and Boston folk will be glad to see this English *Sea Bird* come into her harbor. 'Tis the same craft that has caused so much trouble to fishing boats. I'll bring Anne on board," and John Nelson ran to the schooner's side and called, "Anne! Anne!" A moment later and he lifted his little daughter to the deck of the schooner.

"You are a brave child," declared Captain Starkweather. "This schooner is really your prize, for 'tis by your courage that we have taken her."

The schooner's course was changed, and, the wind increasing, she swept off toward Boston harbor.

" 'Twill be a good tale for Mr. Samuel Adams to hear," said Captain Starkweather, "and you will indeed be proud of your little daughter, John. I doubt not but this will be printed in the Boston papers, and news of it sent to General Washington himself."

It was hardly sunrise when the *Sea Bird,* towing Captain Starkweather's sloop, came to anchor off the Freemans' wharf. John Nelson's hail to a friendly fisherman brought a number of boats alongside, and when he had told them of how the capture was made a chorus of huzzas filled the air. The news was carried to the other vessels in the harbor, and the *Sea Bird* was soon surrounded by small boats. One of these boats pulled for the shore, and its crew spread the news that a little girl and two sailors from Province Town had captured and brought into harbor a fine English schooner. Mr. Freeman heard the news on his way to the wharf, and saw the crew of the *Sea Bird* being marched up the street under a strong guard. The church bells were rung, and when John Nelson and Anne reached shore they were welcomed by cheers.

Rose came hurrying through the crowd.

"Oh, Anne!" she exclaimed. "Here is Mr. Samuel Adams waiting to speak to you! You are the bravest girl in the colony."

" 'Twill be a wonderful thing to tell Amanda," said Anne happily. "Even Amos could hope for no finer adventure."

"There'll be prize money," added Frederick. "I heard my father say that there'll be a large sum for you and your father and for Captain Starkweather."

It was a week later when they sailed once more for Province Town. It was decided that it would be safer to leave the harbor at nightfall, when there would be a better chance of the sloop not being recognized and followed by some watchful craft lurking in the lower harbor. This time the little cabin was nearly filled, for Captain Starkweather was taking gifts to each one of his six boys, beside wonderful packages for their mother, and Anne and her father could hardly wait for the time when Uncle Enos and Aunt Martha should see the set of lustre ware, the fine pewter, and the boxes of figs, dates, jellies and sweets which they were taking to Province Town.

CHAPTER NINETEEN

HOMEWARD BOUND

CAPTAIN STARKWEATHER HAD renamed his sloop. The old name had been painted out, and now, on each side of the boat, in gilt letters on a white scroll the new name *Anne Nelson* could be seen.

The little craft was anchored off the Freeman wharf, and at early twilight Mr. Nelson and Anne said their goodbyes to the Freemans, and put off in the sloop's tender. Captain Stark-weather was on board the sloop, and as noiselessly as possible they made ready to start.

The favoring winds swept the little craft along, and as the sun came smiling up from the far horizon Anne awoke, and was quite ready for the crackers, boiled eggs and doughnuts that Mrs. Freeman had packed for their breakfast.

The long "arm" of land now stretched out as if to welcome the returning voyagers, and the sloop ran in beside the little pier just as Captain Enos and Jimmie Starkweather came down the beach.

"Been watching your craft since sunup," declared Uncle Enos. "What's kept you in Boston so long, Starkweather? We began to worry about you, John, and feared some ill news of our little maid."

Anne did not wait to hear her father tell the story of their great adventure, but ran swiftly up the path toward home. Aunt Martha was standing in the doorway, and as Anne saw the loving smile and felt the kind arms encircle her she was indeed sure that this was home, and that the most fortunate thing that had ever befallen her had been the welcome Aunt Martha had given her two years before, when she had come to that very door asking for shelter.

How much there was to tell! And how Aunt Martha exclaimed over the adventures of her little maid, and thanked heaven that she was safely back in Province Town.

Then when Uncle Enos and John Nelson came up the path, each wheeling a barrow filled with the fine gifts that Anne and her father had brought home, then indeed did Mistress Stoddard declare that it was enough to make one believe in good fairies. And that reminded Anne of Caroline's story, which she had written down in the book.

Captain Enos put on his glasses and looked the book over admiringly.

"It should be in print," he declared; "this book is the finest thing of all, Anne. 'Twould be an excellent idea, Martha, for us to ask the neighborhood in to hear it read."

But Mrs. Stoddard shook her head, and said Anne must not think too well of what, after all, was Miss Rose Freeman's book as much as it was Anne's. "You must not overpraise our little maid," she warned Captain Enos reprovingly. But the book was ever one of Mistress Stoddard's most valued treasures, and was kept with *Pilgrim's Progress* in the big chest.

It was late in the afternoon before all the dishes, pewter, the fine new tablecloths, and the pretty brown cloth for Mistress Stoddard's new gown were unpacked.

"This package is for Amanda," Anne said, holding up a good-sized bundle.

"For Amanda, indeed!" exclaimed Mistress Stoddard. "I'm not too sure that she deserves it. 'Twas she that sent you out into the night, thinking your Aunt Martha hardhearted."

"Amanda did not mean to," pleaded Anne.

Anne sped away down the path toward Amanda's home. Amanda was at the door, and Anne called her name joyfully:

"Is it not fine that I am home! And these are presents for you," and Anne held out the silk sash and pretty dimity. Instead of exclaiming with delight as Anne expected, Amanda covered her face with her hands and began to cry.

"Stop crying, Amanda! You will get spots on the sash," exclaimed Anne; and Amanda's tears ceased instantly.

"Taste of this barley sugar," suggested Anne, smilingly, opening a heart-shaped box and helping herself to a piece. Amanda promptly followed her example; and when Mrs. Cary came to the door a little later she found the two friends sitting close together and talking happily.